# TITANIA
## CHERRY POPPING DADDIES
### BOOK III

# RAISA GREYWOOD

Cover art by Wicked Smart Designs<br>
Cover Photo taken by Furious Fotog<br>
Cover Models: Kevin R. Davis and Lovett Taylor<br>
Editing: Briggs Consulting LLC and Bossy B-Word Editing Services

## DESMOND

Hoping to get some answers, Desmond followed Damian, his twin, into their younger brother Braden's, office. Aside from Damian's darker hair and full-sleeve tattoos, he and Damian were identical with brown eyes and neatly trimmed beards. As usual, Braden was clean-shaven and wearing one of his customary suits.

The suit was probably apropos, considering Braden managed Club BDE. Desmond and Damian were silent partners.

"So, let me get this straight." Damian sat in one of the matching club chairs across from Braden while Desmond took the other. "Delia told you she got an email about the auctions from you?"

"And she thought you set up the auctions instead of giving her and Ivy raises?" Desmond asked.

"That's what she said." Braden scowled and pushed the printed email toward his brothers. "The email went to everyone except the three of us, and it's not in my sent folder. My IT guy, Martin, says the email header was spoofed and routed through a virtual private network."

The Club BDE gossip tree was too well-fertilized to let the auctions die, making it that much harder to put a stop to them.

"Meaning, we can't track it." Desmond studied the email, then passed it to Damian. "Where is Martin anyway?"

"Sick as a dog with some upper respiratory thing, so he's not much use for tracing it." Grimacing, Braden added, "Not that he found anything to begin with, even though I hired him to help prevent this kind of shit from happening. Now, everyone believes the auctions are legitimate because they thought I was sanctioning them."

"And then you made a deal with Killian O'Rourke for information." Desmond rubbed his face and gave his idiot brothers an ugly glare. "It was bad enough for Blake to vouch for his membership. I have no idea what you were thinking when you made a deal with a mob boss. It's like you both were trying to trash the decade Bastian and I spent trying to put him in prison."

Calling each other by their first names was a childish game. Desmond knew it, and so did Damian, but neither one of them wanted to be the first to stop. Hell, Desmond couldn't even remember when it started.

"Did you ever think you might not have found anything on Killian because there isn't anything to find, *Bryce*?" Damian snapped.

"No, *Blake*. I never once thought that," Desmond retorted. "He's as dirty as your hands are after a day in your garage."

"Enough." Braden slapped his desk and glared at his brothers. "Yes, I was pissed at Damien for recommending Killian without telling me who he was, but that's on me for not vetting him as thoroughly as I should have. I hired Martin to close that hole in our onboarding procedure. Nobody, no matter who recommends them, gets a membership, guest pass, or employment without a full background check."

"But—"

Braden lifted a hand to cut Desmond off. "Regardless of our personal feelings, Killian doesn't bring his business into the club, and he's an excellent, safe dominant who has never caused a moment's trouble."

"That doesn't mean he won't in the future," Desmond muttered. "For all we know, he's the one running the auctions."

"Killian wouldn't do that," Damian replied. "Well, he might, but he wouldn't hide it behind Club BDE."

Desmond forced his fists to unclench before he punched Damian in the face. "And you know that because you're such good friends with a mob boss, and completely forgot your fucking twin is a cop?"

"I said that's enough. We have bigger issues on our plate," Braden snapped. "Aside from that, Killian got closer to finding the little asshole running the auctions than anyone else, and he's still pissed about coming up empty."

"Fine," Desmond muttered, giving Damian a poisonous sneer. "We'll agree to disagree."

Instead of replying, Damian rolled his eyes and flipped him off.

"Good." Braden stuffed the printed email into his desk drawer. "Moving on. Damian, before Martin got sick, I had him rush the background check on Rio Jimenez. He came up clean, so I'll make him a formal job offer later today."

"Wasn't he the guy who took down Don Graham after Emily maced him?" Desmond asked.

"Yeah. Rio is my neighbor. He's a stand-up guy." Damian cleared his throat, then added, "And he has no criminal record or dealings with criminals. If he takes the job, he'll be working as a security guard."

After a moment's hesitation, Desmond nodded. "Good. We could use another guard or two. I'll go through my contacts and see if we can scare up one more."

"Thank you, Desmond." Braden rested his elbows on his desk and folded his hands. "At least whoever is running the auctions is paying the participants quickly. The money is put into escrow, and tax forms are going out. It's exactly as I'd have done if I was actually hosting the auctions."

"Do we know the company sending the tax forms?" Damian asked.

Braden cursed under his breath and rolled his eyes. "You get three guesses, and the first two don't count."

"Club BDE's accountant?" Desmond asked, tightening his fingers on the arms of his chair. "Are you fucking serious?"

"Serious as the stroke you look like you're about to have," Braden replied.

"Son of a bitch." Damian got to his feet and paced the office. "When I get my hands on that little fucker..."

They nodded in agreement as Braden went to the sideboard and poured three glasses of scotch.

"Whoever is doing this has intimate knowledge of how the club is run," Desmond said after accepting his glass. "Presumably, if they're sending out tax forms, they're also familiar with our accountant. Have you checked with them?"

"Yes, but the information went to them in those spoofed emails," Braden replied.

"It has to be an employee." Damian sipped his drink and nodded approvingly. "But which one? Aside from Martin, who has computer skills like that?"

A lot of money was changing hands, and even though the auctions weren't technically illegal, nobody liked not knowing where it was going. Although most of it went to the people being auctioned, twenty-five percent was being siphoned into someone's pocket.

"Good question," Desmond said. "Since Club BDE isn't paying the participants, I think the tax forms would be evidence of fraud, but I know we'd all prefer to fix this ourselves. I just wish we could find one lead. That's all it would take."

"We'll get it." Braden rose to his feet. "I promise we'll find whoever is running the auctions and make them sorry they ever fucked with the Elliott brothers."

# THERE'S A MYSTERY AFOOT

TANIA

The money was gone, spent on a quixotic attempt to prove Victor Andersen wasn't dead.

Not that it mattered. Even before his death, Tania's father hadn't come around much.

Mandy, her stepmother—and the person who had spent almost a million dollars on a fruitless search—didn't seem to care he'd been lost in a hurricane seven years prior, or that she still had to make house payments. Although there weren't that many left, they still needed to be paid.

Not for the first time, Tania wished she'd been more insistent on clearing the mortgage before Mandy decided to go off the deep end.

With statistically improbable curves, blonde hair, and wide, guileless blue eyes, Mandy looked more like a fashion doll than a living, breathing human. It would have been reasonable to expect Tania to hate having a stepmother barely five years her senior—especially since Victor spent a grand total of ten minutes introducing her before taking off again for a job he refused to discuss with anyone.

Maybe she should have been pissed at him for giving her a stepmother instead of driving lessons for her fifteenth birthday, but she'd lost the ability to rely on him long before then.

Besides, Victor had, for once in his life, done something right with Mandy.

Despite her appalling lack of common fucking sense—at least where Victor was concerned—Mandy was impossible to dislike.

At first, Tania considered her just one more nanny and tried to ignore her, but it wasn't long before Mandy won her over. She'd been the one to teach Tania to drive, help her choose a university, and navigate the ninth level of hell that was the federal application for student financial aid, even though Tania already had a Sirens of STEM scholarship to cover most of her expenses. It didn't gain her anything except a healthy respect for anyone who didn't end up in rehab after filling it out, but Mandy still did it every year.

With hot chocolate laced with peppermint schnapps and a plateful of burnt cookies, she'd nursed Tania through her first heartbreak and all the rest of her teenage angst too.

She might not have evicted Tania from her own womb, but she was a mom in every way that counted. Even better, she'd given Tania the one thing she'd always wanted. Bianca, her six-year-old half-sister, was the light of her life.

Lord only knew how Victor had managed to marry her, much less keep her. Mandy could have done so much better.

"Mandy, I've said this so many times already, but you need to have Victor declared dead," Tania finally said as she gazed at the bank statement on her laptop screen from her spot on Mandy's luxurious couch in the living room. "He had life insurance, and—"

"No. He isn't dead."

"All right." She relaxed her shoulders and inhaled deeply, trying to keep a rein on her temper. "What's your plan now?"

"I have some ideas. Stop worrying."

Fuck's sake. Mandy was too busy on her phone to even look at her. Thankfully, Bee was napping upstairs and wouldn't have to hear their discussion.

"Stop worrying? Really? You're seriously going there?" Tania rolled her eyes and clenched her hands together to control her urge to wrap them around Mandy's slim neck. "But losing the house is no problem, right? You and Bee can totally move into my one-bedroom apartment. It'll be so cozy."

"That's enough." Mandy lifted her head and her blue eyes glittered like ice. "Bee and I will be fine, and I don't need your negativity right now."

Tania pressed the heels of her hands to her eyes and sighed. "It's not negativity to be concerned over where you and Bee are going to be living in a few months. Victor is gone, and I doubt he'd be happy about you spending your inheritance on a—"

She shut her mouth before she added, *fool's errand,* but Mandy caught what she'd left unsaid.

"Honey, I know you mean well, but—"

"Even if he walked through the front door right now, you spent all the money he left you on private investigators," Tania interrupted. "You did that, and I wish you would wake up and recognize how close you are to losing your home."

"You don't know him like I do. He wouldn't leave us like that."

"The last time I spoke to Victor was at your wedding a few months before he died." Tania softened her voice, hoping she hadn't woken Bee from her nap. "The time before that was my mother's funeral when I was five. So, no, I don't know him, but I do know he isn't coming home again."

"You're wrong." Mandy wrapped her arm around Tania's shoulder and hugged her. "Don't worry about me. I think I have a plan."

"What is it? Can I help?"

"No!" Mandy winced and lowered her voice. "I need to work out the details, but it's going to be okay. Promise."

Meaning, Mandy didn't have a plan at all, and was trying to put off their conversation.

Again.

Giving up, Tania logged out of the bank website and closed the browser, then went to the kitchen for a glass of wine. As much as she wanted to, Tania couldn't help with Mandy's financial issues. Not right away, at least. Although job offers were starting to trickle in, she wouldn't graduate for another eight months. She couldn't even push early graduation in December because she needed the time for her senior project.

Bee was only six, and Tania couldn't stand the idea of her and Mandy losing their home. Unfortunately, there wasn't much she could do about it. Even if she left college and found a job, she wouldn't earn enough to support all three of them unless they sold the gated-community McMansion and bought something cheaper.

She returned to the living room and blinked in surprise as Mandy held up her phone and took a selfie.

Tania sat next to her and caught a glimpse of a website before Mandy hurriedly swiped to hide the browser. The color scheme was dark with red accents and a Gothic aesthetic, and the word *auction* was emblazoned on the banner.

A strange premonition twisted in her stomach, and she closed her eyes to commit the URL to memory. Although it was probably innocuous, there were far too many assholes out there who would take advantage of a desperate woman, and they liked to hide behind slick websites. Whatever it was, Mandy didn't need to be there, but Tania would hold her peace until she could check it out.

"Fancy website. Is it a message board or something?"

Giving Tania a smile that didn't reach her eyes, Mandy rose to her feet. "Something like that. I'm just catching up with some friends. Could I ask you a favor?"

"Sure, anything."

"I'll be... I have to go out of town next weekend. I

know you have school, but could you watch Bee while I'm gone?"

Her Spidey senses tingling hard enough to rattle her brain, Tania nodded. "Sure. I'll take her to the children's museum. It'll be fun."

Taking her sister to the museum wouldn't be a hardship either. It was one of Tania's favorite places in the world.

"Thanks." Mandy squeezed her eyes shut, then tried for another wan smile. "If you don't mind, I'm going to lie down until Bee wakes up from her nap."

"Of course. Sleep as long as you need. I'll take care of her."

Mandy bent to give Tania a tight hug, then kissed her cheek. "Thanks, sweetie. You're the best fairy queen a stepmonster could have."

"Back atcha, Bratz doll."

Mandy laughed softly at the familiar nickname and squeezed Tania's shoulder before trudging up the stairs.

The door to Mandy's bedroom clicked shut, and Tania gave her a few moments to settle in before opening the website on her laptop.

## DESMOND

He poured scotch into a glass and set it in front of the seat across from him, as he'd done for the past seven years. As he put the bottle aside, Braden joined him and Bastian at the small table in Club BDE's restaurant above the pit.

"I always forget what today is until I see that empty chair." Braden cleared his throat and glanced toward the stairs leading down toward the pit where several scenes were taking place. "It's been years, and I still expect to find him doing whip demos."

So did Desmond. Victor's body had never been found, and a part of him still believed his old friend wasn't dead. Or maybe it was just blind hope.

"Here's to Victor." Desmond lifted his glass and touched it to Braden's as Bastian did the same. "May he rest in peace."

"To Victor," Bastian said.

Their moment of silence was interrupted by a ping from Braden's phone. After reading the text, he said, "Damian is running late, but he should be here shortly."

Desmond hid a frown. Whenever he and his twin had to be in the same room, they usually ended up fighting, but he was fairly certain they could behave for a few hours in Victor's honor. Emily, Damian's fiancée, was pretty good at keeping the peace, but she wouldn't be joining them.

The thought of Emily, and of Braden's babygirl, Lottie, reminded him they needed to get a handle on the unauthorized auctions happening under their noses. Although there was a carefully worded disclaimer stating the money was for services instead of sexual acts, a good prosecutor could easily obtain an indictment for pandering. Aside from that, someone who wasn't him or one of his brothers was using Club BDE for their own gain.

Worse, he and his brothers would be on the hook for damages if something went wrong, and he didn't want to think about what would happen if someone was auctioned without their consent.

His brothers had bought Emily and Lottie, and although they'd consented to participate, that didn't mean someone couldn't be sold against their will.

He'd say one thing for Damian. Although he and Desmond were both silent partners in Club BDE and left the management to Braden, Damian had stepped up to the plate to help figure out who was running the auctions.

It was about time he made an adult decision.

"Victor was a valued friend and was one of Club BDE's first members who wasn't related to me,"

Braden said, pulling Desmond from his thoughts. "He was a good man."

"The best of men," Desmond murmured. "It's just hard to imagine him never coming through that door again."

Bastian leaned close and kissed Desmond's cheek, then hugged him tightly, letting Desmond relish the comfort of his best friend and partner.

Braden studied his scotch for several seconds. "I think of inviting Titania and Mandy every year, but it's probably for the best I don't."

Chuckling, Desmond shook his head. "Mandy hasn't been here since before Bianca was born, and I'm pretty sure Victor would come back from the dead to haunt us if we invited his daughter into a kink club."

Bastian and Braden laughed, but Desmond hadn't been joking. Titania was beautiful, with dark hair, hazel eyes, and a curvaceous body that would have every unattached Dom in the state panting after her.

There was no way he'd let her within a hundred miles of Club BDE—no matter how much he wanted to hear her call him Daddy. He hadn't even mentioned his fantasy to Bastian.

They'd talked about finding a babygirl to share. Hell, they'd even shared submissives in the club a time or two. Unfortunately asking a woman to submit to two demanding Daddies for longer than a few hours seemed impossible.

Things hadn't ended well the few times they'd tried. One female partner had taken it upon herself to try to pray their gay away, and another had attempted to pit him and Bastian against each other in the hope of separating them.

If they ever found a woman to share, she'd have to be mature. She'd be over thirty, with a job and a life of her own, and she'd have to accept both him and Bastian, which made things even more difficult.

Their babygirl certainly wouldn't be the daughter of one of his oldest friends—and it didn't matter that Victor was gone. Titania was barely old enough to drink, and thinking of all the things he wanted to do to her made him feel dirty.

Of course, Emily and Lottie were around Tania's age—decades younger than his brothers. Hell, almost twenty years separated Mandy and Victor, so maybe the idea wasn't as far-fetched as it sounded.

Desmond pushed all thoughts of Titania out of his head. Maybe the age gap wasn't so bad, but she was still Victor's daughter.

"Bianca must be getting so big. I haven't seen her since she was a baby," Bastian said, resting his hand atop Desmond's.

"She is. They still live in my neighborhood, and I

see them in passing sometimes." Braden sighed and rubbed his forehead. "Every so often I wonder if I should check on them, but I don't want to impose."

"Titania is in her final year of college, right?" Bastian asked. "She and Mandy came to our house-warming party a few years ago, and I only got to talk to her for a few minutes."

"I'm not sure, but probably," Braden replied. His speculative gaze locked with Desmond's, making him wonder if Braden suspected his feelings about their close friend's daughter.

"I was thinking we could have her, Mandy, and Bianca over for supper," Bastian said. "I guess we can invite them when Titania comes home for winter break."

"It'll be nice to catch up with Mandy," Desmond replied.

He would have loved nothing more than to spend time with Titania, but it was a bad idea. He didn't think he could be that close to her without touching her. At least he wasn't completely despicable. He hadn't once imagined Titania as his and Bastian's babygirl until their housewarming party, and she'd been nineteen at the time.

Ugh, he *was* that despicable. She might have been legally able to give consent, but lusting after her wasn't right.

"What is she studying again?" Bastian asked.

"Aerospace engineering," Desmond answered without thinking, and winced, kicking himself for letting Bastian and Braden know how much he'd thought of her. "At least that was her plan the last time I talked to her."

Braden nodded approvingly and smiled. "That girl will go far in life. Still getting straight A's too, I bet."

Desmond couldn't help thinking Braden was reminding him of why she was so far out of his reach. Hell, he didn't know why he was thinking of it anyway. Bastian wouldn't be interested in her, and unless they both agreed, there would be no babygirl in their bed.

# 2

# FANTASY HAS A PRICE

TANIA

With one eye on the stairs leading to the bedrooms where her sister and stepmother napped and the other on her laptop, Tania brought up the website Mandy had tried to hide.

"Holy shit!" She slapped a hand over her mouth, hoping her entirely too loud exclamation hadn't been heard.

Her eyes narrowed as she perused the site. It was indeed an auction, offering people of all genders, ethnicities, and body types to the highest bidder for a night of fantasy.

Well, the buyer's fantasy, anyway.

There was even a disclaimer at the bottom, saying

that no sexual acts were required, which didn't make much sense for an auction like this, but Tania supposed it got them off the hook for charges of prostitution.

She swiped to navigate to the tab offering virgins and blinked at the average bid amounts. Mandy's photo had been in the MILF category, which had an average bid of around ten thousand dollars. The virgin bid average was much, much higher, and it didn't seem to matter that none had pictures showing the women's faces.

"Well, slap my ass and pull my hair," she murmured under her breath. The auctions were hosted by Club BDE, lending the website some credibility. She'd never been there, but according to the rumors she'd heard around campus, it was supposed to be one of the finest places in the south to get one's kink on.

In exchange for a useless piece of tissue in her vagina—which probably wasn't even there anymore—and a few hours of her time, she could pay off Mandy's mortgage and keep them afloat until she graduated, giving Mandy enough time to find a job of her own.

Folks in the deep-south bible belt had an ugly word for what she was considering, but Tania didn't see things that way. To her, the bigger sin would be to let her sister and stepmother lose their home when it was in her power to stop it.

Besides, given her dating history, she was looking at dying a virgin anyway. Her socially dictated innocence might as well go to a good cause, and it was certainly better than losing it in a crappy dorm room or the back seat of someone's car.

Hopefully, the folks running the auctions wouldn't care about self-pleasure. Tania's battery-operated boyfriend didn't complain about being washed and shoved into her nightstand when she was done with it. Unfortunately, men would probably resist that procedure.

Of course, if the person taking her virginity was one of Victor's friends... Well, having Desmond Elliott or Bastian Carter pop her cherry would be worth six figures. Hell, if she had the money, she'd pay *them* to do it—especially if they let her call them Daddy like the heroes in her favorite romance novels did.

She laughed at the thought, but god, they were gorgeous. Both were muscular and fit with salt-and-pepper hair. Mr. Desmond had a neatly trimmed beard she wanted to pet and was a few inches shorter than Mr. Bastian. Both men had warm brown eyes she felt like she could drown in.

They might have been at least twice her age, but

she'd been crushing on them since she hit puberty. She had no idea how many times she'd gotten herself off thinking about them, but she always felt a little disgusted with herself afterward for objectifying them. Not only were they gay, but they were also in a relationship with each other.

Even if they'd been bisexual, she doubted either of them would have anything to do with her. They probably saw her as a little kid—their friend's daughter. Then again, there had been almost as many years between Victor and Mandy. Maybe, like her father, they liked younger women.

She tried to remind herself of their orientation but couldn't help wishing they were bisexual and looking for a woman to share.

Forcing herself to push the thought of being the meat in their beefcake sandwich deep into her spank bank, she focused on her task. Unfortunately, the website didn't have a phone number. Using the contact form, she sent a message asking for a return call. Surprisingly, her phone vibrated with an incoming call a few moments later. After checking the caller ID, which read Club BDE, she hurried outside.

"Hello?" She sat on the porch swing, making sure she could see the stairs through the front picture window so she could watch for Bee.

"This is Club BDE returning your call," a man said. "You had questions for us?"

"Hi. My name is Tania." She almost gave her last name but stopped herself at the last minute. "I'm calling to verify your auction website."

"May I ask how you found us?"

"It was a close friend. I prefer not to share her name, but she..." Tania crossed her fingers, unable to decide if she wanted her next words to be true or not. "My friend was one of the women you auctioned."

"All right." The man's tenor took on a clipped edge. "I'm sure your friend told you how the auctions work, but I'll sum it up in case she missed anything. The people who auction their services are willing and are legally able to give consent. All buyers are vetted, and all parties must provide health screenings. Protection against pregnancy is the responsibility of the female."

*Didn't that just figure?*

"Does that mean condoms aren't allowed?"

"No. It means the person buying the fantasy may not want to use them or may have a breeding kink. If you choose to engage in sex and don't want a child, I recommend other methods of birth control. Club BDE takes no responsibility for children conceived as a result of our auctions."

Tania pressed her lips together and shuddered,

wondering if there was a reason behind that particular rule. If she decided to go through with selling her virginity, her next stop would be the university health center for birth control, along with the required medical screening. The last thing she needed or wanted was a child.

"What about physical injury?"

"While scenes can often include impact play such as spankings, participants agree in advance that no permanent marks will be left on anyone, and any injury requiring medical care will be reported to the police. You will also be asked to communicate your hard limits."

It sounded like they were trying to keep things safe for everyone, which she appreciated, but she wished he hadn't mentioned spankings. It would be impossible to get rid of the mental image of going over Bastian's or Desmond's knee.

"Fair enough. What percentage does the club take?"

"Twenty-five percent, and you're responsible for the taxes. There's a ten-thousand-dollar fee if you back out after the auction is completed, and the terms of the auction must be met within fourteen days. Are you over eighteen?"

The percentage seemed high to her, but if her virginity sold for the average amount, it would leave more than enough to pay off Mandy's mortgage. "I'm twenty-one."

"Okay. Click the sign-up link at the bottom to set up your own account. Follow the instructions to upload your profile, health screening, and pictures before midnight tomorrow night, and we'll set you up for this Friday."

"That should work for me."

"If something comes up, you'll need to withdraw your profile before the start of the auction, but there will be another next month. Use the contact form on the website or call if you have any further questions."

"Thanks."

After ending the call, she chewed her lower lip, knowing she'd already promised to watch Bee that weekend. She also didn't want Mandy to have to go through with the auction, especially when the amount she'd receive would only keep her and Bee for a few months.

Although the idea didn't sit well with her, she'd have to lie and tell Mandy something had come up. It wasn't too far from the truth and would keep her stepmother out of the auction.

Truly, it was a simple matter of economics involving the perceived value of a scarce resource. A diamond was just carbon formed into a crystalline structure by time, heat, and pressure. They were expensive because diamond brokers marketed them as luxury items instead of industrial abrasives and cutting tools.

Tania wasn't a diamond though. After all, one could only sell their virginity once.

## BASTIAN

He pinched the skin between his brows and scowled at Desmond and Damian, who hadn't stopped sniping at each other since Damian walked in.

Personally, Damian wasn't one of his favorite people either, but neither of them was behaving like a grownup. He was about ready to get out a paddle to teach them both some manners.

When Damian left the table to talk to someone he knew, Bastian leaned close to Desmond. Whispering softly, he said, "Looks like someone is going to have a very sore ass later tonight if he doesn't shut his mouth and quit baiting his brother. Do I need to ask Mistress Rogue to join us?"

Sighing, Desmond squeezed his eyes shut, then shook his head. "You're right, and I'm sorry. He might have started it, but I didn't have to engage with him."

"It's okay." Bastian kissed his cheek. "Thanks for not arguing with me."

"I can't. It's not the place or the time." Desmond finished his scotch, then turned his chair so it faced away from Damian. "Blake can be an asshole all he wants. I should have walked away when he got here."

"It might help if you stopped calling him Blake."

"It's his name." Desmond smirked and accepted a glass of water from their server.

"And yours is Bryce."

He'd never know what possessed Desmond's parents to name their three boys Bryce Desmond, Blake Damian, and Braden Dominic. It was like they wanted their sons to get beat up at school. Maybe it was a family alliteration thing.

More than a few submissives had confused the twins, and even when they didn't, they often mixed up their names.

"I'll stop calling him Blake when he stops calling me Bryce. Sound fair?"

Before Bastian could reply, Damian strode to their table and scowled before tossing his phone between them. "We've got another girl up on the virgin auction."

Bastian pulled the phone close and scrolled through several somewhat grainy boudoir photos of a young woman. "Says her name is Misty. Is that ringing a bell for anyone?"

Although her face was pixelated, she was gorgeous, with short, dark hair and generous curves he wanted to pet. Her ass was round and full, and tapered to a narrow waist. Her only identifying mark was a small tattoo on her inner wrist, but he couldn't tell what it was.

Closing his eyes, he tried not to think about having her between him and Desmond. They'd spent years looking for the right babygirl to share, but she wouldn't be it for them. Purchasing a woman's virginity was no way to start a relationship.

Her short pixie haircut reminded him of Titania Andersen for some reason. Laughing at himself, he almost rolled his eyes. There was no way Titania would be selling her virginity—even if she still had it to sell.

Unfortunately, the idea stuck in his head, and he couldn't help but put her face over the pixelated image. He shifted in his seat, trying to convince his cock to behave.

Victor truly would come back from the grave if he knew of all the filthy thoughts running through Bastian's head.

Titania between him and Desmond, with Desmond's cock in her pussy, and Bastian's in her ass.

Bent over for a spanking. Kneeling at their feet, taking their cocks in her sweet mouth...

*What is wrong with me?*

"I can go through our membership records, but I don't recognize her," Braden said, pulling Bastian back to the matter at hand.

"Let's enlarge the image. Maybe we'll recognize the tattoo." Damian touched the screen then spread his fingers apart until they could see the woman's ink. "Looks like algebra. Who the hell would get a tattoo of an equation?"

"Maybe someone who studied and went to school?" Desmond asked. "That wouldn't be you, *Blake*."

"Fuck you, *Bryce*. You don't know it either."

"I'm thoroughly tired of both of you," Bastian snapped. "Grow the fuck up and focus on finding out who this woman is. Do we know anyone who might recognize the equation?"

Thankfully, they both subsided. Bastian was about done with their bullshit. Although he couldn't take a paddle to Damian's ass, he was more than willing to take his frustration out on Desmond's.

"I'm pretty sure Titania would," Braden said, easing the tension. "Let's take a screenshot and text it to her. Does anyone have her number?"

Damian retrieved his phone and scanned his

contacts. "I have Mandy's. I'll send it to her and let her ask Titania." After forwarding the photo, he added, "We could always Google it, but I have a feeling Titania will give us a better explanation than a search engine."

Desmond crossed his arms over his chest and gazed over Damian's head. "I think the bigger question is which of us is going to bid on her. It's one thing to let people like Mistress Avery auction their services. We don't know anything about this girl, and I don't even want to think about her being in Emily's position."

Mistress Avery did brisk business on the auctions, offering verbal humiliation and torment to her clients. Unfortunately, she didn't know who was running the auctions, but promised to share anything she learned.

"Desmond and I are strapped. We just finished paying for the last of the renovations on our house," Bastian said. "If the bids go over a hundred grand, we'll lose."

"I could toss another hundred thousand into the kitty," Braden said. "It'll be worth it if she knows anything about who's running the auctions."

"We can beat our money out of them once we catch them," Desmond muttered.

Bastian laid a hand on Desmond's knee, unable to disagree.

"Says she's only twenty-one, so we should plan on Misty going for at least three hundred thousand." Damian gazed at the photo, then glanced around the club as if he was looking for Emily. "Bid as much as you need to. I'll cover whatever you can't."

"No." Desmond scowled and shook his head. "We'll figure it out ourselves. I'm not taking your help."

"I'm not helping you, dipshit." Damian leaned toward Desmond and slammed a fist on the table. "I'm helping Misty. If she's in the same position Emily was, I won't have that on my conscience. Deal with it."

To Bastian's shock, Desmond relaxed and nodded, then held out his hand to his brother. "Okay, Damian. Thank you."

# 3

# SECRETS AND LIES

TANIA

"Earth to Titania. Is the fairy queen distracted?"

Hearing her full name on Dr. Pappas's lips was like sandpaper over exposed nerve endings.

Ignoring the titters of her classmates, she kept her expression placid and imagined stabbing her pencil into her instructor's left eyeball. Mercy, she'd die a happy woman if she never had to listen to another of his vapid *Midsummer Night's Dream* references.

With his chunky, black glasses, white short-sleeved shirts, and bowties, he looked like the definition of a *nerd*. The thinning comb-over didn't help.

He wasn't even that old. If she had to guess, Tania would have said he was in his mid-thirties.

He was certainly younger than the two men she shouldn't have been fantasizing about.

"No, sir. I was considering my answer to your question."

Thankfully, she managed to stop thinking about the Club BDE auction for a hot minute and quickly gave her least favorite instructor the answer he wanted. Also, thankfully, the alarm on his phone signaled the end of class.

Before she could escape, he said, "Miss Andersen, a moment of your time, please."

"Bet he's gonna ask to see your wings," Jason, one of her classmates said, looking her up and down.

She flipped Jason off and gathered her things. It was the life of a female engineering student. After her first semester, she learned to walk like the Winter Soldier on his way to kill something, so at least she didn't get pushed around in the corridors anymore, but barely a day went by that someone didn't say something stupid.

She reminded herself that Dr. Gabrielle Knox, the founder of Knox Software, and the source of Tania's scholarship largesse, would frown upon a felony conviction. Then again, she'd heard rumors about how Dr. Knox treated misogynistic douchebags, so maybe not.

*Two hundred and thirty-six point two days until graduation.*

And just a few scant hours before the auction for her virginity opened for bids.

After taking a deep breath in an attempt to keep her cool, she trudged to the lectern at the front of the room. "Yes, sir?"

"Come sit, my dear," Dr. Pappas murmured, gesturing to a pair of chairs. After sitting across from her, he laid his hand on her knee. "I'm having a small gathering at my house tomorrow night. I'd like to discuss our future."

"I'm afraid I don't understand," she lied. Tania understood him perfectly but was willing to let him dig his own hole.

Heck, she'd already gone to Dr. Ng, her department head, three times. Despite the university policy prohibiting fraternization between students and instructors, he'd made it clear she would be committing academic suicide if she complained publicly about sexual harassment against a tenured professor. At almost halfway through her senior year, she was too close to the finish line to risk it.

Then again, Pappas was actually touching her this time. Unfortunately, there wasn't anyone around she'd trust to back up her story. It was also clear he'd pulled the same shit with other female students, but she'd make sure the university heard all about his antics once she had her degree in her hand.

"Well..." He tightened his hand on her knee, and she resisted the urge to kick him in the balls. "I'm sure you're on the hunt for an advisor for your graduate program."

"My scholarship doesn't cover postgraduate work. I can't afford it and it's too late to apply for a grant, so I'll be taking a job right after graduation. If my employer wants me to have a master's degree, they'll pay for it."

"Are you sure? We'd work very well together." He leaned closer, letting her catch a whiff of peppermint from a breath mint. "Imagine what we could publish if we embarked on a mutually satisfying relationship."

*Translation: I'll stick you with an exorbitant tuition bill and make you do all the work, then put my name on the publications. If you sleep with me, I might add you to the credits.*

When his hand moved up her thigh, Tania lost what was left of her patience, and very nearly her lunch. Before she could tell him off, her phone chimed with Mandy's ringtone. "I'm sorry. I have to take this. It's my stepmother."

A flicker of annoyance crossed his face, but he hid

it with a smile. "Of course. I'll email you the party details."

"Thanks, but I'm honestly not interested."

Before he could reply, she grabbed her backpack and strode from the classroom, then accepted the call. "Hey, Mandy. Is everything okay?"

"We're great, but I have a favor to ask."

"Okay. I just got out of my last class for the day, but I'm headed to a study session to work on my project. Can it wait until next weekend?"

Tania still felt awful about lying to Mandy but stifled the guilt. Mandy needed time to recognize Victor wasn't coming home instead of getting horizontal with some stranger before she was ready.

"Oh, it's something easy. I'm going to text a picture to you. Could you tell me what it is?"

When her phone buzzed with the incoming text, she opened the image and gasped, but managed to control her reaction before Mandy heard it.

"Where did you get this?" she asked, gazing at the photo of the tattoo on her inner wrist with a flash of sheer black fabric in the background. The barely healed ink was just over a week old, and Mandy hadn't seen it. Thankfully, the image showed just the tattoo and not the rest of her.

She tried to tell herself the body art wasn't hers, but honestly, who else would have a tattoo of that particular equation in the exact same spot? The odds were ludicrously small. Hell, it was in her own handwriting. Tania had drawn it herself, so unless the artist copied it, it was impossible for the ink to be anyone else's.

The thought of Mandy seeing her in that transparent negligee... Tania winced, wishing she'd been a little more circumspect with the photos she'd uploaded to the auction site, but it had been hard to stop posing once she got started. Since she'd planned to obscure her face, she hadn't bothered with makeup or hair, but the silky nightgown and decadent lingerie made her feel beautiful for the first time in her life.

Add a little sexy Motown and some fantasies of Mr. Desmond and Mr. Bastian, and she went from engineer to ingenue in no time flat.

"Damian Elliott sent it to me, so I could ask you."

Oh, god. Where was a hole to crawl into when she needed one? Was Mr. Damian going to bid on her? She hurried to a bench under a live oak and sat, trying to control her panic.

"Um...I think I remember him," Tania finally said. "He's Mr. Desmond's twin brother, right?"

"Right. I figured you'd remember Desmond and Bastian from their housewarming party a few years ago," Mandy replied. "They were friends with your father."

"Do you know where the photo came from?"

"Damian didn't say. The tattoo is cute though. I could see you getting something like that."

"Tell him..." She swallowed hard and tried to control her breathing before she passed out. "Tell him it's the formula to calculate lift."

She'd gotten the tattoo on impulse and wasn't entirely sure what made her decide on the design. It fit her though. All she had to do was look at it to remind herself of how high she'd soar once she was out of college.

"We figured you'd know what it was. Thanks, sweetie."

"No problem. Give Bee a kiss for me."

Tania ended the call and stared blankly at a pair of squirrels chasing each other across the tree branches. Did she dare go through with the auction, knowing there was a chance Mr. Damian would be the one to take her virginity?

She shook her head, trying to dispel the thought. Unfortunately, Tania couldn't explain how he'd gotten the photo in the first place. If he had it, it probably meant he'd been looking. Feeling a little sick to her stomach, she wondered if she should cancel the auction.

No. There was too much at stake. Even if it was Mr. Damian, she had to go through with it.

*Please, let me be wrong.*

Mr. Damian's hair was darker, without so much gray, but aside from that, he and Mr. Desmond were physically identical. Although she could try to convince herself Mr. Damian was Mr. Desmond if she closed her eyes, her body knew the difference. She didn't want Mr. Damian at all.

And she didn't want Mr. Desmond unless she could have Mr. Bastian too.

God, she couldn't even bring herself to call any of them by name without adding mister to it. Fuck's sake, was she twelve? It didn't even make sense. She'd called her father by his first name for years—not that he was ever around to hear her.

Tania's wants weren't important—especially since she was wishing for the impossible. She had to focus on the big picture and achieve financial security for Mandy and Bee. Pushing down her trepidation, she opened the auction website on her phone and added an item to her list of hard limits.

*Masks required for all parties.*

She didn't have that many limits anyway. Without experience, she had no idea what she liked or didn't, but could say for certain she wouldn't do anything involving blood or human waste. Hopefully, the new addition to her list wouldn't drop her payout too much.

After taking a deep breath, she strode toward the library and tried not to picture herself being fucked by someone who wasn't one of the men she wanted.

❧

## DESMOND

Damian's offer to help pay for Misty's virginity left Desmond in an uncomfortable position, and not even the sensory deprivation scene going on in the pit managed to get his mind off the frustration mixed with gratitude.

At least the restaurant overlooking the club's main play area wasn't crowded, meaning he and Bastian wouldn't be bothered while they waited for the auction to begin. Bastian's presence in the seat next to him also helped calm him down, and thankfully, Braden and Damian had wandered off.

While he was grateful to his younger brother, it stuck in Desmond's craw to accept his help. They'd been at odds for years, and their ongoing fights only got worse when Damian decided to recommend Killian O'Rourke for membership in Club BDE.

Braden might have believed his claims about Killian being a decent guy, but Desmond knew better.

Unfortunately, Bastian was right about their finances. Their Isle of Palms house had needed almost a quarter of a million dollars in renovations and repairs when they bought it, and although they lived comfortably on the income from investments and private security contracts, they didn't have sufficient liquid assets to make their bid successful without dipping into their retirement funds.

He could also see Damian's point. Damian was twitchy after what Emily's father, Don, had done to her, and Desmond didn't blame him for it. None of them liked thinking of any woman in danger.

Thankfully, Don was going to prison, and wouldn't bother anyone for a long time. Don might have once been a friend, but there were some things a man couldn't come back from. Threatening his only daughter and torching her home would do it. At least Emily's mother, Elizabeth, had turned her life around. She was clean and sober, and taking classes while she finished her jail sentence. When she got out, she'd be in a position to make her own way. Hell, maybe Damian could give her a job.

As the scenes in the pit wound down, Desmond kept an eye on the clock marking the time remaining before the start of the auction and told himself Misty wouldn't be the babygirl he and Bastian so desperately wanted.

Despite knowing better, he couldn't help but hope. At the very least, he needed someone to take his mind off Titania.

"I'm proud of you," Bastian murmured, brushing his lips over Desmond's jaw.

"What for?"

"For cowboying up and accepting Damian's help." Bastian moved his hand up Desmond's thigh, coming dangerously close to his thickening cock. "It might even get you out of the punishment you deserve."

Desmond groaned as Bastian dragged a finger down the ridge of his erection and flexed his hips upward, desperate for his lover's touch.

"Ah, ah." Bastian squeezed his balls, then removed his hand. "I didn't say you were off the hook for being an asshole. This will give you something to think about until we get home."

Desmond grumbled under his breath but knew better than to protest. Besides, they both needed to focus on the upcoming auction and get a bid in when it started.

"Ten minutes," Bastian said when Desmond didn't reply. "This is going to sound weird, but that girl looked familiar."

"Oh? I thought you didn't recognize her."

"I didn't." Bastian nodded when their server

offered to refill his water glass. "Her haircut kind of reminded me of Titania."

Desmond burst out laughing and had to cough to clear his throat. "Titania Andersen? Are you high?"

"Good question." Bastian sighed and rested his elbows on the table. "We haven't seen Titania in two years, but I'd swear Misty has the same haircut and color as hers."

Frowning, Desmond pulled his phone close and opened Misty's auction page. "I mean, maybe? It's kind of the same cut, but a lot of women have short brown hair, and we have no idea what Titania looks like now."

Despite his words, he couldn't stop looking at Misty. She was curved in all the right places, and the transparent nightgown left nothing to the imagination. Her generous breasts were on display and topped with stiffened nipples. He could even see the neatly trimmed hair on her mons.

Unfortunately, now that Bastian had mentioned it, he couldn't unsee Titania in the woman's place.

Swallowing hard, he scrolled back to the top of the page in a desperate attempt to quell his arousal. Of all the sick things to think about...

"I have to be wrong," Bastian said, pulling Desmond from his thoughts of Titania in their bed. "Titania doesn't have any ink."

"It's been two years. She could have more ink than Damian by now." Desmond stilled and scrolled down to the photo of the woman's wrist. "He said the tattoo was the formula for lift. Titania is studying to be an aerospace engineer."

Bastian blinked and paled. "You don't think it's her, do you?"

"God, I hope not. I'm also curious about why she added the bit about masks to her list of limits. Maybe we should ask Mandy if Titania has a tattoo."

"No. We don't want Mandy to know a thing about these auctions or wonder why we're curious. With Victor gone and her having to take care of Bianca alone..." Bastian shook his head. "That can't happen."

"It's not Titania," Desmond said, unable to decide whether to hope he was right or pray he was wrong. "Victor would have done right by them, and she has a scholarship for school. She doesn't need the money and wouldn't have any reason to auction herself. Besides, she'd have recognized her own tattoo when Mandy showed it to her."

"Who's to say she didn't?"

"Are you trying to convince me it's her?" Desmond tried not to think about the fantasies he'd already entertained about his oldest friend's daughter.

"Mostly, I'm trying to convince myself we're not bidding on her." Bastian waved their server down and ordered a few plates of chicken wings. "It doesn't make sense. They might both be twenty-one and have the same hair, but they can't be the same person."

"Right." Desmond hesitated, then added. "Titania is gorgeous though. Have you ever—"

"No. She's sexy as fuck, but she's also Victor's daughter. We can't—" Bastian cut himself off and exhaled softly. "We shouldn't even think about it."

"But you are," Desmond replied.

A muscle twitched in Bastian's cheek. "So what if I am? It's just a fantasy that will never come true."

Bastian entered their bid when the auction opened, scowling when they were outbid almost immediately. Desmond pushed his irritation at having to ask for help aside and silently thanked his brothers. At the rate the bids were climbing, he and Bastian would have never won by themselves.

"What are we going to do with Misty once we win her?" Bastian asked.

"Ask her if she wants to be our babygirl?" Desmond snorted out a dry laugh. "Honestly, I haven't thought that far ahead."

Bastian studied him for several seconds. "If we like her, we could see if things work out. Maybe we haven't given younger women a fair shake because we decided we'd only look at women over thirty."

Pulling his attention from the rapidly escalating bids, Desmond stared at him, but couldn't think of a single thing to say. He knew Bastian better than anyone. If he hadn't been interested in her, he wouldn't have made the offer.

"Maybe."

Would it be so wrong to at least ask her?

Leaning close, Bastian took his hand. "If she says no, we cancel the auction and let her go."

"What if she's in a position like Emily was? We can't not help her."

"Des, we're retired cops. We can fix problems like that without giving her..." Bastian glanced at the bid amount and winced. "Two hundred grand already. Fuck."

"And if she says yes?"

"We do what she lets us do and figure the rest out later."

## ❧ 4 ❧

## CONTRACTUAL OBLIGATIONS

TANIA

Some situations simply called for wine, and watching people bid on a chance to fuck her was high on the list.

She poured more of the cheap, overly sweet red into her NASA coffee mug, then grimaced as she drank it down. The wine wasn't helping the butterflies in her stomach, but it was doing the job she intended and left her calm enough to sit still while the clock ticked down on her auction.

There wasn't room to pace in her tiny apartment anyway. The only good thing about it, aside from its proximity to campus, was that she didn't have to deal with a roommate.

"C'mon, people," she muttered when the bidding

stalled. "Don't leave it at a prime number. That's just bad juju."

Deciding to get something besides wine into her stomach, she grabbed a takeout container of leftover chana masala from the fridge in her tiny kitchen and stood over the sink to eat it cold.

Prime number or not, the bid was well over what Mandy owed on her house. Of course, there was still the twenty-five percent the auction would take and taxes to account for, but the net would be enough to keep Mandy and Bee in their home until Tania graduated and found a job.

After finishing her meal, she tossed the empty takeout container into the trash and went back to her desk to watch the last few moments of the auction.

The bids had gone up another thirty thousand in her absence. As she watched, the timer flashed to zero and the page refreshed to show a banner at the top.

*Winning bid placed by 2KnottyDaddies.*

She blinked and let out a somewhat hysterical laugh, thankful no one was around to hear her. Maybe her buyer had an omegaverse kink, but the implication that there was more than one gave her pause.

It also meant her buyer probably wasn't Mr. Damian.

Shivering, she tried to forget her fantasies of Mr.

Bastian and Mr. Desmond. As much as she loved menage stories with crossing swords, it wasn't realistic. They'd be horrified if she called them Daddy, and even if they were looking for a third, she wasn't their type.

Then again, Mr. Damian *had* seen her tattoo...

Nope. It wasn't possible. The artist had probably shared a photo of his work, and Mr. Damian had found it online somewhere. He had a lot of ink himself, and there was absolutely no connection between Club BDE and the Elliott brothers. She just couldn't picture any of them going to a kink club.

Pushing the idea of Mr. Bastian and Mr. Desmond bending her over a spanking bench out of her head, she poured another splash of wine into her mug and drank it. An email alert sounded from her laptop, making her swallow wrong.

Once she finished coughing, she deleted the junk advising her that she needed to pay Bitcoin to keep her porn addiction private, then opened the important one.

Under the heading, *Auction Contract and Details Inside*, was the winning bid. The money would be held in escrow until both parties signed off on the contract. Even subtracting taxes and the auction percentage, it was enough to pay off Mandy's house and cover Bee's school tuition for a few years.

It also wasn't a prime number. Tania knew she was being superstitious, but everyone needed something to be weirdly OCD about.

There were even instructions from the... buyers.

*Hello, Misty,*

*We are Daddy D and Daddy B. We first want to explain that you are under no obligation to accept the terms of the auction.*

*Full disclosure: We are bisexual males in a committed relationship with each other. Although we would like to share you, you will never be forced into a sexual act, and if two buyers isn't something you want, there will be no hard feelings. If you decide to back out, we will pay the $10,000 penalty.*

Damn it. It was like they knew what would get her off. Daddy D and Daddy B was exactly what she called Mr. Desmond and Mr. Bastian in her fantasies.

*Regardless of your choice to accept or refuse the terms of the auction, if you are in danger, homeless, or experiencing food insecurity, please reply to this email or call the number at the bottom. Your safety is very important to us.*

*We believe a woman's first time should be special, and if you accept us, we promise to do everything in our power to make sure you have a wonderful experience.*

*Swoon.* Christ, they were ticking all her buttons. A trickle of moisture dampened her panties, and she bit back a whimper of arousal. Between their concern for her safety and their words about making her first time special, she was about ready to slip her hand into her yoga pants just to take the edge off. They were even bisexual. It was like she'd picked them out of a catalogue. Hopefully, her vibrator was charged. It would be getting a workout.

*To that end, we're giving you the choice of location for our evening. You may choose one of Club BDE's private rooms, or we can reserve an Airbnb or hotel room. You may also choose to drive your personal vehicle or use a car service provided by the auction. Our schedule is flexible, so we'll leave the time and date up to you as long as it's within the fourteen-day limit.*

*Before you accept, we have some requests.*
*We understand your need for anonymity. However, we will be sharing a meal to give us a chance to get to know each other. Choose a mask which allows you to eat. Also, please let us know of any preferences, food sensitivities, or allergies.*

*Wear a skirt or dress. It need not be formal. You may wear stockings, but no tights or panties. A bra is optional. If you are unable to purchase a dress or the mask, we'll take care of it.*

*If you agree to penetrative sex, we will be wearing condoms from a sealed box. You may choose additional contraceptive measures as well.*

*Although we prefer your intimate areas to be waxed or shaved, we'll leave your personal grooming up to you.*

*Most importantly, you must edge yourself at least once per day until our meeting. This means you should touch yourself until you're ready to come, then stop before you climax. You must also email us when you've done so.*

*We look forward to meeting you.*

*Best,*
*Daddy D and Daddy B*

Tania fanned herself, wondering if she was about to spontaneously combust. It took every ounce of her self-control to stop herself from dialing the number to invite them over. Sadly, doing so would put her in the *too-stupid-to-live* category. It was one thing to meet strange men for sex in a private kink club or hotel, and quite another to let them know where she lived. Besides, her double bed probably wasn't big enough for three people.

She hit the icon to reply but didn't immediately start typing. Instead, she drank the last of her wine straight from the bottle and slipped her hand down the front of her pants.

The minute she touched her clit, Tania's belly tightened, and she gritted her teeth, trying desperately to force her climax back. She'd never come so close to orgasm so quickly but couldn't bring herself to disappoint her new Daddies. Whining softly, she pulled her hand free and began to type.

## BASTIAN

"Do you think Misty will say yes?" Desmond asked as he backed into their garage.

The door squeaked as it closed, reminding Bastian to fix it. Despite spending a fortune on renovations, it seemed like they were forever finding something in need of repair. Thankfully, they'd gotten to the point where most of them were small annoyances instead of big problems.

"I don't know."

"Maybe the bigger question is whether we want her to say yes." Desmond walked around the front of Bastian's car and went up the steps into the kitchen, leaving Bastian to follow.

"Having second thoughts?" Bastian got two glasses from the cupboard and filled both with water and ice from the fridge dispenser.

Desmond grimaced and took a sip from his drink. Although he didn't want to admit it, he couldn't lie to Bastian. "Depends. Will you think I'm a sick bastard for imagining Titania's face in place of Misty's?"

"We discussed this before the auction started." Bastian set his glass aside, then cradled the back of Desmond's head before taking his mouth in a teasing kiss. His cock thickened and he pressed himself against Desmond, letting his partner feel every inch of his need. He gentled his embrace, then added, "I guess we're both sick bastards."

Desmond chuckled and shook his head. "Fair enough. We just have to remember to call her Misty instead of Titania."

"I still wonder why she's auctioning her virginity."

After sitting on a stool at the breakfast bar, Desmond shrugged. "As long as she's not in danger, it's not really our business. We just have to do what we promised and show her a good time."

"Still..." Bastian sat next to him and laid his phone between them. "We should check to see if she responded. I can't help worrying."

"Me too."

Bastian logged into the auction site, knowing he and Desmond wouldn't rest until Misty confirmed her safety. Thankfully, there was a message waiting.

*Daddies D and B,*

*To set your minds at ease, I'm not in any danger, homeless, or experiencing food insecurity. I may live on ramen and take-out, but that's mostly because it's safer for everyone if I don't cook. I have a decent apartment, no debt, and no problems meeting my expenses.*

*All of that must make you wonder why I'm auctioning my virginity. I will only say that I'm doing this for a friend, and that I'm not under any duress. The individual I want to help is also not in any danger, etc.*

Bastian glanced at Desmond and chuckled when he sighed in relief. "Well, that takes care of our biggest concerns."

"Assuming she's telling the truth. I really want to know about the friend she mentioned."

"Same." Bastian leaned close to Desmond and rested a hand on his knee as they kept reading.

*I'm glad to hear your schedule is flexible. The only free day I have within the two-week time limit is next Saturday from six o'clock until midnight. I'd like us to share our evening in one of the private rooms at Club BDE. I don't need a ride or help with the dress and mask, but I appreciate the offer.*

*Yes, to the condoms, please and thank you.*

"Independent little thing, isn't she?" Desmond asked, smiling as he read. "I wonder what she does for a living."

"Dunno. I don't get the feeling she's in a rush to get the money." Bastian tried to control the hope growing in his chest. Despite her young age, Misty couldn't have sounded more perfect if she tried, and he liked that she appeared able to take care of herself. Unfortunately, he still wondered about her friend. It didn't sit well with him to know there might be a second person at risk.

*To answer your question regarding our meal, I don't have any allergies or food sensitivities. I'll eat anything I don't have to cook myself.*

*Anyway, on to your requests. Yes, to all of it, but I really hope we can make Saturday work because I had my hand in my pants the minute I finished reading your email. I mean, two bisexual Daddies? Where do I sign up? Heck, I should be paying you!*

*2KnottyDaddies? I don't know if you're into rope or omega-verse, but I'm down with either or both. Mercy, y'all are making me wet already, and I haven't even met you.*

*It's as if you stepped out of my fantasies like Lisa in that ancient movie* Weird Science. *I'm beginning to wonder if those people sending emails threatening to share my porn history have actually been watching me.*

*Also, I'm kind of a nerd and have no verbal filter. Sorry in advance if I've made you uncomfortable.*

He and Desmond burst out laughing. After catching his breath and wiping tears from his eyes, Bastian said, "Hey, maybe we should auction ourselves. Might give us enough to put in that infinity pool we've been wanting."

*Before you ask, I didn't let myself come, but I'm pretty sure I won't have enough self-control to do it for long. Please, Daddies, don't make me wait.*

*Best,*

~~Misty~~ *Miss T*

"We should spank her for calling *Weird Science* ancient," Desmond said.

Bastian's smile faded as he studied the email. "Victor used to love those eighties movies, and that one specifically. It's really strange she mentioned it."

"Yeah, I remember. Mandy said he even sent Titania a DVD of *Sixteen Candles* for her sixteenth birthday." Desmond frowned and scratched his beard. "It's probably nothing. The cable channels show those old movies all the time."

"True." Bastian finished his water, then put their glasses in the dishwasher, unable to stop himself from wondering. It was very odd for such a young woman to mention that particular film.

Worse, she'd changed Misty to Miss T. The correction made it even harder to stop himself from imagining Titania in bed with him and Desmond.

Desmond wrapped his arms around him and slid a hand down his stomach to stroke Bastian's cock. "Let's go to bed, Daddy B."

"Good idea." He took Desmond's hand to lead him to their bedroom, then sat on the loveseat in front of the fireplace. "Get undressed. Slowly."

Desmond smirked and unbuttoned his shirt to

reveal his trim abdomen dusted with crisp salt and pepper curls. Moving ever so slowly, he laid the shirt on the blanket chest at the foot of their bed, then slid his belt through the loops of his jeans as he toed off his shoes and socks.

The muscles in his arms flexing, Desmond unbuttoned his jeans and pushed them down his lean hips, revealing his thick erection. Bastian's mouth watered, and he crooked a finger at his partner.

"We'll discuss your punishment later. Kneel in front of me so I can fuck your throat."

"Yes, sir." Wearing nothing but a cocky grin, Desmond obeyed.

# PAINFUL REVELATIONS

TANIA

"**M**iss Andersen, could we talk?"

She let out her breath, then turned to face Dr. Pappas. The man had some balls to be coming for her after nearly a week of being edged until her brain cells floated in a soup of frustrated arousal.

Not that Pappas knew any of that.

It had crossed her mind more than once to cheat and let herself come, but she never did. Her Daddies had asked for that one thing, and she didn't want to disappoint them. Besides, one measly orgasm from her own fingers wouldn't assuage the aching need deep in her core, and she doubted her trusty vibrator was up to the task either.

By Wednesday, she'd given up on the auction messaging system and used the phone number they'd given her to text them when she touched herself. They might have asked for once a day, but they got more.

A lot more. And she wouldn't get relief for another whole day. She hadn't even seen the Daddies, and had no idea what they looked like, but that didn't seem to matter to her body. Heck, she'd ducked into the ladies' restroom between classes more than once.

They seemed delighted to hear about her desperation, which drove her desire for them even higher. Having her pubic hair removed hadn't helped, and the group texts with both of them made it even worse. Everything was too slick... too sensitive, and she couldn't help imagining one or both of them licking her silky pussy.

Not wanting to spoil the surprise, she hadn't yet told them of her trip to the day spa. She even had a sexy dress and a mask that would cover the top half of her face and had already gotten her health screening. Luckily, the timing had been perfect for her birth control shot to be immediately effective.

"Is this regarding my coursework?" she finally asked.

Dr. Pappas reached for her hand, then apparently

thought better of the idea, and didn't touch her. Maybe her complaints to Dr. Ng hadn't been ignored.

"You seem distracted, dear. Is my class finally getting the better of you?"

Christ. If Dr. Pappas had taken his eyes off her tits long enough to notice, she wasn't hiding her need for her Daddies as well as she'd thought.

"I'm fine." She turned to leave, but he caught her hand. After pulling away, she added, "Thank you for your concern."

"That's good to hear. I'd like to discuss our future relationship."

"Interesting."

After licking his lower lip, Dr. Pappas smirked at her. "What is, my dear?"

"Are you offering to pay my tuition, sir?"

"Excuse me?" His smile faded and he frowned in confusion. "What do you mean?"

"Well, since you apparently weren't listening to me when I told you I couldn't afford grad school, you must be offering to pay my tuition."

"I... Well..." A bead of sweat trickled down his temple.

"As I told you last week, we don't have a future or a relationship. I still can't afford to attend grad school, and I don't have time for dating. Even if I did, it wouldn't be with one of my instructors." She picked up her backpack and slung the strap over her shoulder. "And I'm still not interested."

"Don't forget you need my class to graduate."

Slowly, Tania turned to face him, wondering if he was saying what she suspected. Did he honestly think it would work?

Who was she kidding? Of course he did. He didn't even seem to care that there were still students in the classroom.

"I'm aware. I also have a ninety-eight percent without benefit of a curve."

His eyes glittered spitefully as a faint smile ghosted across his thin lips. "You still have a midterm and final to go, and they'll be quite difficult. I'll also be one of the judges for your senior project."

Tears burned her sinuses, threatening to spill from her eyes, but she wouldn't give him the satisfaction. Instead of screaming her rage, she walked out, pushing past Jason in her haste to get away before she did something that might get her arrested, or worse, thrown out of school.

She hated herself for running too. After over three years of standing up for herself, she was reduced to scurrying away like a mouse running from a cat. She especially hated that she'd done it in front of an audience.

"Tania! Wait up!"

She broke into a jog, ignoring Jason as she crossed the quad toward the parking garage. He wouldn't have anything productive to say. In fact, she could almost picture his delighted sneers. The old boys' club was alive and well in academia, and she wanted no part of it.

It was also still prominent in some industries, and definitely hers, but she wouldn't have to stay in a toxic work environment. Transferring to a different university wasn't a viable option—not when she was almost halfway through her senior year—and with her luck, one of her new instructors would be equally heinous.

Tania considered going to Dr. Ng again, but it was clear he wouldn't do anything, and she wasn't stupid enough to expect Jason to corroborate her story. What was the point of even trying?

God, she wished she could talk to her Daddies. Except they weren't. Although she looked forward to their texts and was beginning to like them, they were paying for her virginity and nothing more. After their date, she'd never see them again.

It was a transaction—not a date. Calling it that implied friendship, or at least a common interest in something. There wouldn't be conversations in coffee shops or over a meal, no movies, football games, or concerts.

No... nothing.

A cold tear trickled down her cheek as she tossed her backpack in the trunk before getting into her car. She hauled in a breath and tried to pull herself together before she backed out of her parking spot.

To her surprise, she saw Jason as she drove to the garage exit. He shouted her name and waved frantically for her to stop, but she pretended not to notice him and went home. He was the second to last person she wanted to see.

The minute the door to her apartment was closed and locked behind her, she fell into bed and pulled the covers over her head, letting her tears soak her pillow. She'd taken off her shoes, at least, but didn't undress or bother with whatever leftovers were in her refrigerator. Her stomach would probably revolt if she tried to eat.

Her phone buzzed with an incoming message, and without looking at it, she silenced the notification. There was no one she wanted to talk to, and she didn't want to read a text from the Daddies when she had no desire to play their stupid little edging game anymore.

All she had to do was meet them at Club BDE, get her cherry popped, sign off on completion of the agreement, and walk away. She didn't have to like the Daddies, and although it would be a bonus if she enjoyed herself, it wasn't required. She had her vibrator for that.

Maybe once she got rid of the hormones flooding her brain, she could figure a way out of the situation with Dr. Pappas.

Everything would go back to normal. It just had to.

DESMOND

"Do you think she'll show?"

Bastian shrugged and checked his phone, then gazed across the crowded club. "She still has ten minutes."

"Yeah, but she hasn't messaged us since yesterday. Do you think she—"

"Des." Bastian turned to face him and rested his hands on Desmond's shoulders. "We already talked to Braden, and he agreed to let her in without a background check so we can ensure her safety. If she doesn't show, we'll ask Ray at the department to search her phone number and do a wellness check. Try not to worry."

"Yeah, I..." Desmond frowned at the sound of

raised voices coming from a station across the main play area, then turned to face the disturbance.

Shane, a submissive who usually spent most of his club time collecting gossip while he passed out candy corn, stood toe to toe with a man dressed in old-guard leather that didn't match his white button-down shirt, glasses, and thinning brown hair. Shane's ferocious scowl was completely at odds with his usual cheerful demeanor, and when the man reached for him, Shane knocked his hand away.

Before Desmond could think to intervene, Shane tilted his nose into the air and stalked off, his sculpted ass twitching in gold lamé pants paired with a lacy shirt under a corset vest. He detoured to Vivian at the reception desk to whisper something in her ear, then glared over his shoulder at the man.

"Wonder what that was about," Bastian murmured.

"Yeah. Been a long time since I've seen Shane about to throw down with someone. Want to check it out?"

"I think he's okay. The leather wannabe isn't following him." Desmond smirked, then added, "Remember what happened the last time some asshole thought he was an easy mark? We were sweeping up teeth for hours."

Shane might be a sub, but he was nobody's doormat. Although it took a lot to set him off, he had a nasty tendency to break bones when he was disrespected. Despite that, he was one of the kindest men Desmond had ever met and didn't start fights. New submissives were always sent his way for mentoring, and he often stood up to protect them from abusive Doms.

Desmond made a note to bring the leather wannabe to Braden's attention. With the auctions putting them at risk, they didn't need a clueless baby Dom causing trouble.

He'd never worried about new people coming in before, but every stranger was a potential threat now, and if the leather dude managed to piss off Shane, he didn't need to be in the club.

Out of the corner of his eye, he saw a curvaceous woman in a black dress sidle toward the reception desk. She kept her head down, but he saw the edges of feathers on the side of her head as she tried to fix a mask in place. Although many people wore masks to Club BDE, Desmond stilled and focused on her, wondering if she was Miss T.

"Titania, darling!" The leather wannabe grabbed her arm and swung her around to face him.

Her plump lips—the same ones he'd imagined wrapped around his cock more times than he cared to count—parted in shock. The mask fell from her fingers, and she jerked free, then backed away from the wannabe.

The dress hugged Titania's sumptuous curves, revealing a woman grown instead of the girl Desmond remembered. Skillfully applied makeup highlighted her chiseled jaw and cheekbones, and her full mouth was painted scarlet.

Most damning of all was the inked formula on the inside of her wrist, visible when she lifted her hand as if to ward someone off. Desmond shook his head, trying to make sense of what he was seeing.

Victor wouldn't have left Titania in a position to need to sell her virginity, and he couldn't understand why she'd go so far to help a friend as she'd claimed.

"Oh, god." Bastian grabbed his arm, his fingers digging into Desmond's triceps. "No."

He jerked out of Bastian's grip and dashed across the club, desperate to get her to safety. Before he could reach her, Titania gazed at the man in horror and covered her mouth with a shaking hand. Shane positioned himself between her and the leather wannabe and slowly shook his head.

"Don't," he murmured. "Just don't."

The man sneered and drew himself up in an attempt to make himself look bigger. "Get out of my way, faggot."

Ignoring him, Shane turned to Titania. "Okay,

sweetheart. It's time for you to go. I'll keep him from following you."

Desmond eased his way past the wannabe and reached for her hand. "Titania, you shouldn't be here."

"No shit." She glanced at Bastian and took a step backward toward the door. "This is the fucking worst night of my life."

Before he could reply, she darted outside and vanished into the dark.

"Titania, wait! We need to discuss our future," the man shouted.

When he attempted to follow, Shane clotheslined him and slammed him against the wall. "First off, my sexual orientation is none of your business," he purred. "Secondly, the lady didn't look like she wanted anything to do with you. You want to follow her, you're gonna do it in a body bag."

"We'll see her to her car," Bastian said. "Hold the asshole until she's gone."

"No." Shane gazed at him dispassionately and tightened his hold on the wannabe until he squeaked. "Sorry, Daddies. If she wanted you, she'd have stuck around, so you'll need to take your big dick energy somewhere else."

"Shane, it's okay. We know her," Desmond replied.

"I. Said. No." He winked, then added, "If you could see your way clear to ask Mistress Rogue to give me a scene, I might be convinced to let you keep your cute faces all pretty and unbroken."

As much as Desmond appreciated his protectiveness for the club's female subs, he needed to get to Titania. Unfortunately, tangling with Shane wasn't on his to-do list tonight and would probably end up with him and Bastian in traction.

Besides, they had other ways of finding her.

"Fine," he finally said, forcibly stopping himself before he chased her down and paddled her ass for putting herself at risk.

"Braden is on his way," Bastian said. "We'll get this asshole banned."

"You can't ban me!" the man shouted. "Do you know who I am?"

"I sure do," Braden strolled closer, showing teeth in an unpleasant smile. "You're a banned former member who decided it was okay to call another member ugly names and grab a woman without her consent. Your name doesn't matter."

## FLIGHT DOESN'T MEAN
## ESCAPE

TANIA

*Just fucking perfect.*

Pressing her foot down on the accelerator, she merged onto I-26 heading northwest out of Charleston. Her hands shook and tears burned in her sinuses, but she managed to get on the expressway without killing herself.

"Let me count the ways I can fuck up my life," she muttered as she passed the I-95 interchange that would have taken her to school. She'd have to go back but couldn't face it just yet.

If her situation hadn't been so dire, she might have laughed at the sight of Dr. Pappas in cheap leather pants and a vest over his short-sleeved white dress shirt. God, he looked ridiculous, but his presence in the club raised a lot of questions she wasn't sure she wanted answered.

Had he followed her? She shivered and swallowed hard before remembering he'd gotten there before her. The thought of him with an impact toy was unsettling enough. Besides, unless he hacked her phone or email, there was no way he could have known she'd be there.

Then again, his absurd outfit meant he'd done at least a little planning before going to Club BDE.

Dr. Pappas wasn't the only one she wanted to avoid. She definitely would have dodged Mr. Bastian and Mr. Desmond before they spotted her.

Daddies D and B, indeed. How could she have been so damned stupid to miss the connection? Mr. Damian had asked about her tattoo, and he was Mr. Desmond's brother.

Tania didn't know what was worse. Actually, she did. She could avoid Bastian and the Elliott brothers forever and ever, amen, but she'd have to face Dr. Pappas three days a week until the end of the semester if she wanted to graduate. There was still the issue of him being on the judging committee for her senior project too.

She shivered and tried to think. Her scholarship didn't have a moral turpitude clause, but the school did. It went without saying that Dr. Pappas would threaten her with exposure if she didn't agree to be his graduate assistant, but he'd also been in the club, and she had zero qualms about calling his dumb ass out. After all, if he hadn't been there, he wouldn't have seen her.

Unfortunately, he was tenured, and she was an undergrad. He'd get a slap on the wrist and a wink-wink, nudge-nudge, and she'd get expelled, despite having done nothing wrong.

"Boys will be boys. Close your mouth and open your legs. Don't complain when they call you a slut for doing what they want because they'll call you a bitch if you don't, and lie about it anyway," she mocked. "You'd be so pretty if you smiled."

*You'd be so pretty with a knife in your chest.*

Fuck's sake, she couldn't even go to the grocery store without some asshole telling her to smile. She scrubbed a hand over the carefully applied smoky eye she'd learned from YouTube and screamed her rage to an uncaring sky.

"I don't want to be pretty!" She stomped on the accelerator and screamed again. "I don't want to fucking smile, and boys should grow the fuck up and be men! What stupid ass shit is it to spend six figures to be a woman's first lover anyway? It's like they're dogs pissing on fire hydrants."

Teeth bared, she swerved through traffic, passing

slower vehicles in a desperate attempt to get away from the shitstorm of her life.

The blue lights flashing behind her, with accompanying sirens, were just a passing annoyance that didn't surprise her in the slightest. In fact, it was almost mundane.

What was a speeding ticket in the grand scheme of things?

She pulled over, angling her car to protect the trooper. Instead of lamenting her fate, she grabbed her registration and insurance card from the glovebox and her license from her purse.

Once she had her documents in hand, she lowered her window and waited for the trooper to lean down and peer at her.

"Ma'am, do you know how fast you were going?"

"No, sir." She handed him everything he'd eventually ask for but didn't look at him. "I have pepper spray, but no firearms or other weapons, and you have permission to search my car. If you could just give me the ticket, I'll be on my way."

"Ma'am?"

"What?" She forced herself to look at the surprisingly young officer, whose nametag read E. Reyes. "I'm sorry. I don't know what else to give you. I've never gotten a ticket before."

He cleared his throat and narrowed his eyes at her

smeared makeup and the reddened marks on her arm from where Dr. Pappas grabbed her. "Are you safe?" he finally asked.

"Define safe." Tania sighed and leaned against the headrest. "Sorry. I'm fine. Just give me the ticket, please."

"Here, take this." He pressed a card into her hand and straightened. "It's about twenty miles west and has private security. Nobody will get to you there."

She glanced down at the card containing the name and address of a women's shelter and sighed before handing it back. "This isn't for me, but thank you for offering."

"Ma'am..." He leaned down and rested his elbows on the door. "They can help you."

"No, seriously, I'm good." She hesitated, then added, "I'm a college student. One of my professors is trying to coerce me into being his fuck toy slash grad assistant, and I kind of did something stupid, but I'm not in danger of him hurting me."

He glanced at her license and shook his head. "Ms. Andersen, you might think he won't hurt you, but there are all kinds of hurt."

"Tell me about it." She gave him a wan smile, then added, "It's going to be okay. Do you know why?"

"Um...why?"

"Because I met someone tonight who is truly

kind." Tania laid her hand atop his and her smile warmed. "Just out of the blue, I met a South Carolina state trooper who gave me the address of a women's shelter instead of a ticket, and didn't tell me I'd be prettier if I smiled while he steals my work for his own gain. Meeting him gives me hope that not everyone with a Y chromosome is a dick."

"Ouch, but you didn't meet me quite out of the blue." He chuckled, then added, "You were doing ninety-five in a seventy zone."

"Whoops." She squeezed his hand, then let him go. "Now, about that ticket..."

◈

## BASTIAN

"Dr. Marinos Pappas." Desmond threw a sheet of paper on his desk. "Titania has a class with him."

He rubbed his eyes and tried to focus on the information. They'd been up too late with Braden going over Club BDE's membership. "What do we know about him?"

"Braden's background check is pretty thorough, and there wasn't much to find." Desmond lowered himself into a chair on the other side of Bastian's desk and sighed. "He's in his first year of tenure. No issues aside from a few students complaining about his grading policies."

"Hmm." He drummed his fingers on his desk, then turned to gaze out the window at the sun rising over the beach. "Any criminal record?"

"Just a couple of traffic violations, and nothing requiring a court appearance." Desmond pulled his chair around and sat next to him, then took his hand. "I wish I knew what he meant when he mentioned talking to Titania about their future."

"You think they're seeing each other?"

Bastian tightened his fist on the arm of his chair until the leather creaked, then forced himself to relax. It wasn't his business who she dated. Hell, they'd even paid the cancelation fee for the auction, and still didn't know why she needed the money.

He tried to brush his disappointment aside. He and Desmond had promised Victor they'd take care of Titania—not take her to bed—and he had no right to wish they hadn't canceled the auction. Unfortunately, he couldn't control his jealous rage at the thought of that asshole touching her. Bastian hadn't missed the reddened fingerprints he left on her arm and had to forcibly push the memory away before he hunted the bastard down.

"Doubt it." Desmond topped off their coffee cups, then returned to his chair. "Judging by the look on her face when she saw him, he was the last person she wanted to see."

"True, but it might have been because she was stepping out on him to meet us."

"No." Desmond took out his phone then scrolled through the messages she'd sent. "We asked her if she was seeing anyone, and she said she didn't have time to date."

"She also might have been lying. Hell, she might not even be a virgin."

"You're kidding, right?" Desmond snorted and turned to glare at him. "We've known that girl since she was in diapers. Has she ever lied to either of us?"

"I—"

"Hell, Bastian, she never got so much as a detention the whole time she was in school, and I seriously doubt she'd be stupid enough to date one of her instructors. Why are you determined to think the worst of her?"

Bastian pressed his lips together and gazed at the coffee in his cup as if it held the answers to all his questions. Desmond had a point, and it didn't feel right to think Titania would do something so underhanded. However, it wouldn't be the first time a woman lied to them—and Desmond got hurt every time.

"I don't know," he finally said. "She was never

prone to lying when she was a kid, but how do you explain what Dr. Pappas said?"

"There's an easy way to find out." Desmond pulled him to his feet and dragged him from the office. "Let's get dressed. We're going to her apartment to ask."

It was no great challenge to get her address and her car's license plate number. He didn't feel all that guilty for invading her privacy either. Victor would have wanted him and Desmond to keep his daughter safe—even if she was lying.

That's what he told himself as they took I-95 north to her university anyway. If he was wrong and she wasn't trying to pull a fast one, she needed their help to get out of whatever the situation was with Dr. Pappas.

Bastian found street parking half a block from Titania's apartment building. It seemed secure enough, with a locked entrance, and well-lit parking, and was the type of place the daughter of a cop would choose.

"There isn't a buzzer," Desmond said. "Do we call her?"

"It's either that, or camp outside the door until she comes out." He detoured to the parking lot to look for her vehicle and found it parked under a halogen light mounted on the side of the building. "Looks like she's home."

They returned to the front entrance, and Bastian's ears pricked when he heard a lanky young man with dishwater blond hair shout Titania's name into his phone.

"Call the cops if you want, Tania. I'm not leaving until you talk to me."

"Christ," Bastian muttered, wondering if history was repeating itself. "Does the girl have a magic pussy, or what? She must have a damned revolving door to her bedroom."

Desmond stiffened, then slowly turned to face him. "I'm going to forget you said that instead of breaking your fucking face. Regardless of what you think, she's Victor's daughter. If you can't—"

"What the fuck, Jason?" Titania's angry screech was punctuated by the door slamming behind her. She wore a faded blue T-shirt covered in what looked like grease stains, sweatpants cut off at the knee, and socks with flip flops. Her hair stuck up in messy spikes and her eyes were swollen with dark circles under them.

"Hey, Tania, I—"

"No. I'm not some asshole's ornament, and I don't owe you a goddamned smile. I don't have to be nice, or even talk to you if I don't want to, and you don't get to—"

Bastian blinked at the stream of fury coming from her mouth. What had happened to her? The Titania he remembered was soft-spoken and shy and wouldn't have stood on a street tearing into a young man like that.

"God, you're a bitch." Jason rubbed his face and his shoulders slumped. "I just wanted to tell you I reported Dr. Pappas for what he said, and I talked Hassan and Owen into doing the same."

"I—" Her lips parted, and she blinked. "I'm sorry. What did you say?"

Titania and Jason hadn't seen them, and he wanted to drag her away from the young man to get some straight answers. Before he could move, Desmond grabbed his hand and pulled him to a stop, then silently shook his head. Together, they ducked behind a tree to listen.

"You drove right past me after it happened," he muttered, scowling at her. "I was going to tell you then."

"Why did you do that? You don't even like me."

"I really don't. You're kind of mean." Jason shrugged, then added, "But it was so gross, and then I thought about some dickweed pressuring my girl-friend into being his grad assistant with benefits, so here I am. I also reported all the times I heard him proposition you."

"Wow. I—"

"And then for him to double down after you told him you couldn't afford grad school…" Jason shook his head. "Anyway, I hope it helps."

No wonder she'd looked so panicked when she saw Dr. Pappas. Judging from her reaction, and Dr. Pappas's comment about their relationship, Bastian wouldn't put it past him to threaten her with exposure to force her to comply either.

His stomach soured with guilt. Desmond had been right all along, and he'd misjudged her. Even if she hadn't heard any of the nasty things he'd said, he owed her and Desmond an apology.

However, he wasn't wrong about Dr. Pappas. Hopefully Jason's report would solve the problem, but if it didn't…

He and Desmond were more than up to the task of making him rethink his harassment of Titania.

# 7

# UNEXPECTED VISITORS

TANIA

"Wow." She pulled Jason into a tight embrace, hardly daring to believe he'd actually helped her. "I don't know what to say except thank you. I'd also like to buy you supper. I can invite Hassan and Owen too."

She let out a slightly hysterical giggle, then added, "Hell, I'll invite the whole damned class."

"I talked to everyone else, and we decided we'll keep him from bothering you in class, but you don't owe us shit." He extricated himself from her hug and flushed. "Just... you know, maybe pretend you think the rest of us are actually human and worth talking to once in a while."

"I will. Promise, and I'm really sorry for going off

on you. It's been a day, but you didn't deserve that. Are you sure I can't take you out? I owe you big."

"Nah. I'm good." He winked, then added, "My girlfriend wanted me to ask you something though."

"Oh?"

"She wants to know if you'll help her with calculus. I tried, but I'm a shit tutor."

"I'll help as much as she wants until she gets a passing grade. It's the least I can do."

"Cool." Jason scribbled his girlfriend's name and number on an old receipt and gave it to her. "Anyway, I'm taking off. See ya."

Jason was right. She was a bitch. That hadn't been her intent when she decided to stand up for herself. One could be assertive without being unkind.

For a single moment, she considered telling Jason she'd found Dr. Pappas at Club BDE but changed her mind. With luck, Dr. Pappas wouldn't bring it up, and she really didn't want the news spread all over campus. Jason might have done her a really big favor, but it wasn't in her best interest to trust him too far.

She could be nice to Jason without giving him her innermost secrets.

With a last wave, he got into a small sedan and drove away.

Sighing with relief, she turned to go inside to get cleaned up and put on something that didn't make her look homeless. Hopefully, Jason's report would do the trick and get Pappas off her back.

Before she could open the door, the hair on the nape of her neck prickled as the last person she wanted to see spoke.

"Titania."

Slowly, she turned to face Mr. Bastian. She should have known her weekend of shit wasn't over, and she absolutely hated that he and Mr. Desmond looked so perfectly put together in casual trousers and pressed shirts. She hadn't showered, and still wore what she'd put on after throwing that damned black dress into the trash. Heck, she hadn't bothered removing her makeup.

Despite knowing they were probably furious with her, she lifted her chin. "Why are you here?"

Mr. Desmond tilted his head toward the door. "Let's go inside before we talk."

"Fine." Although she didn't want them in her apartment, she led them up the stairs and opened the door to let them in. Instead of inviting them to sit, she added, "I'll pay you back for the auction cancelation fee. I tried to pay it last night, but my account was already settled."

Mr. Desmond sat on the edge of her futon couch as if he expected it to collapse under him. "Interesting."

"Very interesting," Mr. Bastian replied as he sat next to Mr. Desmond. "Why would you need to auction your virginity if you have that kind of money available?"

She actually didn't have the money. She'd planned to put it on her credit card, then get a part time job to cover it.

"First of all, I don't have to share my reasons. Secondly, it's none of your business."

"Titania..." Mr. Bastian reached for her hand, then sighed when she moved out of reach. "We want to help. Whatever it is, your father would have wanted us to do that."

The anger she thought she'd successfully quelled rose up, hot and poisonous, and she couldn't stop the words. "Yeah, dear old Victor was so damned concerned about our welfare that he decided to die without leaving Mandy a corpse to bury. She's so convinced he isn't dead that she spent every penny of what he left trying to find his dumb ass. I did the auction to earn enough to pay off the mortgage on her house."

Mr. Bastian straightened and shared a look with Mr. Desmond. "Titania, how is this possible? Your father wouldn't have left you without—"

"The old bastard left plenty—except the one thing we needed." She scowled, wishing it was late enough in the day for a glass of wine. "If he'd just left a body like a normal person, Mandy wouldn't have spent almost a million dollars on private investigators."

"Honey, he was your father," Mr. Desmond said. "Could you show him some respect?"

Tania burst out laughing and shook her head. Respect was the last thing Victor deserved. She just wished she could stop the words. There was no reason for her to unload on Mr. Desmond and Mr. Bastian, but it was like they'd opened the floodgates on all the things she couldn't say to Mandy or one of her few friends.

Maybe it was better this way. Once she got rid of them, she wouldn't have to talk to Mr. Desmond or Mr. Bastian again. It wasn't like they'd come around to the house to see Mandy and Bee, and hell would freeze over before she set foot in Club BDE again.

"Really? You're coming for me with that? At best, Victor was a sperm donor. He barely waited for my mother's body to get cold before he vanished. I didn't see him for years until he married Mandy."

"Titania—"

"You know what's worse?" She scraped her hands through her tangled hair and glared at Mr. Desmond. "She actually loves the bastard, and I'm pretty sure he married her so he wouldn't have to keep paying a nanny to take care of me. He certainly didn't give a shit about forcing her to parent someone so close to her age."

"Hey, sweetie. It's going to be okay." Mr. Desmond caught her and put his hands on her shoulders, but she couldn't take comfort from it. "We can help you."

"He couldn't..." After jerking free of his touch, she paced the tiny apartment and tried to pull herself together before she burst into tears. "Look. It's not your problem. We'll be fine."

Before she could protest, they squeezed her into a hug between them. The tears she thought she could keep at bay trickled down her cheeks and she choked on a sob.

Worse, her stupid body still wanted them, and being in their arms was everything she'd ever dreamed of. They wore the same aftershave with hints of pine and leather, and the sound of their beating hearts filled her ears.

"We've got you, Titania. It's going to be all right," Mr. Bastian murmured into her hair, his powerful arms wrapping her even tighter in his embrace.

She wanted to be there forever, but she couldn't pawn her issues off on them. She was a freaking grownup—or she would be in less than eight months anyway. Despite whatever misguided posthumous promises they'd made to themselves on her dead father's behalf, she and Mandy weren't their responsibility.

"Look. I said it's not your problem." She pulled away and wiped her eyes, then went to the door and opened it. "Please, just get out. I'll deal with it myself."

❦

## DESMOND

With every word Titania spoke, his anger grew, both at Victor, and at Bastian for misjudging her so harshly.

How had they failed to see the mess Victor left in his wake? He was their friend, and although he'd tried to take care of Titania, Mandy, and Bee, Mandy's financial irresponsibility left Titania in the same position Emily and Lottie had been in before Damian and Braden had claimed them—broke and suffering because of their parents' behavior.

And just like Emily and Lottie, Titania was trying to clean up the mess by herself. Desmond didn't blame her for being furious, but he wasn't about to leave her. If Bastian wanted to be a dick about it...

Well, they'd discuss it later. Titania was more

important. He crossed the room and embraced her before closing the door. Ignoring her struggles, he marched her back to the couch, then pulled her down to sit next to him.

"Sweetheart." He cupped her cheek and gently turned her face until she was looking at him. God, even with smeared makeup and unwashed hair, she was about the prettiest thing he'd ever seen. "We're not leaving until we have a plan to take care of Mandy and Bee."

Bastian sat on the couch next to her and wrapped his long arms around her and Desmond. "And then we're going to talk about Dr. Pappas."

Squeezing Desmond's arm, Bastian nodded imperceptibly, making Desmond release the tension tightening his belly. He hadn't been looking forward to what had promised to be a stupendous fight with his partner and best friend.

"Ew." She shuddered but didn't try to get free. "Dr. Pappas is the last person I want to think about, and I'm not going to discuss Mandy and Bee with you. I said I'd take care of it."

Damn it. He still wanted to paddle her ass, both for putting herself at risk with the auction and for her snark, but he couldn't when all she'd wanted was to help her family.

His cock twitched and he tightened his jaw in a

desperate attempt to keep his erection from growing at the thought of spanking her cute butt until it was red and she was crying his name.

"How?" Desmond asked, once he thought he had himself under control. "Do you have a plan?"

"Not at present. The auction was the best I could come up with." Sighing, she shook her head. "Since that won't work, I'll get a part-time job or something."

"Let's forget about the auction and Dr. Pappas for the moment." Bastian set his phone on the coffee table, which was a piece of old shelving set on cinder blocks. "I'm more concerned about getting Mandy and Bee stable without you having to sacrifice your future. Do you know how much is left on the mortgage?"

"About fifty thousand, but really, this isn't your—"

Shaking his head, Bastian laid his hand over her mouth. "Babygirl, I know you mean well, but one more argument will buy you a spanking. Stop being so damned independent and let us help."

After batting his hand away, she wriggled free and stood with her hands on her hips. "Why do you even care?"

His face fixed into implacability, Bastian rose to his feet and stalked her, not stopping until she was backed up against the kitchen counter. He got into her space, crowding her until she swallowed hard and looked up into his eyes.

"Babygirl, until Dr. Pappas showed up, you were willing to give us your innocence. You spent a week tormenting us with how many times you edged yourself at our command. I'd say that makes us your Daddies, at least temporarily."

Her cheeks flushing scarlet, she looked away. "That was then. This is now. I'd like you to leave."

"No." Desmond crowded her from the other side, trapping her between him and Bastian. "That's not how this works. We're not going to touch you inappropriately, but you're going to sit still and listen while we work out a plan to take care of Mandy and your sister."

"And after that, we'll deal with Dr. Pappas for you," Bastian added. "So, obey your Daddies, sit your cute butt down, and behave."

"Fine!" Scowling, she pushed past them and dragged a kitchen chair into the living room. After seating herself, she folded her arms. "Let's get this over with."

Her decision to sit apart from them didn't go unnoticed, but Desmond let it slide. It was probably the best choice anyway. He wasn't sure he could have stayed so close to her without letting his libido get the better of him.

Glaring at Titania as if he expected her to disobey and was looking forward to punishing her, Bastian tapped the screen on his phone and set up a conference call with Braden and Damian, putting it on speaker.

Braden answered first. Before he could speak, Bastian said, "Hey, Braden. We have a situation. You're on speaker, and we're waiting for Damian to pick up."

"Okay. First: Have you or Desmond talked to Titania? Mandy doesn't know where she is, and she isn't answering her phone."

"We found her," Desmond replied. "That's what we need to talk about, but let's wait for Damian."

"Is she with you?" Braden asked.

"Yeah." Desmond lifted a hand to stop her before she could speak. "We're at her apartment with her. She's not going anywhere."

"Good." Braden let out an audible breath. "Young lady, do you have any idea how much trouble you're in?"

"Oh, for fuck's sake." Titania rolled her eyes and sighed. "It's not like Tweedles Dee and Dum are going to let me leave my own home. Can we just get on with this so they can go away?"

# 8

# SUPPER AND SORE BOTTOMS

TANIA

"**B**raden, we'll have to call you back."

Without waiting for an answer, Mr. Bastian ended the call. He didn't give her time to move or react before he jerked her from her uncomfortable kitchen chair and hauled her face down over his lap.

His hand crashed against her ass in a painful spank, followed by a storm of blows like he was beating a drum.

"Bastian!" She howled in anger mixed with pain, and when she tried to escape, Desmond trapped her legs to hold her still. "What the fuck? Ow!"

"Young ladies shouldn't swear."

*Whack. Whack. Whack.*

Desmond followed up with, "And they need to be respectful to the people trying to help them."

*Whack.*

"Oh! Ow! That fucking hurts!"

She'd always imagined them spanking her, but her fantasies were less pain and more sexy times. What they were doing shouldn't have been sexy.

No, she couldn't say she enjoyed getting a punishment spanking, Except...

Somehow, she did.

Bastian's hand on her ass hurt but felt strangely good at the same time. Her pussy dampened as the heat from her punished bottom went deeper into her core, and every time he spanked her, the movement rubbed her needy center against the hard muscle of his thigh. She bit back a moan, knowing it was the absolute worst time to tell a man who seemed hell bent on beating the sass out of her that his punishment wasn't doing what he'd intended.

"A punishment spanking is supposed to hurt." Bastian delivered several hard blows to the tender crease between her ass and thighs. "Young ladies should definitely not put themselves at risk in an auction for their virginity. Do you have any idea what could have happened to you?"

Desmond knelt and grabbed her hair to make her

look at him. "And they should always come to their Daddies when they need help."

She could let go. Release all the tension she'd held since she was five and Victor introduced her to the first in a long line of transient nannies while he went out and did whatever he did with his life.

Giving in to Desmond and Bastian was a single step, and sounded easy on the surface, but she'd given her trust so many damned times already.

*Will I see Dad on Christmas morning?*

Tania was ten before she finally stopped asking that dumbass question. Although Victor never let a holiday go by without presents, expecting him to show up when she opened them was as much a childhood fantasy as Santa Claus.

Bastian and Desmond cared enough to call her out for being stupid when she put herself up for auction. They chased her down at school, offered to help with Mandy's house, and with Dr. Pappas.

Then there was the man at the club with the corset and gold pants. He might have looked too submissive to protect her, but she hadn't missed how Dr. Pappas backed down from him.

Aside from the state trooper, who hadn't given her the ticket she deserved, the man in the gold pants was another person who cared what happened to her, and he didn't even know her.

Would it be so bad to let Bastian and Desmond in?

No, but also yes. It would be one thing if they couldn't help. She'd be no worse off than she was now, and she couldn't expect them to subsidize the mortgage on Mandy's house, much less pay it off. Unfortunately, trusting them would be giving them a way to hurt her like Victor had done for so many years.

Bastian tightened his fingers on her abused ass as Desmond kissed her forehead.

"Babygirl..." Desmond's voice softened, and he wiped a tear from her cheek. "Let us help you. Please."

With that one word, the sobs came, thick and choking as she cried for all the hurts, all the isolation, and all the times she'd needed her dad when he was too self-absorbed to care.

She cried for Mandy, who, like her, was lost in a world that didn't give two shits if she lived or died. She bawled her heart out for Bee, who would never know a father who should have loved her.

And most of all, as Desmond and Bastian cuddled her in their laps and tried to soothe her with soft touches and softer words, she cried for herself.

Letting everything go, she closed her eyes and let them hold her as she drifted into exhausted slumber.

The scent of cooking food and the sound of low voices woke her.

Did her oven even work?

She blinked and sat up, squinting at the setting sun through her bedroom window. Unsurprisingly, Bastian and Desmond had tucked her into bed.

Her belly rumbled as she tried to remember the last time she'd eaten more than a handful of chips. Was it two days ago or three? Her clothes fell in a trail as she trudged to the bathroom to shower off the grime left from her meltdown and a truly heinous weekend.

It had been too much to hope Desmond and Bastian were gone. She just wasn't that lucky and didn't need the smell of cooking food or the sound of their conversation to tell her they weren't going to leave her alone.

Despite her nap, she was too tired to even be embarrassed over them spanking her.

After cleaning up, she dressed in yoga pants and her favorite cotton sweater, then trudged from her bedroom to face the music.

"Hey, babygirl. Did you have a nice nap?" Desmond asked from his spot in front of the stove, which apparently did work. He slid a skillet forward, then back, tossing mushrooms into the air before catching them expertly.

"Um, yes?"

Bastian poured a glass of wine and gave it to her. It was an actual glass, which she didn't own, and there definitely hadn't been such an expensive vintage in her fridge. "Supper will be ready in a few."

## BASTIAN

Desmond checked the temperature of the prime rib roast, then left it to rest before adding a splash of wine to the sauteed mushrooms.

"Holy—" Titania glanced at him and winced, obviously remembering her spanking. "Holy sugar. I didn't know my oven even worked. Everything smells delicious."

"Thanks. There's steamed asparagus and rolls too." Desmond gave the mushrooms another toss, then jerked his head toward Bastian. "You could help Daddy Bastian with the salad."

Out of the corner of his eye, Bastian watched her flush as she cleared her throat. He hid a smirk, wondering if she'd call him Daddy as Desmond suggested.

"I know I didn't have actual food like this in my fridge," she finally said. Lifting her glass, she added, "Or this wine."

She hadn't even had real silverware, much less anything else she'd need to prepare a meal. They'd only found a few plastic spoons and forks, which had obviously come from takeout meals.

"You didn't." Bastian handed her a tomato and a kitchen knife. "I watched over you while Desmond went for food."

"We're going to discuss your eating habits too, babygirl." Desmond slid the mushrooms into a bowl and topped them with chopped parsley. "Three bottles of grocery-store wine, one expired yogurt, and a takeout container of something I think might have been fried rice isn't going to nourish you."

Her diet was another thing Bastian wanted to spank her for, but she'd already told them she didn't cook. Besides, given her course load, she probably didn't have time.

"It was lo mein, I think." She glanced at the bowl and blinked. "Did you buy me dishes too?"

"I went home and grabbed some stuff." Desmond pulled the rolls from the oven and transferred them to a cloth-lined basket. "I was going to buy everything you needed but remembered you don't cook."

"I can make ramen at least." She lowered her head

and cut up the tomato, then dumped it into the salad bowl. "Um... you didn't have to do this. It's really nice, but I could have ordered in."

"Would you have?" Desmond opened her cupboard, revealing a mostly empty bag of potato chips and a few cups of instant noodles. "Or would you have eaten a handful of stale chips and called it supper?"

She sniffed and looked away without giving him an answer, letting him know Desmond had guessed correctly.

Bastian handed her a peeled cucumber, which she dutifully chopped and added to the salad. As he gave everything a toss, he said, "For tonight, you're going to let your Daddies take care of you, and that includes a nourishing meal."

"I'm going to buy you a slow cooker and help you with meal prep, so you don't have to spend so much on takeout." Desmond pulled asparagus from the steamer and arranged the brilliant green stalks in a serving dish.

"Um..." She carried the finished salad to the tiny kitchen table, which was already laid with plates and silverware. "I mean, that's really nice, but—"

"Sit down, Titania," Bastian said. "You don't have to be so independent all the time. Let us take care of you."

She flushed pink and parked her cute butt in a chair, then scowled when she seemed to realize how quickly she'd obeyed. Before she could argue, he carried the vegetables to the kitchen table while Desmond sliced the prime rib. Once everything was laid out, he used tongs to fill a bowl with salad and placed it in front of her.

Giving them a suspicious glance, she started eating. As if she'd been starving, she finished the salad and dove into the rest of her meal.

Bastian watched her silently, the urge to continue taking care of her growing stronger with every bite she took.

It was bad enough that she lived like a squatter in her own apartment. The only thing that didn't look like it came out of someone's roadside junk pile was the computer workstation, complete with multiple monitors mounted on the wall and a very expensive desk chair that he'd pulled into the kitchen, so they'd have a third seat at the small Formica-and-chrome table.

He and Desmond hadn't had much better while they'd been in college, but he couldn't stand seeing his babygirl living like that.

Then again, judging by the label on her closed laptop, she'd prioritized her expenditures. Her furniture might have come from dumpster diving, but she'd spent a healthy chunk on her computer—which, considering her major, wasn't so surprising.

He and Desmond could fix her situation. All they had to do was...

Bastian shook the thought away. Assuming she agreed, which he highly doubted, moving her into their home was a step he wasn't sure he and Desmond were ready for.

Although the idea tempted him, Titania would be right to refuse, as it would increase her commute to classes. Then again, they were both retired, and could drive her to school.

Fuck. Why was he even thinking about keeping her? She was too young, for one. No, he and Desmond were too old. It might have been okay for Damian and Braden to hook up with women half their age, but Bastian couldn't help thinking Emily and Lottie would be widowed long before they were ready.

He didn't want to think about having children at his age either. Would Titania even want them? Certainly not any time soon. She hadn't even started her career.

They ate in silence, with Bastian keeping his thoughts to himself, watching Tania carefully to make sure she ate every bite.

After patting her lips with a napkin, she finished

her wine, then said, "Thank you. That was really good."

"We're glad you enjoyed it," Desmond said as he helped Bastian clear the table. "We'll clean up in a bit, but we're going to talk first."

"There's nothing to talk about." Titania folded her napkin and laid it on the table. "I really appreciate the food, but it's time for you to leave."

# 9

# THE FIRST KISS ISN'T ALWAYS THE SWEETEST

TANIA

Bastian sighed and pinched the skin between his brows. "Christ, it's like you want us to spank you again."

As much as she wanted to relieve the pressure on her punished bottom, she resisted the urge to shift her sore butt in her seat. It wouldn't do to show them her discomfort, and she refused to let them see how much Bastian's words affected her.

She especially refused to show them how much she wanted a fun spanking instead of one for punishment.

"I don't want that," she finally said. "But I'm asking you to look at it from my perspective. I could have justified using the auction money for Mandy's house if it came from a stranger, but I can't do that with you. It's not your responsibility to clean up Mandy's mess."

Bastian, who was sitting in her desk chair, shook his head. "That's where you're wrong, sweetheart. I know you don't think much of your father, but he was our friend. He would have wanted us to take care of you, Mandy, and Bee."

"And..." Desmond reached across the table to take her hand in his larger one. "It's our fault for not stepping in before now."

"Why?" she asked, honestly mystified. "He's been dead for years, and frankly, you both knew he left me with nannies more often than not."

He shared a glance with Bastian, then cleared his throat. "We spoke with him about a month before he died. He... Well, since he's gone, we might as well tell you the rest."

"What rest?" She plucked a roll from the basket and tore it into pieces, more out of something to do with her hands than hunger. "What else is there?"

"Victor left the police force and went deep undercover with another agency after your mother died," Bastian replied. "We don't know anything about his assignment, or why he married Mandy, but we do know she isn't aware of what he did. He asked us not to say anything to either of you."

Her breath left her lungs and she fell back against her chair like someone had punched her.

"Holy shit." She swallowed and tried to keep her supper where it belonged. "They never found his body. Do you think Mandy is right?"

"It's possible," Desmond admitted. "We don't know."

Bastian stood and plucked her from her chair, then returned to his seat and cuddled her in his lap. It felt good, but her anger grew with each passing second.

"What did he say?" she finally asked. "I want to know what he said to you."

"He asked us to look after you," Bastian replied. "Then he said he'd be in touch when he could."

"So, he's probably living it up in WITSEC. Maybe he has a new family he actually sees over the breakfast table every morning." Straightening, she pressed the heels of her hands into her eyes. "God. What a fucking mess."

"Sweetheart, it's going to be okay," Desmond said.

She wriggled free of Bastian's octopus arms and went to the sink to rinse their dishes. They could have waited, but she needed time to sort out her emotions. Was he safe somewhere, as Mandy believed? Maybe he couldn't contact them because it was too dangerous.

*And maybe he just didn't want them anymore.*

Tania pushed the thought aside, refusing to listen to the little girl inside her who just wanted her father. Whatever Victor's reasons were, she had to let go of her lingering hurt and disappointment. Whether he was alive or not, nothing would bring him back, and she couldn't let her bitterness spoil her future.

"If I get a part-time job, I can maybe stretch out the time before the bank forecloses until I graduate," she finally said, schooling her voice into a calmly even tone.

"Well, about that..." Desmond took a plate from her and set it aside. "We've got Mandy's house payments covered."

"Did I not just tell you I didn't want that?" she snapped, resisting the urge to throw a dish against the wall. She would have if they hadn't been Bastian's and Desmond's. "What part of it's not your responsibility did you not understand?"

Without warning, Desmond's hand cracked against her ass, sending dark pain coursing into her core. He grabbed her shoulders and spun her to face him.

"Your father asked us to look out for you." When she tried to break free of his hold, he grabbed her chin and forced her to look at him. "No matter what you think, that makes you our responsibility, and we're not going to let you do this yourself. Get the fuck over it."

Desmond's brown eyes glittered with anger as if he was forcibly holding himself back from turning her over his knee. "Got it, babygirl?"

"I…" Feeling like a bug pinned to a display board, she swallowed hard. "Yes, Daddy."

"Goddammit." He squeezed his eyes closed, then opened them as he gripped the back of her neck and pulled her into a searing kiss.

The taste of him, like spice and wine, and deep, scorching need, consumed her. Whimpering softly, she sank her hands into his salt and pepper hair, relishing the soft strands under her fingers. He groaned and picked her up, setting her on the counter before wedging his big body between her thighs.

"Tell me to stop, babygirl." He kissed a path along her jaw and nipped the tender skin under her ear. "Say you're too young and tell us not to touch you."

Stopping would have been the smart thing. She could have done as Desmond said, except they weren't too old for her. They were just right, and she'd wanted them for years.

Besides, she'd already proven she wasn't smart when it came to her Daddies. She wanted *them*—not their money. Explaining that could be a problem for future Tania.

"No." She wrapped her legs around Desmond's hips as Bastian stroked her back, his intent gaze focusing on her lips swollen from Desmond's kisses. "I'm not going to do that, Daddy."

For once, Tania was going to take what she wanted.

❧

DESMOND

The devil on his shoulder yelled at him to tear Titania's stretchy pants from her body and bury his face between her legs, but the angel on the other side shouted for him to stop.

She was too young.

*No, she isn't. Little Titania is* all *grown up.*

He and Bastian wanted too much. No one would agree to having two dominants for more than a few hours.

*Are you sure about that?*

Fuck, yes, he was sure. Well, pretty sure. She'd mentioned wanting two Daddies in her first message to them, but they hadn't talked about it, and he seriously doubted she'd been imagining two men her father's age.

*Hard to say that when she has her legs wrapped around your waist and calls you Daddy, ain't it?*

The devil on his shoulder might have been louder than the angel, but she was still Victor's daughter. He and Bastian shouldn't be touching her at all.

"Yes, Daddy D." Titania crossed her ankles behind his back and laced her fingers in his hair, driving all the reasons he shouldn't kiss her out of his head.

"Titania…" Bastian touched her jaw to make her look at him. "The auction is over. You don't have to do this."

Desmond couldn't decide whether he wanted her to agree or hoped she wouldn't.

"Call me Tania." Straightening her spine, she lifted her chin. "You spanked me, refused to leave when I asked multiple times, and won't let me handle Mandy's mortgage by myself. You're both a literal pain in my ass, but I seriously doubt you'll force me to have sex with you and Desmond. I'm doing this because I want to."

Before Bastian could reply, she snaked her hand behind his neck and pulled him into a deep kiss. Bastian groaned and wrapped his arm around her waist, kissing her hard as her free hand crept under his shirt.

He pulled away and wiped his mouth. His expression stricken with guilt, he said. "Tania, we can't do this."

"Why not?" She stroked his chest and worked at his belt buckle, then scowled when he removed her hand.

"Because it's wrong."

"Again, why?" She dropped her legs from around Desmond's waist and slid to the floor, then stepped into Bastian's space.

"You're Victor's daughter," Bastian replied.

"And half our age," Desmond added.

Tania was an adult, only a scant few years younger than her stepmother. She was intelligent and strong and could communicate what she wanted. Would it be so wrong to give in to her desires?

"And?"

Bastian shook his head and took a step away from her. When she tried to follow, he held up a hand to stop her. "Isn't that enough?"

"No." She leaned against the counter and crossed her arms over her chest. "I've fantasized about you and Daddy D for years. Did you know that? Did you know you and Desmond were my first sexual fantasy? I'm feeling pretty stupid now, but you might as well know I always wanted both of you, and I do not give a single fuck about your age."

"Tania—"

"Who the hell gets to decide what's wrong or right anyway?" she interrupted. "Society? Why do random people we don't know get a say in how we live our lives?"

Swallowing his protest, Desmond steeled himself under Tania's questioning gaze. Although he and Bastian wanted a babygirl to share, they both had to agree.

It was clear Bastian wasn't going to accept Tania no matter what she or Desmond wanted. Desmond would have given almost anything for a do-over. He shouldn't have touched her in the first place, and knowing she'd wanted them all along made refusing her that much harder.

And now...

He'd have only the memory of her taste on his tongue, and the faint scent of her lemony soap.

"Sweetheart..." Desmond took her hand and rubbed her knuckles, unsure of who he was trying to comfort. "We just want you to be happy."

"That's a lie." She jerked out of reach and scrubbed angry tears from her eyes.

"Your father wanted us to keep you safe, honey. I doubt that included us touching you," Bastian replied.

"Victor is dead, and he didn't give a shit about me

when he was alive." She pushed past Desmond, then went to the door and opened it. "You want me obedient and quiet, just like Dr. Pappas does, and just like him and Victor, you don't care whether I'm happy or not. I want you both to leave. Now."

"We still haven't talked about Mandy and Bee," Bastian replied, making Desmond want to slap the back of his head. "Honey, you can't take the responsibility on all by yourself."

"Mandy and Bee are my problem—not yours. I also asked you to get the fuck out." Her face lost all expression, and she tapped the screen on her phone. "I suggest you do it now before I call the cops."

Knowing she was too angry to listen, Desmond grabbed Bastian's arm and tugged him from the apartment. She slammed the door behind them and snapped the deadbolt into place with an audible click.

"That went well," Bastian muttered.

Desmond strode past him and went downstairs to their vehicle, then got behind the wheel. Without giving Bastian time to fasten his seatbelt, he stomped on the accelerator and drove away.

"Did you lie to me?" he finally asked, not looking at Bastian as he got on the expressway headed home. "Were you blowing smoke up my ass when you said you fantasized about her?"

He was willing to let Tania go if Bastian didn't

want her in their lives, but he wouldn't be lied to—especially not by the man who was supposed to be his ride or die. But fuck, it hurt.

"No, but I..." Bastian rested his hand on Desmond's thigh and squeezed gently. "I want to make her come until she's screaming our names, but I also want to keep her locked in a room lined in velvet, so nothing ever hurts her."

"I don't see Tania letting us do the velvet-room thing."

Bastian barked out a laugh. "Yeah, no. Fuck, she's so young, and I feel like absolute shit when I think about what I want to do to her."

"And?"

He caught Bastian's scowl out of the corner of his eye and almost laughed.

"Fuck you." Bastian sighed and his jaw tightened. "I can't help thinking she's Victor's daughter, you know?"

Desmond thought about that too, but he couldn't come up with a resolution.

"The thing is..." He hesitated, then added, "Judging by what Tania said about him, I'm wondering if we need to forget Victor and listen to her."

"I'd like to say he raised a strong daughter, but he didn't. He didn't do shit for her. She became strong on her own, and..." Bastian exhaled softly. "And you're right. I need to start thinking of Tania as a grown-ass woman who can make her own decisions."

Desmond relaxed and loosened his tight grip on the steering wheel. "So, what's our next step?"

"Well, getting arrested isn't on my agenda for the evening, so we'll give her a few days to calm down, then try to talk to her again."

Silently, Desmond took the exit toward Isle of Palms, giving himself time to think. "Do you want her to be ours?" he finally asked.

"I do." Bastian took his hand and squeezed gently. "God help me, I do."

"And what happens until we can talk to her?"

Straightening in his seat, Bastian gave him a feral grin. "We shadow her cute ass and keep her safe. Nothing will touch our babygirl."

# HELP FROM AN UNLIKELY SOURCE

## TANIA

**E**very step toward Dr. Pappas's classroom sent dread into her stomach until she thought she might be sick.

It was already midafternoon, and so far, she'd gotten no sideways glances, no sudden invitations to Dr. Ng's office, or anything else that might have made her think Dr. Pappas had told everyone he saw her at a sex club.

Didn't mean he wouldn't use it as blackmail. He was probably waiting for just the right opportunity.

Tania considered darting into the restroom to give herself time to calm down, but the closest one was the one she now refused to use. She'd spent too much time edging herself in the corner stall and didn't need the reminder.

She wanted Daddies who would give her comfort and support. Instead, she got overly controlling assholes who thought they could dictate her life and choices.

Not. Happening.

They could kindly fuck right off. Thankfully, she'd never see them again.

And it hurt way too much to think about them or what might have been.

Knowing she couldn't delay any longer, she trudged in and took her seat, but didn't look at Dr. Pappas.

"So good of you to join us, your majesty," he said, giving her an ugly smirk. "Did you have a nice weekend?"

Before she could reply, Jason, Owen, and Hassan moved to surround her. Owen took the seat in front of her, while Jason and Hassan took up positions on her right and left.

"What are you doing?" she whispered.

Owen did not whisper and stared at Dr. Pappas as he spoke. "If Dr. Ng isn't going to help, we will."

To her shock, the rest of the students moved until she was seated in the center of a crowd of young men. Although she hated needing their protection, she'd be forever grateful to her classmates. Tears burned and she sniffed in a desperate attempt to keep them at bay.

"Don't you dare cry," Hassan murmured. "It'll be really freaking weird, and you're not going to let him see that he's gotten to you."

"He isn't getting to me. Y'all..." She choked out a watery laugh. "I'm taking all of you out for drinks tonight."

"Also weird," Jason muttered. "We don't like you, remember?"

Before she could reply, Dr. Pappas said, "If you're quite finished playing musical chairs, shall we get started?" He gave her an ugly glare, which she returned with interest. In an act of what had to be sheer spite, he tossed a stack of paper on Owen's desk, then added, "Surprise pop quiz."

Owen frowned as he took one before passing the stack to his neighbor. "Dr. Pappas, this is material we haven't covered in the lectures."

"Do you have a problem with that, Mr. Nakamura?"

Shaking his head, Owen pressed his lips together and went silent.

"At least the dickweed curves," Hassan muttered under his breath.

To their credit, none of them seemed to blame

Tania, but she wasn't about to delude herself and say Dr. Pappas wasn't hitting the class with an unfair quiz to punish them for protecting her.

For a moment, she considered going to Dr. Ng, but doubted it would help. After ignoring documented sexual harassment, he wouldn't give two shits about an unfair quiz.

The quiz paper finally made it to her, and she scowled. Owen was right. She suspected Dr. Pappas had planned the quiz for much later in the semester, probably as a warmup for the final.

Although she'd studied ahead, it was going to be a challenge, and more than a few of her classmates were barely keeping up as it was.

She lifted her head and smiled at him, baring teeth. "Since you already know we're all going to fail, we're having a surprise group project."

"Excuse me?" His face flushed with anger; Dr. Pappas put his hands on his hips. "There will be no talking during a test."

"The test you know we won't pass without Tania's help?" Jason asked. "Dr. Ng might not be willing to say anything to you about what you're doing to her, but I think he'll have a lot to say about this."

"Maybe I should tell Dr. Ng where Miss Andersen spends her weekends." He licked his lips, then stepped to the side where he could see her. "I'm sure he'd love to hear all about it."

Her blood iced, but she didn't dare let him know he'd gotten to her. "I—"

"Nobody cares what a nerd with no social life does with her time," Jason snapped. "She's a crazy cat lady in training, and you know she's the only one weird enough to have studied ahead."

*Wow, Jason. Tell me what you really think.*

He wasn't exactly wrong, but Tania's building didn't allow pets. She'd get a kitten or two eventually.

"Fine." Dr. Pappas shoved his laptop into its case and zipped it shut. "Class is canceled."

Without another word, he walked out.

"What a fucking tool," Hassan said.

"Amen to that," someone replied. "I'm gonna bounce and get something to eat."

"Actually, it's an opportunity," Tania murmured before her classmates could leave. "Who wants to shove this quiz right up his skinny ass?"

"I could think of something a lot more painful to put there." Owen turned in his seat to face her. "What's on your mind?"

"Gentlemen, let's get to work." She opened her laptop and found the correct section in her online textbook. "We're going to finish this quiz and slip them under his office door."

## BASTIAN

As he and Desmond followed Dr. Pappas to his office, he hid a smile under the brim of his ball cap. It seemed Tania already had protection from the little asshole, but they were going to make sure he remembered the nondisclosure agreement he'd signed when he applied for membership to Club BDE.

Once again, he thanked his lucky stars Dr. Pappas had shown what kind of person he was and got himself banned before he touched a submissive.

Bastian almost stayed behind to keep an eye on Tania, but decided she'd be fine. Although Jason hadn't been exactly complimentary, he and the rest of the students had stood up for her.

"Dr. Pappas," Desmond said as they caught up to walk alongside the smaller man. "A moment of your time, please."

"Office hours are tomorrow between three and four." Without looking at them, he twisted a key in the lock and pushed the door open, then spun to face them when Bastian put a hand on the wood to prevent him from slamming it in their faces.

"You!" He paled, then backed away from them to

reach for the phone on his desk. "I suggest you leave before I call security."

"We won't be staying long," Bastian replied as Desmond slid an envelope containing a copy of Dr. Pappas's signed agreement from his jacket pocket. "We're simply here to give you a reminder of the NDA you signed when you applied for membership to Club BDE."

Dr. Pappas barked out an ugly laugh, then snorted in derision. "I'm banned, remember? I fail to see how—"

"No member, former member, or guest, regardless of membership status, may reveal the identity of any guest or other member of Club BDE to outside parties," Desmond interrupted, reading from the page. "Failure to abide by the terms of this agreement will result in legal penalties outlined below."

"I'm assuming you understood this document when you signed it," Bastian added before Desmond could read them aloud. "Is that not your signature?"

"Fine." Scowling, Dr. Pappas grabbed the sheet of paper from Desmond's hand and crumpled it into a ball. "You've made your point."

"And yet you threatened to expose Ms. Andersen five minutes ago." Desmond studied him for a moment, then cocked his head to the side. "So, either you didn't read the agreement before you signed it, or you think Club BDE won't sue you."

"That would be an unwise assumption," Bastian said. "They have the money for a very expensive lawsuit. Do you?"

"By the time Club BDE's lawyers got done with you, Ms. Andersen would never have to work again." Desmond dropped the empty envelope on the desk. "Oh, and one more thing."

Dr. Pappas swallowed hard and looked away. "What now?"

"Ms. Andersen has already expressed her refusal to attend graduate school and has declined a personal relationship with you. Your harassment of her stops. Now."

"Further," Bastian added, "you will score her work and that of her classmates fairly. You will not punish them for protecting her from your unwanted advances."

"Excuse me?" Dr Pappas drew himself up and sneered. "How dare you accuse me of—"

Bastian held up a hand, suddenly tired of the bullshit. "Those young men, who, I might add, showed more maturity and ethics than you possess, heard you threaten her grades if she didn't agree to your fucked-up bargain."

"And we personally watched you attempt to force

them to take a quiz you hadn't prepared them for," Desmond added. "We also watched you throw a tantrum when they decided not to play your infantile little games."

After looking them up and down, Dr. Pappas sniffed. "You're both obviously too old to be students. Why do you care so much about her?"

"We served on the police force with her late father." Bastian met his gaze steadily. "Count yourself lucky we haven't told his coworkers about you."

"Yet," Desmond added. "I wouldn't want to be you if they find out what you're doing to the daughter of one of their own."

A bead of sweat trickled down the professor's temple and he licked his lips, betraying his nerves. "Fine. You'll get what you want. I'd like you to leave."

"Gladly, but one more piece of advice," Bastian said. "Ms. Andersen is under our protection. One of us will be escorting her to and from your class, and we'll be waiting right outside the door. I suggest you remember that."

Without waiting for him to reply, they strode from the office and returned to watch over Tania.

"Think we put the fear of God into the little asshole?" Desmond asked as they seated themselves across from the open door leading into the classroom.

Bastian nodded, but before he could reply, they heard groans from the classroom.

"God, this is fucking impossible, Tania," someone said. "I want to go back in time and punch past me in the face for deciding to be an engineer."

Carefully, he and Desmond crept to either side of the door to watch. Gathered in a tight circle with Tania at its center, the small group of students frowned at the sheets of paper in front of them.

"Aw, c'mon, Theo. Graduation is in two hundred and twenty-five point eight days. You got this."

"Why am I not surprised you counted? Weirdo."

"Bite me, Jason. If you had to put up with Pappas talking to your tits every other day, you'd be counting too."

"Ouch." After a beat of silence, Jason said, "We're sorry we didn't do something sooner."

"Thanks, but I'm sorry you got dragged into my mess."

"There shouldn't have been a mess at all," someone said. "I hope he gets fired soon."

"Me too, Owen. So, so much." Tania sighed, then smiled. "Anyway, y'all promised me beer and pizza, and I'm hungry. Let's do this and send Pappas a fancy fuck-off. Oh, and take a picture of the quiz so we can use it to study for the final."

Bastian put his hand over his mouth and swallowed a laugh as he returned to the bench on the other side of the corridor. Desmond sat next to him, then leaned close and whispered, "She's gonna be okay."

He nodded but didn't reply. Taking care of Dr. Pappas for her was the easy part. They still had to convince her to accept their help with Mandy and Bee and persuade her to take a chance on two old men who wanted her more than they wanted to breathe. Bastian doubted it would be so simple.

❧ 11 ❧

# CALL ME MAYBE

TANIA

Two hours later, she was reasonably confident they'd all get at least a C, and if they didn't, they'd have proof of unfair grading practices to take to Dr. Ng.

"Hey, Queen Tania." Hassan loaded his books and laptop into his bag. "You still on for pizza?"

"And don't say you need to study or take care of your cats, weirdo." Jason nudged her from her chair. "Be a normal human for a few hours and have supper with us."

"I don't have a cat."

"That doesn't make you less weird," one of her classmates countered. "Besides, we learned more from you in a couple of hours than Pappas has taught us all semester."

She laughed and slung her backpack over her shoulder. "Aww. It's like you guys actually like me."

Tania wasn't sure how she felt about her newfound popularity. It was nice to finally be accepted, but she didn't know if she could trust her classmates' sudden willingness to help.

"Please." Owen pushed her to the door. "We're just bribing you into helping us with Pappas's class."

She laughed and followed them from the classroom. Strangely, two men sat on a bench near the water fountain. Both were reading paperbacks and had baseball caps pulled low over their faces.

For a moment, she thought they looked like Desmond and Bastian, but shook the ridiculous notion away. After their fight over the weekend, she doubted they'd speak to her—much less stalk her on campus. The thought of never seeing them again hurt more than it should have, but she couldn't let herself miss what would never happen.

They were too busy throwing Victor's name in her face to see her as a real person, and that was on them.

"Caruso's okay with everyone?" Hassan asked. "It's close enough to walk."

"Ooh, yes. They know what it means when I say extra anchovies." After laughing at the retching noises that ensued from her peers, Tania added, "Y'all are Philistines."

"How can you be so smart and so weird at the same time?" Owen asked. "It's unnatural."

"Hey! At least I don't like pineapple on my pizza. Talk about unnatural."

Everyone laughed, and they fell into comfortable conversation as they walked. She inhaled deeply, enjoying the warm fall evening. It had been forever since she'd taken the time to slow down and enjoy a meal with friends, and even longer since she'd taken an evening walk.

Although she was perfectly safe surrounded by her classmates, her spine tingled as if she was being watched. Deciding to ignore the uncomfortable sensation, she moved toward the center of the group and stayed there until the tantalizing aroma of spices, tomatoes, and garlic from Caruso's open patio reached her nose.

Her stomach growled noisily, making Theo chuckle.

"I guess you really are hungry," he said as he held the door for her.

"Thanks." She moved deeper into the restaurant to give everyone room to follow her inside. "I forgot my lunch and didn't have time to go home for it."

"Welcome to Caruso's," the hostess said. "The patio is free if you want it."

"Perfect," Jason said, "and three pitchers of your draft beer special, please."

"Sure thing." After seating them and checking everyone's ID, she hurried away for their drinks.

Throughout the meal, Tania kept telling herself she was having fun. Caruso's pizza was amazing, and her classmates were quickly becoming friends—despite their protests and good-natured teasing.

Why, then, did she feel so empty inside?

Worse, she knew what was missing. She wanted to share a pizza with her Daddies, but that was impossible for too many reasons to count.

Actually, she could count them. There were two, and their names were Bastian and Desmond—the big jerks. They just *had* to go all morally superior on her, and decide she was too young to know what she wanted.

Tania ate another slice of pizza and tried to focus on her new friends. Desmond and Bastian didn't get to live rent-free in her head anymore.

"Anything else I can get you?" the server asked once they'd demolished their food.

"I'm stuffed," Theo said. "You good, Tania?"

"Yes, thank you. It was delicious." She leaned

down to get her wallet from her backpack, but he moved it out of her reach.

"It's our treat. We owe you for helping us."

"Yep," Jason added. "Split the check twelve ways and leave out the crazy cat lady in training."

"I already told you I don't have a cat, dork," she retorted.

"That's why you're in training!"

Shaking her head, she joined in their boisterous laughter and let them have their way. After the bill was paid, they walked outside. To her surprise, Theo offered her his arm.

"Can I walk you back to your car?"

"Oh, you don't have to, but I appreciate the offer."

"Nope." He tucked her hand into the crook of his elbow. "I spent too much time trying to ignore what Pappas was doing to you, so you're going to let me pretend to be a gentleman."

"I... wow. Th—"

"And don't say thank you. You're a human being and shouldn't have to put up with that bullshit."

Too surprised to speak, she let him escort her toward campus.

When they were out of sight of their classmates, Theo cleared his throat and said, "Just out of curiosity, what are your plans for after graduation?"

"Getting a job." She nudged him with her shoulder and smiled. "And an apartment where I can have a cat."

"Same, but with a dog." He guided her to a bench in a small park, then pulled her down to sit next to him. "Would you go out with me?"

After a split second of shock, she considered the idea. Why shouldn't she go out with Theo? Although she didn't know him very well, he was geeky-cute with tousled brown hair and thick, horn-rimmed glasses perched on a narrow nose. The muscles under his long-sleeved t-shirt proclaimed he didn't spend all his time at a computer desk like she did. He was also really sweet and had the prettiest gray eyes.

Besides, it was obvious Bastian and Desmond didn't want her. They just wanted to run her life and appease their guilt over shirking a responsibility that wasn't theirs to begin with. Heck, she didn't know why she was still letting them take up space in her head.

When she didn't immediately reply, Theo grimaced. "Wow, could I be any more awkward? I'm sorry. Forget I said anything."

"No. It's okay, but we both have the course load from hell. Our dates will be study sessions."

Looking horrified, he shook his head. "I didn't mean now! God, not until after graduation. Can you imagine trying to date with our senior projects still hanging over our heads?”

“Right? I have no idea how Jason is managing to keep a girlfriend.”

“They moved in together at the start of the year so they could see each other more than once a week. He’s gonna ask her to marry him after graduation.”

“Yeah, that makes sense.” Deciding to *yeet* her not-Daddies out of her head, she kissed his cheek. “I’d love to go out with you.”

He blinked and gave her a brilliant grin. “Really? Wow. Um—”

“The twelfth of June, six o’clock at Caruso’s.”

“That’s...” He helped her to her feet, and they continued walking toward her car. “Two hundred and thirty-two point two days away.”

“Sounds like a date to me.”

Take that, not-Daddies. With luck, she could make herself believe a date with someone else was the right choice. Maybe, just maybe, six months would be enough time to get Desmond and Bastian out of her head.

## DESMOND

"Des, you cannot beat the kid up for asking Tania out," Bastian whispered from their hiding spot just a few yards away from where that snot-nosed brat Theo was hitting on their woman.

Knowing Bastian was right, he scowled and kept himself still. "Doesn't mean I don't want to."

Unfortunately, Theo was exactly the man Tania should have been dating. He was her age, and seemed every bit as focused on his education as she was on hers. They would be a perfect couple.

Besides, she wasn't theirs yet. Although they'd taken care of Dr. Pappas, they still had to convince her to accept their help with Mandy and Bee—not that she had much choice since everything was already arranged. The external shit was the easy part though.

Convincing her to forgive them for being dumb-asses would be a lot more challenging.

When Tania continued down the street with the kid who would look much better with a black eye, Desmond and Bastian kept to the shadows and followed at a distance.

"If he kisses her, I make no promises," he muttered as Tania and Theo reached her car.

"Shh."

Thankfully, Theo only gave her a hug and a quick peck on the cheek, then like a damned gentleman, waited until she drove away before going to his own vehicle.

Desmond hated the kid already.

"Let's go," Bastian said. "I want to be waiting in front of her apartment building when she gets there."

"Yeah."

Not for the first time, he wished they'd made her listen instead of letting her throw them out. Of course, as angry as she was, he didn't doubt she'd have called the police as she'd threatened.

Thankfully, the traffic lights seemed to understand their haste and they managed to be standing in front of the entrance to her building before she got home.

When they saw her car, Bastian said, "Let's get out of sight. I don't want her to see us and keep going."

"Good idea."

Quickly, they moved to stand in the concealment of some potted trees and waited for her to approach. Before she could put her key in the lock, Desmond said, "Hey, Tania."

She screamed and brought her keys up, aiming a can of pepper spray at them. Thankfully, she put her hand down when she saw them.

"Christ, Desmond! You scared the crap out of me. What the hell is wrong with you?"

"Sorry. We didn't mean to startle you," Bastian said, "Do you have a few minutes to talk?"

"If I agree, will you both go away afterward?"

Slowly, Desmond nodded. "If that's what you want, yes."

"Good." She glanced at the time on her phone, then gazed at them expectantly. "You have five minutes."

"Can we go inside to talk?" Bastian asked. "You might want to sit down."

"No." She tapped the phone screen a few times, then added, "I set a timer. You have four minutes and fifty seconds."

Yep, she was still mad. Thankfully, they had enough sense not to tell her they'd been stalking her all afternoon. He doubted she'd take it well. Hopefully she wouldn't argue about them watching her in Dr. Pappas's class.

He glanced at Bastian, then said, "Damian, Braden, and I are splitting Mandy's mortgage payments until you graduate."

"And before you yell at us, we're using the money we intended for the auction, which would have gone to Mandy anyway," Bastian added.

"I asked you not to do that."

"We know, but we told Damian and Braden, and…" Taking a risk, Desmond closed the distance between them and took Tania's hands. "Trust me, we had to fight hard with my brothers to keep them from paying it off completely."

"It was a compromise, Tania." Bastian moved to stand behind her and rubbed her shoulders. "Mandy won't lose her house, and you won't have to worry about making the payments until after you graduate."

"We felt we had to tell Damian and Braden because they contributed funds to your auction, but we also wanted you to know your feelings mean something to us, and that we're listening," Desmond added. "It's not quite what you wanted, but Damian is a stubborn ass."

She laughed and rubbed her face with shaking hands. "Meaning I shouldn't be surprised if he pays off the mortgage anyway, right?"

Desmond scowled but nodded. "We tried, sweetheart, but he's a little twitchy after his fiancée's father hit her before setting her home on fire."

"Oh, my god." Tania laid her hand over her mouth and softened her defensive stance. "Wow. I thought I had a shitty sperm donor. Is she okay?"

"Emily is fine, and her father is going to prison for a long time," Bastian replied.

"Good." Her shoulders drooped and she sighed.

"You win. I'll talk to Mandy and make sure you get the login credentials to pay it online."

"Honestly, Damian and Braden will probably pay off the mortgage, call it your graduation present, and refuse to hear another word about it. We just don't want you to be blindsided when it happens." Bastian glanced over her shoulder at her phone. "If you give us another five minutes, we have other news for you."

Smiling, she rolled her eyes. "Sure, but let's go inside. It's getting chilly."

Desmond hid a sigh of relief but didn't allow himself to relax. They weren't out of the woods with Tania yet. It would take time before she let him and Bastian into her bed—and more importantly, into her life.

"Great." Bastian took her backpack while Desmond got her keys and unlocked the door. "After you."

When they reached her apartment, she slipped off her shoes and directed Bastian to drop her backpack on the desk. A box containing the dishes Desmond had brought over rested on the kitchen table.

"Do either of you want anything to drink? I don't have much, but I can make a pot of coffee."

"We're good." Bastian sat on the futon and patted the seat next to him. "Have a seat. I have a feeling you're not going to like this part, but it was necessary."

"Oh?" She squeezed herself next to him to make room for Desmond. "That sounds ominous, but I'll try not to have another screaming meltdown."

After they each took one of her hands, Desmond said, "We went to campus and had a little chat with Dr. Pappas."

"Ugh." She leaned back against the couch and squeezed her eyes shut. "I have no idea if that will make things worse or better, but I really wish you'd have let me handle it."

Desmond forced himself to stay still. It took every ounce of his control to resist the urge to pull her into his lap for a cuddle. She smelled so damned good, like lemon candy, and he wanted to kiss the wrinkle on her brow until it went away. When he thought of a better way to relax her, he pushed the idea from his dumbass head. They still had to talk about the massive elephant in the room—meaning the age gap between them.

"Sweetheart..." Bastian squeezed her hand and brought it to his lips, then brushed a kiss over her knuckles. "You didn't say so, but we knew you'd be worried about him telling everyone you were at Club BDE."

"We brought a copy of the nondisclosure agreement he signed to remind him of the penalty for invading a guest's or member's privacy," Desmond said. "Before we could show it to him, he did actually threaten to expose you."

"You were watching, I assume." She frowned and chewed on her lower lip. "I thought that was you and Bastian I saw sitting on the bench near the water fountain."

"It was a business decision." Bastian turned slightly to face her. "Damian, Braden, and Desmond share ownership of Club BDE. It's a lot cheaper to remind people than it is to sue them. We also spoke with Dr. Pappas about his harassment. He promised to stop, but either Desmond or I will be escorting you to and from his class until the end of the semester."

"Hmm. I should be surprised to hear the Elliott brothers own the club, but I'm not."

She went quiet for several seconds, making Desmond wonder what she was thinking. Although he wanted to believe she'd accept them watching over her, he wanted more. He wanted him and Bastian to be the people she went to with her problems instead of trying to take care of everything by herself.

"Tania?" he asked. "What's on your mind?"

"I'm feeling some kind of way right now." She leaned back and crossed her arms, gazing at a blueprint of an airfoil hung over her desk. "Part of me is glad I won't have to deal with his shit anymore, and another part is really angry you didn't let me fight my own battles. And most of the rest of me is relieved because I wasn't doing such a great job handling it on my own."

She rose to her feet and got a reusable bottle of water from the fridge, then settled between them once more. "Honestly, I think I'm more upset that I didn't get to watch. Were there humiliations galore?"

"So many." Desmond scooted to face her then kissed her gently. "But we want you to know we're listening. We're not taking over your life, and we don't want to violate your consent, but we need you to understand that we can't watch you struggle."

"Fair enough." Tania stroked Desmond's beard and he resisted the urge to moan at the gentle touch. "I get it, and I'll try not to be such a bitch anymore."

Before he could reply, Bastian said, "And since you're a good girl and will let us escort you to and from class, you'll get to see it every day."

# 12

# CALL US DADDY

TANIA

She pulled away and stood before Desmond could kiss her again, then faced him and Bastian with her hands on her hips.

"We're not doing this again. You don't get to tease me, then turn around and tell me I'm too young for you."

They glanced at each other before Desmond spoke. "All the things we told you are true. We're over twenty years older than you, and even if things work out and we stay together, we're going to die long before you do."

Wanting to look at Desmond and Bastian while they talked, she grabbed a pillow from the futon and sat cross-legged on the floor. She had a feeling this was going to be a long conversation but wasn't sure she had it in her to convince them.

Truthfully, Tania didn't think she should try—no matter how much she wanted to. "I could get hit by a bus tomorrow and make it a moot point."

"We were also very close to your father," Bastian added, ignoring her comment.

God, Tania wished the bastard was still alive so she could bitch slap him. She'd gone months at a stretch without even thinking of Victor, and now she couldn't get rid of him. If she had to hear his name one more time...

*Hey, Dad. Surprised I'm actually calling you that? Yeah, I won't do it again if you kindly fuck off and stop haunting me!*

Knowing there was a reason Victor hadn't been around didn't stop her anger. Well, she wasn't angry at Victor as much as she was at Desmond and Bastian for insisting on bringing him up. It didn't seem to matter that he wasn't the man Bastian and Desmond thought he was. They put him on a pedestal anyway, and fucking would not shut up about him.

Actually, she *was* still pissed at Victor. Whatever he'd been doing couldn't have been important enough to make him essentially abandon her.

"I think Victor would have wanted me to be happy, but I have no idea because he wasn't around long enough for me to ask him. He also married a woman only a few years older than me, so I'd say he doesn't have a lot of room to judge our choices."

"What do you think Mandy would say?" Desmond asked.

"She'd congratulate me." Tania lifted her chin. "I still think she could have done so much better, but Mandy also chose to marry a man twenty years her senior who only stuck around long enough to get her pregnant."

"Ouch." Desmond grimaced but nodded. "Victor was one of my closest friends, but I understand where you're coming from."

"I don't think you do because you're still seeing me as a child in pigtails, which I haven't been for years." She straightened her spine and blinked back a few tears before they fell. "I get that you have baggage with Victor, but it's not mine to carry, and you shouldn't be hauling it around either. He's gone, and I refuse to let a dead man have a say over how I choose to live my life."

Bastian opened his mouth, but before he could speak, she uncrossed her legs and rose to her feet. "I've wanted you and Desmond since I was nineteen, and I mean both of you at the same time. I'm comfortable wanting you, and you have no idea how thrilled I was to learn you're bisexual and that my fantasies of being shared by my two Daddies might actually come true."

"Tania—"

"I'm not done, Bastian, and you aren't listening." she interrupted. "I've read modern romance, and I'm not talking about the books where sex happens in the dark and behind a closed door. Those don't fit me or what I want. I want all the sword-crossing goodness. I want the power exchange, and the Daddy Dom, and all the rest."

"We didn't know." Desmond glanced at Bastian, then added, "I can't believe you've thought about us sharing you."

"I think about a lot of things. One or both of you might have hypertension or high cholesterol, and you probably wear reading glasses. You won't have the recovery time of a twenty-year-old, and your fertility might be diminished. I don't give a shit if you avail yourselves of little blue pills or use toys to make me come. Do both if you want."

"Christ." Bastian glared at her. "It's like you looked at our medical records. How did you know Desmond's blood pressure is high?"

"Wild guess. Just don't color your hair like Braden and Damian do. Their dye jobs look ridiculous, and I want you just the way you are."

"Brat," Desmond muttered.

"You can't spank me for being right." She smirked, then sobered. "I also know I'll lose you when I'm in my sixties if I'm lucky enough to keep you that long. I'm aware that if we have children, our grandchildren will probably never meet their grandfathers."

She swiped at a trickle of moisture under her eye at the thought of losing them, but she needed to make them understand. People got as much time as they got, and she refused to contemplate the what-ifs when everything she'd ever wanted was within her reach—if her Daddies had the balls to accept her.

"There is one thing I will no longer do. I'm not going to argue with you anymore. I deserve better than being forced to convince you to love me. I deserve men who will ignore all the background bullshit because I'm the most important thing in their world, and I fucking deserve men who will love me as much as they love each other."

"We would be your first, honey," Bastian said. "You've barely had a chance to date other people, and it would be wrong of us to take that away from you."

They still didn't get it. She wondered if she should talk to Mandy and see if she had any advice for dealing with older men who needed to get their heads unstuck from their asses. There had to be some trick to it, but she wasn't going to fight anymore.

Without answering, she went into her bedroom

and got the toys from her nightstand. Enjoying their matching looks of surprise, she ignored the twinge of embarrassment and dropped one in each of their laps. "Technically, the rabbit you're holding was my first, Bastian. I was hoping you and Desmond would be my second and third."

"What? No butt plugs?" Bastian asked, making Desmond scowl at him.

"I figured one of you would want to boldly go where no man or toy has gone before," she retorted before snatching the vibrators from them. "Look. If you and Desmond aren't willing to take a chance, forget the bullshit, and see if I'm your person, I need you to leave."

BASTIAN

Tania was right about all of it. She shouldn't have to convince them, and no matter how much Bastian had liked and respected Victor, he didn't need to be in their bedroom.

Strangely, letting go of his worry about what Victor would have thought took a weight he hadn't realized he was carrying off his soul. He'd miss Victor, but maybe he missed the friendship they used to share before Victor went undercover.

At least he and Desmond wouldn't be at risk of getting punched in the face like Emmett Duvall had done to Braden when he learned about Lottie's and Braden's relationship.

Victor was gone, and against all the odds, had left a legacy in a beautiful, intelligent, and incredibly strong young woman who knew what she wanted and wouldn't settle for anything less.

She absolutely deserved better than two men who stupidly refused to see her as an adult rather than the teenager they remembered, but she wanted him and Desmond anyway.

And what their babygirl wanted... she got.

"We've fantasized about you too," he murmured, stalking her slowly to give her a chance to change her mind. "Ever since you came to our housewarming party when you were nineteen."

"We told each other to make sure we didn't call you Titania when we met up with Miss T." Desmond moved toward her and neatly trapped her between them.

Bastian traced a finger down the tendon under her ear, making her shiver. "It was your face we saw on those sexy as fuck pictures you uploaded to the auction website."

"We imagined your voice calling us Daddy." Desmond followed Bastian's touch on her neck with kisses, then cupped her cheeks. "I'm sorry I didn't listen to you. Will you forgive us for being idiots and let us be your Daddies for real?"

"Bastian..." She chewed on her lower lip, then met his gaze steadily. "I'm not throwing blame, but you seemed the most resistant to a relationship with me. I'd like to know why."

"It's because I wasn't listening either." She blinked at his quiet reply, but he held up a hand before she could reply. "It wasn't just you I wasn't hearing. I was listening to all the reasons why we shouldn't be together, and ignoring how happy we could be if we just gave it a chance."

"I—"

He cradled the back of her head and kissed her, letting his tongue slip between her plump lips. She tasted so damned sweet, and the fragrance of her lemony soap filled his lungs until he didn't want to breathe unless the air carried her perfume.

When she whimpered, he gentled their kiss and smiled at the haze of arousal in her hazel eyes. "Do you forgive me?"

She shook her head as if to clear it, then said, "Yes. On one condition."

"Name it, and it's yours," Bastian replied.

"The next time the ghost of sperm donors past rattles his chains in your heads, kick his ass to the curb."

"We're so sorry, sweetheart." Desmond rested his forehead against hers. "When he asked us to look after you, we had no idea you felt that way about him."

Truthfully, if Bastian had known Victor had essentially abandoned Tania for so long, he'd have stepped in and kicked the shit out of him.

Her gaze softened and she stroked Desmond's beard. "I'm not asking you to forget him. You can respect him and cherish your friendship, but he's not allowed in my bed."

"There's only room for the three of us," Bastian promised. "No one else."

Speaking of which, he'd have to figure out a way to get rid of Theo for her. Or maybe he could trust her judgment and let her do it herself. It wasn't as if she didn't have her head on straight already, but stopping himself from wanting to take care of all her problems wasn't going to be easy.

She stretched up on her toes and kissed him. Groaning, he pulled her close, letting her feel his thickening erection against her abdomen as she slid her tongue into his mouth and teased him.

"God, yes. That's what I want."

"Tell us." Desmond caught his eye and jerked his chin toward her bedroom. "Tell us all the things you want your Daddies to do to your gorgeous body."

"I want you to eat my pussy." She walked backward toward her bedroom as she pulled her hoodie over her head and dropped it to the floor. Her lacy bra met the same fate, revealing generous breasts topped with dusky peach nipples. "I want to watch Bastian suck your cock."

"Oh, babygirl, all that and more." Bastian followed her and caught the sock she tossed at him. "We—"

"I'm not done." She tossed another sock at Desmond, then shimmied out of her jeans. "I want your cock in my pussy while Desmond fucks your ass, and I want to watch it all. I want to see your faces when you come. I want you to call my name, and I want you to make me scream yours."

The breath left his lungs and all the blood in his body went straight to his dick. He couldn't even complain about her skirting the edge of topping from the bottom. She probably didn't know what it meant, and he loved that she was willing to communicate what she wanted.

After clearing his throat, Bastian said, "Oh, babygirl, we—"

"Still not done." She lifted her hand in a come-hither motion, beckoning them to follow her into her bedroom. "Did you know the rabbit is named Bastian? I call the g-spot vibe Desmond. Did you know I already call your names when I get myself off with them?"

Bastian laid a hand on his chest to still his pounding heart. "Fuck, babygirl. You're killing us."

"Good, but I'm not letting you stroke out yet." She bit her lower lip, then sucked a finger into her mouth before circling her turgid nipples with the damp fingertip. "See, I've had a lot of time to think about this, and I have a very vivid imagination. I want you to put me on my knees and call me your dirty girl. I want to feel your hands on my ass when you spank me. I want you to tease me until I beg, and I want to feel your cocks deep in my throat. I want you to take me to Club BDE and teach me how to be my Daddies' babygirl."

"Fuck, yes," Desmond hissed, reaching for her.

"I want it all." She held her ground and slipped out of her lacy black panties to reveal her smoothly waxed mound, forcing Desmond to stop and stare at her with hunger in his eyes. "And you're going to give it to me."

# 13

# YOU'RE OUR DIRTY GIRL

TANIA

Instead of replying, Desmond swept her into his arms and carried her into her bedroom, startling her. She wasn't exactly small, and the gesture made her feel all kinds of ways that probably weren't in the feminist handbook.

Tania felt cherished and protected and loved being held in Daddy Desmond's strong arms, but a quiet voice inside her wondered why she couldn't have just walked into her bedroom. Of course, despite her collection of naughty books about Daddy Doms, she had no idea how the dynamic actually worked.

That wasn't entirely true. She knew how it

worked in the Stella Moore books she consumed like crack, but how would it manifest when she had two Daddies?

Maybe it was normal for them to carry her around.

Did she need to be a brat? Bratting sounded fun, but it seemed like planning proper shenanigans would be a big investment of time. She couldn't wait to find out, but not until after they gave her what she wanted, and definitely not until after graduation. It was going to be hard enough to squeeze them into her schedule as it was, but she'd make it work.

*Or maybe I could just ask if they want a brat when we aren't in the middle of sexy fun times.*

"All the things you've been imagining..." Bastian said as Desmond lowered her to the bed. "You are so, so dirty, babygirl."

"And we think you need a spanking." Desmond sat next to her and patted his lap. "Over my knee, sweetheart."

"Are you spanking me because I told you what I want?"

"No. You're not allowed to stop asking us for what you want." Bastian placed his warm hands on her shoulders and pushed gently until she was face down over Desmond's lap. "We're spanking you because we want to see your pretty bottom turn nice and pink."

Electric shivers danced along her spine as Desmond stroked a single fingertip down her back, and moisture pooled between her thighs.

"And we're not going to stop until you beg us to lick your sweet pussy until you come." Desmond rubbed her butt firmly, making her squirm under his touch.

"Ah, ah." He delivered a sharp swat to the lower curve of her bottom. "Good girls don't fidget."

"Who said I was good?" Using Desmond's thigh for leverage, she lifted her torso off his lap, then channeled her inner Evie Stuart from that Golden Angel book she'd salivated over. "I'm not letting you spank me because you think I deserve it. I'm letting you spank me because I want to know if I like it."

"You might want to rethink your sass, sweetheart." Bastian fisted a handful of her hair and tugged until she lifted her head, forcing her to look into his brown eyes. "Do you need me to give your mouth something else to do while Daddy D spanks you?"

Desmond delivered rapid spanks to her bottom, covering her flesh with blows in a random pattern until she tingled, and her core throbbed with heat. He didn't spank as hard as Bastian had, but they weren't punishing her this time.

This spanking was meant to arouse all of them, and she was a definite fan.

Tania couldn't stop herself from stealing a peek at the bulge in Bastian's slacks—not that she wanted to. Her mouth watered with anticipation as she tightened her fingers in the fabric of Desmond's trousers and parted her lips.

"Fuck." Bastian whispered the curse, and his hand shook as he freed his erection. He was bigger... thicker than either of her toys.

She pushed her trepidation aside. Maybe the toys weren't an approximation of Bastian's cock, but Tania trusted her Daddies to make her first time good for her. Besides, judging by the size of Desmond's erection poking into her side, they wouldn't leave her disappointed.

A droplet of pre-cum seeped from the crown of Bastian's cock, and she whimpered, enjoying the sting as he tightened his fist in her hair. Although Tania had never given anyone a blow job before, she couldn't wait to try it.

And she definitely couldn't wait for them to return the favor after her spanking.

"Yum." She lapped at the pearly liquid, tasting salt and his clean male essence. "So good, Daddy."

Before he could speak, she swirled her tongue around the plump glans, then took his shaft deep into her mouth. He bumped the back of her throat, making her swallow before she gagged. A few tears sprang into her eyes, but she didn't look away from his face as she suckled him.

She didn't watch Bastian because he asked her to. Tania wanted to see the need in his expression. Her inexperience didn't seem to matter, and even though she was the one over Desmond's knee getting her butt warmed, she felt powerful.

"Fuck, yes." Slowly, as if giving her time to adjust, Bastian fucked her mouth with leisurely strokes. "Des, doesn't Tania look pretty with my cock in her mouth?"

Strangely, being called pretty by Bastian didn't make her want to jab an icepick into his forehead. Maybe it was because of how his hand trembled as he touched her face. He meant it to be complimentary and couldn't know the word triggered her.

For a moment, Tania considered telling them, but decided she liked it when her Daddies called her pretty.

"Gorgeous." Desmond spanked her hard on the crease between her ass and thighs, making her moan around Bastian's cock. Desmond squeezed her heated flesh, then pushed his hand between her legs and circled her clit with his finger. "Our babygirl's pussy is soaked."

"Mmm. Give me a taste," Bastian replied.

Desmond held up his hand, and Bastian sucked the glistening moisture from his fingertips. After licking Desmond's hand clean, Bastian cradled the back of his neck and pulled him into a searing kiss.

Watching her Daddies together was everything Tania had dreamed of for way too long. Whining around Bastian's cock, she spread her thighs apart and tried to rub her pussy against Desmond's leg, desperate for something—anything—to give her what she needed.

❧

## DESMOND

Tania let Bastian's erection slide from her mouth, and said, "God, yes."

Bastian nipped his lower lip and kissed him harder, stealing his breath. His cock throbbed every time Tania's squirming body pressed against his shaft.

It hadn't helped that she lifted her ass for another swat when he spanked her.

Desmond still couldn't get over everything she said. Had she really been fantasizing about him and Bastian? Tania's claims might have been hard to believe, but she had too many well-considered rebuttals to brush her feelings aside as the fantasies of an infatuated young woman.

Hell, she'd named her vibrators after them—which blew his mind. He supposed that meant he and Bastian had already been her first. In fact, it was better that she had some experience. Desmond hadn't been looking forward to hurting her.

"So fucking hot." Taking advantage of Desmond's inattention, Tania climbed from his lap and knelt on the bed, her gaze fixed on him and Bastian. "Do you know how long I've been waiting for this?"

Bastian chuckled softly and gentled his possessive kiss. "First things first. Does anyone have condoms?"

"We all have recent health checks," Tania replied, "and I got a birth control shot, but there's a sealed box in my backpack."

"And just why do you have condoms in your school bag?" Desmond asked.

"I bought them just in case you forgot them for our meeting at Club BDE." She climbed off the bed and scurried from the room, then returned quickly with the box of condoms.

"Smart. Set them on the nightstand, please." His lips twitching into a smile, Bastian leaned against Tania's dresser and crossed his arms over his chest. "But it's my turn to watch a show. Des, what was the first thing Tania wanted?"

"I want my—"

Bastian lifted his hand to cut off Tania's words. "Stand up, Des. Titania, I want you to undress him slowly while he tells us what your first thing was."

Tania's hands trembled as she unbuttoned his shirt. Every glancing touch sent another electric pulse of need into Desmond's cock, and dripping pre-cum dampened his boxer briefs as she kissed a path down his chest before unbuckling his belt.

Before he could even think to touch her, Bastian snapped, "Hands at your sides, Desmond. Don't make me ask again for you to tell us what Tania wanted."

"Our babygirl wanted us to—"

"Wait." Tania tugged Desmond's arm and pulled him toward the door. Stretching up on her toes, she whispered, "Is this how it is? You're submissive to Daddy Bastian?"

"I'm a switch. That means—"

"You're both dominant and submissive."

Desmond laughed softly and nodded. "Yes. Bastian is the only person I submit to. When I feel the need to dominate someone, I'll find a consenting submissive at the club." He smiled at Bastian and turned her to face him. "Sometimes, he'll dominate us, and other times we'll dominate you."

Slowly, Bastian moved closer and pressed a soft

kiss to Tania's forehead. "Is that something you want?"

"Yes." She narrowed her eyes and unzipped Desmond's slacks. Without warning, she squeezed his cock almost hard enough to hurt. "But no more consenting submissives. I don't share my Daddies."

Desmond wondered if Tania had a switchy side as well, but before he could ask, Bastian smiled and slapped her butt, making her squeak in protest. "Fair enough, but you must never forget we're both your Daddies, babygirl. Desmond will paddle your ass for misbehavior as fast as I will."

"And that leads us back to what we were doing." Desmond let his hands fall to his sides. "I believe you were told to undress me while I tell Bastian all about how I'm going to eat your sweet pussy until you scream for us."

"Mmm." She slid Desmond's shirt down his arms and let it fall to the floor. "Don't let me stop you."

He wondered what she'd think of his salt-and-pepper chest hair but kept his focus on her face. She'd already made her opinion on having Daddies twice her age more than clear and he was done arguing against it.

Thank god he'd never gotten into the habit of coloring his hair like his brothers. He wouldn't put it past her to shave his head in his sleep.

"I'm going to lick the juices from you while I tease your clit." The words exploded from him in a rush as she tugged his slacks down and tossed them across the room. "I'm going to buy you a butt plug to get you ready for us, and I'll fuck you with it while I suck that pretty clit until you scream. You'll fight when I force you to climax over and over, and I'll tie you down to hold you still."

Her eyes widened and she licked her lips. "I—"

"I'm going to make you sit on my face so Bastian can spank your perfect ass while I eat you until you're screaming our names. And then..." Desmond circled her throat with his fingers but didn't attempt to cut off her air. "And then I'll do it all over again until you're crying because the tears of our beautiful baby-girl make my dick hard. You have no idea how much I love making innocent little girls cry for their Daddies to give them relief from our torture."

"Oh, god."

"Don't call for a deity, Titania. They can't help you now." He tightened his grip on her neck, forcing her to lift her head. "When you can't breathe or speak, or remember your own damned name, you'll remember ours. Your magnificent mind will be filled with us until you can't think, and only then will we fuck you."

Her throat moved under his hand as she swallowed, and Desmond was delighted to see a touch of fear in her gorgeous hazel eyes. For a moment, he wondered if he'd gone too far, but she softened against him and nodded as well as she could.

"Do you want that, babygirl?" Bastian asked. "You told us what you wanted, but you should have been careful about what you wished for."

# 14

## THE SECOND KISS IS THE SWEETEST

TANIA

*Holy crap.*

Although she couldn't dispel the sudden trickle of fear, Desmond and Bastian were everything she'd wished for. She wasn't even afraid of them. Not really.

They wouldn't hurt her. Actually, they might, but she was willing to bet she'd like it.

Tania was afraid of what they'd make her feel. She'd asked for it though. She just *had* to fuck around and find out what having two Daddies would mean— and it was better than she'd ever dared imagine.

She cleared her throat and Desmond loosened his hold on her neck. "Yes, Daddies. I want that. I want everything, and I really want both of you."

Bastian tucked a stray lock of hair behind her ear, forcing her to remember how breathing worked so she could inhale his aftershave. Although she didn't recognize the scent, Desmond and Bastian both smelled of pine, leather, and maybe a touch of patchouli combined in a sensuously thick fragrance that made her core twitch with need.

For all she knew, they shared the product. Either way, they were getting it for their birthdays forever.

"Good girl, Titania."

The sound of her full name didn't irritate her like it did when Dr. Pappas said it. It was as if Bastian and Desmond used it to help her find a different mindset. Tania was focused on academics and didn't have time to date. Titania was their babygirl. She belonged to her Daddies, and they belonged to her.

Of course, she still had to figure out a way to fit time with them into her schedule but knew without asking that they would understand when she couldn't.

"Did I do a good job telling Titania about how I'll go down on her, sir?"

"You did very well, Des."

Bastian took her hand, and her knees wobbled as she followed him to the bed. Thankfully, she managed to sit before she fell over. When she tried to position herself so Desmond could do what he promised, Bastian shook his head.

"We have one small detail to discuss before anything happens, babygirl."

Pushing down a twinge of nerves, she asked, "What detail?"

"Which of us will be your first?" Desmond sat next to her, then lifted her hand to his lips and kissed her knuckles. "It's your choice, Tania, and there won't be any hard feelings."

Desmond meant well, so she tamped down her exasperation at being asked to choose between her Daddies. She believed Desmond thought letting her decide which of them would take her virginity wouldn't cause issues, and maybe she was over-thinking things as usual, but choosing one Daddy over the other didn't sound like a healthy way to start a relationship.

"No. I refuse to make that decision. Which of you is the oldest?"

"I am." Bastian reached for her hand and frowned when she eased out of reach. "Babygirl—"

"I said no." She glanced at the ceramic ashtray on her dresser where she kept her keys and loose change. It was one of those "so ugly it's cute" seventies-era art class projects she'd bought for fifty cents at a yard sale. After grabbing a quarter, she said, "Daddy Bastian, call heads or tails."

He blinked, then laughed softly. "A coin toss?"

"I won't pick one of you over the other. A coin toss is a random, binary event."

"A what?" Bastian asked.

*Ugh. What is wrong with me?*

Her Daddies were intelligent and well-educated, but she should have known better than to throw out statistical analysis to a layman. Talk about unsexy. "There are only two outcomes from a coin toss, and I have two Daddies."

"Why didn't you just say that?" Desmond asked, obviously trying to hide a smile.

"I did." When Bastian snickered, she scowled. "And quit teasing me. I know I'm a nerd, but you both understood what I said."

"But it's so much fun." Desmond quit trying to hide his smile, and seeing the wide, happy grin on his face nearly stopped her heart.

*He's so pretty when he smiles.*

It wasn't just the smile though. His delight shone in the deep lines on his forehead and the wonderful crinkles under his eyes. It was the tone of his voice and the way he leaned close to share her space. Despite her distaste for the phrase, she could see herself asking him to smile for her. He would mean it too and wouldn't bare his teeth just to shut her up—like she did to every idiot who asked her to smile for them.

She'd smile for her Daddies and wouldn't need to be asked for one.

After getting her mind back on the business of having her cherry popped, she stuck out her tongue at Desmond. "Daddy Bastian, heads or tails?"

"Heads."

Tania tossed the coin up and caught it out of the air, then opened her hand to reveal the outcome. "Heads it is."

"We should have played rock, paper, scissors, lizard, Spock to pick who called the toss," Bastian replied, gazing at her steadily as Desmond chuckled.

"And I'm the nerd in the room?" She rolled her eyes and dropped the quarter into the ashtray. "Could you two be any more Gen-X?"

Instead of replying, Bastian swept her off her feet, then carried her to the bed and tipped her face down over his lap. When she squirmed to get free, he wrapped his leg around her calves to hold her still.

"Our naughty girl needs a spanking, Des."

"Definitely, sir." Desmond's erection tented his boxer briefs with a deliciously significant bulge as he petted her backside. "She needs a very thorough spanking for being a brat."

Maybe bratting wasn't such a challenge after all.

BASTIAN

"Be still, little one." Bastian squeezed her plump bottom, then spanked her when she wriggled against his cock.

"I'd rather get to the popping-of-cherries portion of the evening." She turned her shoulders so she could look at him and arched her brow. "I'm not getting any younger here."

"So impatient." He let his hand fall to the lower curve of her ass, delivering a stinging spank, followed by several more.

She tried to kick her feet, but he tightened his hold on her legs. "Ouch, Daddy! I'll be good!"

"Uh huh." He turned his attention to her upper thighs, his spanks bringing a pink flush to her skin. "Babygirls always say that when they're being spanked."

He wasn't giving her a punishment spanking though, and his blows weren't hard enough to truly hurt her. She'd been patient long enough, and it was time to give her what she needed.

And past time for him and Desmond to claim their babygirl. Although he still worried they were too old for her, he'd wasted too much time fighting the inevitable. Every minute they shared was precious and he wouldn't squander a single one.

His cock throbbed with the need to be deep inside her. Gritting his teeth against the urge to throw her to the bed, he gave her a few more gentle swats, then rubbed her reddened flesh briskly. "Des, go see what else our naughty girl has in her nightstand."

"Wait!" She struggled to get free, but he laid a hand in the center of her back to hold her still. "There's nothing in there."

"Hmm." Desmond crossed his arms and put his fist under his chin. "Sounds like you're protesting an awful lot over nothing, sweetheart. Why is that, I wonder."

Without waiting for her to answer, he opened the drawer and chuckled as he held up a steel butt plug, still in its packaging, and a small bottle of lube. As he took the toy into the bathroom to wash it, he said, "Looks like someone was thinking ahead."

Bastian closed his eyes and took a deep breath in a desperate attempt to stop himself from nutting like a teenager. After calming himself, he helped Tania stand, then turned her to face the bed.

"Bend over, little one. Elbows on the mattress."

Swallowing hard, she hesitated and glanced at them both. "Um... I kind of thought butt stuff would come later?"

"It is later, and as you said, we're not getting any

younger," Desmond murmured as he exited the bathroom with the plug and a few clean towels. "Did you think we'd neglect your bottom?"

After clearing his throat to hide his laughter at her shocked expression, Bastian said, "I also didn't say which cherry I'd be popping."

"Holy shit. I don't... I mean, I can't..." She squeezed her eyes shut and blew out a breath from between pursed lips. "I can't believe this is really happening."

"It's really happening." Bastian pushed gently on her shoulders to encourage her, then nudged her feet apart. He had no idea how many times he'd dreamed of Tania bent over and open for him, but the reality was better than he'd ever imagined.

He couldn't wait to show her off at the club.

Leaning close, Desmond whispered, "Are you sure you want this? Once it's done, we're not letting her go."

"I do, and I'm sorry I was such a jackass about it." He pressed a kiss to the corner of Desmond's mouth. "She didn't deserve me sticking my head up my ass, and neither did you."

And he gave not a single shit about what Victor might have said. Victor would always be one of his closest friends, but he was gone, and it was time for Bastian and Desmond to move forward with Tania.

Bastian held out his hand and let Desmond cover his fingers with the slippery lubricant. "Put some on her hole, Des. Use plenty."

"Yes, sir." Desmond palmed Tania's ass to spread her cheeks apart, then let a steady trickle of lube fall to her crinkled opening.

"That's cold!" She tightened her muscles and squeaked when Bastian slapped her ass. "What was that for?"

"Relax, sweetheart. Don't tense up," Bastian replied.

Still wearing his boxer briefs, Desmond knelt on the bed next to her head and rubbed her back and shoulders. "We don't want to hurt you."

"That's right," Bastian crooned as the tension left her spine. He circled her opening with a fingertip, then slowly eased it into her. She lifted her head and gasped as the tight ring of muscle relaxed to let him in. "That's our very good girl. You're doing so well."

"I—" Tania groaned and pressed against Bastian's hand, taking his finger deeper into her puckered hole. "Oh, god. That feels amazing."

"Just imagine Bastian fucking you there." Desmond tangled his hand in her hair and kissed her. As he trailed his lips down her throat, he added, "And imagine me fucking your pussy at the same time."

"Yesss." She tightened around Bastian's finger, and

he added a second, stretching her in preparation for the plug.

"Play with her, Des." Slowly, Bastian eased his fingers from her back passage. "I'll be right back."

After washing his hands, he stripped down to his boxer briefs and coated the plug with a generous dollop of lube while he watched Desmond tease their babygirl. Fuck, she was gorgeous, and he'd never tire of listening to her whimpers of need.

Tania lifted her head when he approached and licked her lips as her gaze traveled over his body.

"See something you like?" he asked, resisting the urge to suck in his gut. He might not have a six-pack anymore but judging by the gleam in Tania's hazel eyes, she appreciated the view.

"I see lots of things I like, Daddy."

"Good." Imagining his cock in place of the toy, Bastian teased her with the tip of the plug before pushing it slowly past the tight ring of muscle. She whimpered softly and grimaced, making him stop when she tightened against the intrusion.

"Breathe, sweetness," Desmond murmured as he stroked her clit. "Breathe and push out."

Moaning, she arched her back as the plug slid into place. "Feels so good. I want more."

"That's our girl." Bastian helped her stand, then

positioned her on his lap facing away from him, with her legs on either side of his.

"On your knees, Des." Bastian opened his legs, forcing Tania to spread her thighs apart. "Eat our babygirl's pretty pussy while I play with her tits."

"About damned time," Desmond muttered. Without waiting for a reply, he knelt and buried his face between Tania's legs.

"Oh! Yes, Daddy. That's..." She gasped and buried her hands in Desmond's hair, holding him to her. "Fuck, yes!"

Bastian pinched her nipples and rolled them between his fingers until they were stiff points. "Has anyone ever licked your pussy, babygirl?"

"I..." She cried out and her back arched as Desmond pushed a finger into her. "No, Daddy. Not ever."

"Good." He slid a hand under her thigh and twisted the plug, making her gasp in pleasure. "Des, suck on her clit while I fuck her with this toy. We need to get her ready for us."

# FANTASY COME TRUE

TANIA

She had a feeling she knew what Bastian meant about getting her ready for them. Her deepest, darkest, most perverse fantasy was about to come true, and she'd finally get to experience double penetration for herself.

Talk about getting thrown into the deep end.

The plug filled her as Bastian pumped it in and out, sparking undiscovered nerve endings to life inside her while he used his free hand to play with her nipples. She felt his hard cock against her bottom and tried to rub against it, making him hiss out a curse.

Desmond sucked on her clit and pushed a finger into her pussy. She tried to clamp her thighs around his head, but Bastian held her open, letting Desmond do whatever he wanted.

He curled his finger, somehow finding that one perfect spot inside her that made her see stars. Tania tightened her fists in his hair but wasn't sure if she was hanging on for the ride or holding him close. He rumbled his approval and alternated between sucking her clit and circling it with the tip of his tongue, seeming to know exactly how to drive her ever closer to the precipice without letting her have the orgasm she so desperately needed.

"Do you like what Des is doing to you, Titania?" Bastian pinched her nipple hard, and the lightning strike of painful pleasure shot deep into her core.

"Fuck, yes!" She let her head fall back to Bastian's shoulder, allowing the myriad of sensations stoke the fire rising in her belly.

Every touch of their callused hands... The crisp hair on Bastian's chest against her back, and Desmond's beard tickling her inner thighs... The scent of them...

She'd never get enough of her Daddies, or of how they made her feel.

"How does our girl taste?" Bastian asked, holding her tightly against him.

"Mmm." Desmond pulled his fingers free and

licked her pussy to catch every drop of her arousal. "Delicious, sir."

She whimpered as her core clenched around nothing. "Daddy, please."

"So impatient." Desmond swept his tongue over her clit and stood, then kissed Bastian.

Unwilling to be left out, Tania wrapped her arms around Desmond's waist and kissed a path up his neck to his ear. His soft beard tickled her face and she inhaled, relishing his scent and the feel of his strong body in her arms.

"And greedy." Laughing softly, Bastian lifted her chin with a gentle fingertip, allowing Desmond to take control of their kiss. "Taste yourself on Desmond, babygirl. Taste how delicious you are."

The salt and musk of her arousal consumed her senses as Desmond slipped his tongue into her mouth and cupped the back of her head to hold her still, while Bastian slid his hand down her belly to rub her clit. Tania squirmed in Bastian's lap, desperate for more.

"So sexy," Desmond whispered. "Our babygirl is so damned hot."

"Yes." Bastian growled the word in a raspy voice, then cleared his throat. "Make her come, Des. I want to see her explode."

As Desmond slid from her embrace and lowered

himself to his knees, Bastian twisted the plug in her ass. She tightened around it and cried out when Desmond sucked her clit into his mouth and lashed it with his tongue.

"Oh, god!" Tania's belly cramped and tightened with desire, and she moaned breathlessly when Desmond pushed two fingers into her and pressed against her g-spot.

"That's right, sweetheart," Bastian crooned, the words tickling her ear. "Come for your Daddies."

A storm of pleasure stole her wits and her vision darkened as her core spasmed around Desmond's fingers. She cried out, belatedly remembering she had neighbors when someone pounded on the wall from the adjacent apartment.

Desmond trailed kisses up her stomach, then claimed her mouth, letting her taste herself on his lips once more. Held between them, with the scent of her cum filling her lungs, she'd never felt so cherished or wanted.

From behind her, Bastian kissed her throat, then nipped her ear. "That's our very good girl."

With Desmond's help, he lifted her off his lap and held her close while she stood on wobbly legs. The plug still lodged firmly in her backside shifted with her movements, awakening her arousal. Shivering, she bit back a whimper of need.

"Tania..." Desmond caressed her cheek, then touched her chin to make her look at him. "Whatever happens next is your choice. We can stop now if you want."

Her heart did an odd sort of lurch in her chest at the concern in his brown eyes.

"No." She swallowed and licked her lips, hoping they couldn't see how nervous she was. There was no reason for her anxiety either. Technically, she had sexual experience, even though it wasn't with a person. "I want everything, and I want my Daddies to be my first lovers."

"Then that's what you'll get." Bastian went to the nightstand and opened the box of condoms before getting several from the package. "Des, lie down on your back."

"Yes, sir."

His gaze never leaving her, Desmond stripped off his boxer briefs and dropped them to the floor. Smiling at her, he crawled to the middle of the bed before lounging against the pillows. He grasped his thick cock and stroked himself, making liquid desire trickle from her core. Her mouth watered for a taste, but Bastian stopped her before she could position herself between Desmond's legs.

"Ah, ah, babygirl." Bastian pointed to a spot at the

edge of the bed. "It's my turn. You did say you wanted to watch, right?"

Without waiting for a reply, Bastian lowered his head and swirled his tongue around the crown of Desmond's cock. Groaning, Desmond closed his eyes and laced his fingers through Bastian's hair.

"Oh, fuck," she whispered. "That's so hot."

"Play with yourself while Daddy Bastian sucks my cock, babygirl. We want you wet and ready for us."

## DESMOND

Spreading her thighs, Tania sat back on her heels and trailed a hand down her belly to her smooth mound. With two fingers, she rubbed her clit, while she used her free hand to play with her nipples. Despite what Bastian was doing to his dick, Desmond couldn't take his eyes off her.

Fuck, she was gorgeous. Her skin flushed pink with arousal and she parted her lips on a needy whine, but she didn't stop watching them.

His balls tightened and he gritted his teeth in a desperate attempt to keep himself in check before he shot his load into Bastian's mouth. Bastian would likely beat his ass for coming without permission, but he didn't care about that, or about the fact that they barely fit on her small double bed.

Desmond didn't want to disappoint Tania.

As if he knew how close Desmond was, Bastian squeezed his balls, then lifted his head, stopping the slow, delicious torture. Turning to Tania, he said, "Show us how wet you are, baby."

Slowly, she lifted her hand to reveal fingertips glistening with moisture. Giving them a naughty smirk, she sucked them into her mouth, then pulled them free. "I'm very wet, Daddy Bastian."

"Good girl." Bastian reached for a condom and tore it open. "Watch how to put a condom on and make Desmond like it."

"Can I try?" She laid down next to Desmond, putting her face way too close to his throbbing erection.

"You can put one on me later," Bastian replied. "Watch first."

"I'm going to go on record and say I'll like it whenever Tania touches me," Desmond said.

"Behave." When Tania giggled, Bastian tapped her nose. "You too, babygirl."

"Yes, Daddy Bastian." She winked, then crossed her eyes, and stuck out her tongue. "I'll be good."

"Brat." Despite Bastian's stern tone, Desmond

could tell he was trying desperately not to laugh at Tania's antics. "Pay attention."

After pulling the condom from its wrapper, he centered it over the head of Desmond's cock, then pinched the tip and slowly eased the latex down his hard shaft, squeezing as he went until Desmond had to hold his breath to keep himself from coming too soon.

"Fuck, yes." Despite his efforts to hold still, his hips surged upward.

"Ah, ah." Bastian's grip tightened around the base of Desmond's shaft, and he twisted his lips into a cruel, sadistic smile. "Naughty."

"Yes, sir." Desmond let out a breath and relaxed his fists before he tore holes in Tania's sheets.

"Good. Proud of you, sweetheart." Leaning close, Bastian claimed his mouth in a gentle kiss. "Ready for our girl?"

"He's very ready," Tania interrupted as she nudged Bastian to the side and straddled Desmond's hips. Even through the condom, the wet heat of her scorched him, forcing him to stillness before he slammed his cock into her welcoming channel.

"You think so?" Bastian asked.

"I do." She lifted her chin and boldly met Bastian's eyes as she rubbed herself against Desmond's cock. "You've teased us long enough, Bastian."

*Oh, shit.*

Although Bastian smiled and let Tania take control, Desmond recognized the evil gleam in his eyes. Instead of warning her, he pressed his lips together and tried not to laugh. Bastian probably wouldn't do anything tonight, but poor Tania had a reckoning coming.

"And you have been a very good, very patient babygirl." Bastian tucked a lock of hair behind her ear and traced her jaw with a gentle fingertip. "Look at you, just hovering over Desmond's cock until you have permission."

"Give permission already!" She panted harshly as a sheen of perspiration dampened her forehead.

"All right." Bastian reached between their bodies and grasped the base of Desmond's cock to hold him in position for Tania. "Take him inside you but go slow."

"God, yes." Her lips parted and she let her head fall back as Desmond's cock found her entrance.

"Such a good girl." Desmond held her hips, forcing her to take her time. "You look so beautiful with my cock in your pussy."

"Ah, feels so good." She hissed her pleasure, but his heart twinged at the slight tightening around her eyes as she slowly lowered herself until he was fully inside her. "Fuck, yes."

Bastian got to his knees and grabbed a condom and the lube before kneeling behind her. "Lean forward, babygirl. It's time for me to pop your other cherry."

Hesitating, she nibbled her lower lip before obeying. Desmond embraced her and stroked her back, hoping to calm her nerves. He rocked his hips, fucking her slowly. Bastian met his eyes and smiled as he sheathed his erection.

Without warning her, Bastian removed the plug from Tania's ass and dripped fresh lubricant on her exposed bottom hole. After coating his shaft with more lube, he positioned himself at her back entrance.

"Relax for us, Tania." Bastian's jaw tightened and the tendons on his neck stood out in sharp relief, clear evidence of how close he was to the edge. "Breathe out and let us take care of you."

Desmond lifted her slightly, wanting to make Bastian's entry more comfortable for her. "We'll go slow, but tell us to stop if it hurts."

"I..." She closed her eyes and took a deep breath, then let it out. "I will, Daddy Desmond. I'm ready."

"Good girl." Desmond tightened his hands on her hips and held her still while Bastian eased his cock past the tight ring of muscle until he was deep inside her.

He and Bastian had shared women before, but Tania wasn't some random club submissive. She was theirs, and every gasp, every tightening of her inner muscles made the experience even more profound.

"Ah! I..." Her eyes widening, she lifted her head. "Wow, that feels—"

"Are you okay?" Desmond cupped the back of her head, forcing her to look at him. "Do you need us to stop?"

"Don't you fucking dare!" Her movements jerky and uncoordinated, she rocked between them. "Give me more."

"God." Bastian closed his eyes and gritted his teeth as he tried to keep himself still. "You feel so damned good, babygirl."

"I would if you two would move," she countered, glaring over her shoulder at Bastian.

Desmond grabbed a handful of her hair, and pulled her into a brutal kiss. He didn't stop until she whined and relaxed, her body going motionless under their firm control.

"We'll have lessons on why bratty little girls shouldn't top from the bottom another day," Desmond said, forcing her to look at him. "For now, you need to remember to be careful what you ask for."

# 16

# BE CAREFUL WHAT YOU WISH FOR

TANIA

Once again, she just *had* to fuck around and find out.

She'd read enough erotic fiction to know what topping from the bottom meant, so she didn't even have the excuse of not understanding the term. Always, without fail, it got the hapless submissives more than they bargained for.

And now... now, she had Desmond's *another day* to look forward to.

However, the dread mixed with anticipation couldn't take her mind off what her Daddies were doing to her body. As if they were speaking telepathically, they moved her like a rag doll, rocking her between them as they fucked her holes.

They didn't even give her time to breathe, much less beg for the relief they wouldn't give, and she'd been so, so wrong about their endurance. Her Daddies did not need little blue pills. Like, at all.

Holy hell. They were bound and determined to fuck her unconscious.

"Play with her clit, Des," Bastian said as he slid deep into her while Desmond slid out.

Desmond pinched the swollen nub between two fingers. "I think we can make her come at least four times."

"I'm thinking five." Bastian circled her throat with one large hand and tugged her upward. After kissing a path down her neck, he added in an entirely too relaxed voice, "Loser gets to do the dishes for a week."

"Oh, god." Her vision darkening, she shuddered helplessly with a violent climax, but they didn't stop. "I... Please!"

"Poor baby," Desmond crooned, his eyes sparkling with wicked intent. "Do you need six?"

*Here lies Titania Jane Andersen... She went out with a bang. Literally.*

Bastian stilled and nipped her shoulder, then licked the bite to soothe it. "You know what, Des? We forgot something."

"What did we forget?" Desmond thrust inside her, making her swallow a scream.

Bastian thrust inside her, nearly making her swallow her tongue. "We forgot to give Tania a safeword."

Dark pleasure coiled inside her as he filled her back passage again. The first pinch of discomfort was long gone, leaving only the desire for more.

"Careless of us." Desmond lifted her head until she was looking at him. "Say red if you need to stop, and yellow if you want to slow down."

When she didn't reply, Desmond pulled her hips down and thrust inside her. "Tell us you understand, babygirl. It's important."

"I..." She took a deep breath and tried to focus, but her mind wasn't having it. "I understand. Red to stop, yellow to slow down."

"There's our good girl," Bastian whispered, kissing the back of her neck. "Come for us again."

Her body obeyed as if she was Pavlov's dog. Tania shuddered and a few tears fell as another climax wracked her soul. Strangely, the word that would stop everything refused to be spoken.

"Don't cry, babygirl." Desmond kissed her hard, leaving her lips swollen and sore. "We're not even close to being done with you."

He massaged her clit as Bastian surged into her, pulling another orgasm from her helpless body.

How the hell were they still going?

"Des..." Bastian's soft murmur caressed her, covering her like a warm blanket. "Let's give her one more."

They rocked her between them, slowly and ever so gently, without the demanding thrusts of before. She spiraled into another orgasm and cried breathlessly as they eased her down with kisses and soft touches. Their whispers telling her what a good girl she was soothed her into somnolence and she barely noticed when Bastian pulled his cock free and laid her between them.

Her pussy and ass ached but felt good at the same time. As she shifted into a more comfortable position, her thighs rubbed together, sending a weak pulse of renewed arousal into her core. Sadly, she was too tired to do much about it.

"Shh, sweet girl," one of them said. "Your Daddies have you, and we're not letting you go."

"Me either." Her eyes drifted shut and she dozed, barely noticing when one of them cleaned her with a warm, damp cloth.

"I'd like to help her take a shower, but the stall isn't much bigger than her bed," Bastian said, his voice barely above a whisper.

"I saw that. She's pretty much out anyway." The bed rocked as Desmond moved closer to the edge of the mattress, bringing her with him. "I think there's room for all three of us if we squeeze in tight."

"Stop talking, Daddies. Sleepy now."

They both laughed as Bastian climbed into bed to spoon her from the other side. After kissing her brow, Bastian tucked her against his chest. "Rest well, babygirl. We've got you."

⁊

## BASTIAN

Instead of answering, Tania yawned and fell asleep almost immediately, leaving him to wonder if he and Desmond had made the right decision to take her as their own.

Although he agreed with everything she'd said, he couldn't help the guilt at debauching Victor's daughter. She was so damned smart and would soon have the whole world at her fingertips. They didn't have the right to stifle her dreams or make her choose them over her future.

Except... She hadn't chosen. She'd fucking scheduled their first meeting like she was planning a military invasion, and tossed a coin to pick which of them would take her virginity. Technical manuals and blueprints littered her living space, clear evidence of her determination. Despite knowing they hadn't liked her; she'd even talked her classmates into studying with her.

Of course, they'd changed their tune with her offer to help. He understood their initial dislike though. Tania could be a bit prickly on occasion.

Aside from that, he and Desmond wouldn't consider making her choose between them and her education. In fact, they'd give her everything she needed to succeed—including protection from her instructor's unwanted advances. They both had time to make sure she ate and rested. Hell, they could even do her laundry and clean her tiny apartment.

If he thought about it, Tania was perfect for them. They'd thought their woman would have to be older to have enough life experience and independence to match them, but they'd been wrong.

Thankfully, Tania didn't have to beat them over the head to make the message sink in. Well, not too much anyway. Even her tendency to top from the bottom was endearing rather than annoying—and it gave him a reason to spank her cute butt. Then again, it might be fun to have another switch in the dynamic he shared with Desmond—as long as they both understood who their dominant was.

Tania didn't need them at all. She was financially stable, on track for her degree, and probably already had companies clamoring to hire her. Unlike more than a few of the women he and Desmond had considered, Tania took care of her own business—sometimes when it wasn't her burden to carry. He might have wished Victor had done better by her, but she'd taken the hand she was dealt and come up with a royal flush.

The thought reminded him to set up a meeting with Mandy and the Elliott brothers to discuss Mandy's finances. Although his heart ached for her, it was time for her to come to terms with Victor's death and move on. Tania might be able to take care of herself, but Bee was only six.

Once he was sure Desmond and Tania were asleep, he slipped from the bed, then crept silently into the living room after closing the door behind him. It was late, and there was no point in disturbing them with the call he wanted to make. He went into the kitchen and made a cup of coffee, smiling as he poured water into the espresso machine taking up most of her counter space.

Tania definitely prioritized her expenses, which he appreciated.

As the machine rumbled, he tapped the icon for Ray, his contact on the force, to get him started on a deep dive into Marinos Pappas's history. Bastian's gut told him his behavior toward Tania wasn't his first foray into sexual harassment, and although he trusted Martin's background check as far as it went, nothing compared to a professional investigation.

When the call connected, he didn't waste time with pleasantries. "Hey. This is off the books, but I need you to give me everything you can find on Dr. Marinos Pappas. He's decided to make a pest of himself to Victor Andersen's daughter."

"Seriously?" Ray laughed, then coughed before clearing his throat. "Is the dude high or just stupid?"

"Probably both. Crawl up his ass. I want to know everything starting with when his mama's doctor slapped his butt and cut the cord."

"You got it, brother. I'll get the boys in his neighborhood to make their presence known too."

"Good. Thank you."

"No problem." Ray hesitated, then added, "How is little Titania anyway? She doing okay?"

He resisted the urge to tell Ray how *not* little Tania was. "She's good. All grown up and in college now."

"Good. That's great. Text me his address. It might be next week before I get the info you want, but anything for Victor's kid."

"Thanks."

Bastian ended the call and rested his elbows on the counter as he waited for his coffee to finish brewing. It was one thing to track a predator, but unless he could find evidence that didn't come from her classmates or the dean Jason mentioned, Tania would be forced to deal with him until she graduated. Hopefully, Ray would come up with something Tania could take to her university.

Before he could call in another favor for private security when he and Desmond couldn't watch her, his phone chimed with an incoming call. He answered without looking at the number and poured his coffee.

"Bastian Carter."

"Hello, Sebastian. I thought you might pick up."

His blood chilled at the caller's faint Irish accent, and he set his mug aside to reach for a sidearm he didn't carry anymore. "Killian."

"The one and only. Tell me. How is Ms. Andersen doing?"

"None of your damned business. You shouldn't know she exists at all, and if you even think of touching her—"

"Perish the thought," Killian purred. "I don't poach, and it's more than clear you and Desmond Elliott have her well in hand."

"You're watching her." Not for the first time,

Bastian wished they'd found something on Killian, but they hadn't managed to get so much as an unpaid parking ticket. "What do you want?"

"I find myself in the position to repay a somewhat significant debt, and I'm not one to allow accounts to remain unsettled."

The thought of Tania being anywhere near Killian's radar sent rage coursing through his body, but he forced himself to calm down and listen.

"And? You don't owe me shit. My fondest dream is to—"

"Aye, I'm aware. You want me imprisoned. Your deliciously sexy partner called me..." Killian chuckled, then added, "Oh, right. I remember now. Desmond said I give cesspools a bad name. However, the debt I owe isn't to you or Desmond, or even to the lovely Titania. It's to Victor Andersen."

"Victor wouldn't have talked to you unless he was reading your Miranda rights."

"Ah, but he did. I was able to give him certain information regarding someone much worse than me, and in return, he helped me out of a rather sticky situation. For that, I'm offering Ms. Andersen my protection if you choose to accept it. Of course, I don't need your permission to watch over her, as I've done it for several years already."

"Fuck off, O'Rourke. Don't come near her."

"As you wish, but as a good faith gesture, check the document I've sent to your email."

The call dropped, and against his better judgment, he brought up his email app and opened Killian's document. As he scanned the file containing Dr. Pappas's history, Bastian wondered if his presence at Club BDE had spurred Killian into acting.

Killian O'Rourke might look better in prison orange, and Bastian would wait for confirmation on the information he'd sent, but if it panned out, he'd consider Killian's debt to Victor paid in full.

# 17

# BACK TO THE REAL WORLD

TANIA

"**S**top squirming, babygirl," a soft voice whispered. "I'll paddle your ass if you push me out of this bed."

"Mmm." She nestled her face against Bastian's chest and didn't open her eyes while Desmond snored softly behind her. "Shh. Sleepy, Daddy Bastian."

There was no better place than to be spooned between her Daddies, and Tania had no intention of getting up until she had to—even if her bed was way too small for three people. Her Daddies probably had a king, and she planned to move into it the minute she graduated.

Well, assuming they wanted her to move in with them. They hadn't discussed it. She was probably getting ahead of herself, but it was hard to be patient when everything she'd ever wanted was within her reach.

He laughed softly and kissed her shoulder. "Sleep as long as you need. We'll be here."

"M'kay." As she tucked her head under the sheet, she asked, "What time is it anyway?"

Before he could reply, her phone chimed from the charging dock on her nightstand. She groaned and reached over him to grab it, then scowled when she saw Jason's name on the screen.

She swiped to accept the call, then said, "I'm sleeping, Jason. What do you want?"

"Um...did you forget our study session for the midterm? You're like twenty minutes late."

"Shit!" She scrambled to get up and accidentally jabbed her knee into Bastian's chest, making him grunt. "I'm sorry. I overslept. Give me two minutes and I'll get into the virtual classroom."

As Tania stumbled to her dresser for clothes, she tripped over a shoe and went sprawling. Her phone skittered across the floor, making her crawl to retrieve it. "Goddammit!"

"What happened? Are you okay?"

*Just peachy, thanks. I got my brains fucked out by two scorching hot Daddies is all. Nothing to see here.*

She glared at her Daddies, who were both awake

and trying not to laugh at her. She stuck out her tongue at them, then said. "I'm good. I just forgot to set an alarm. Thanks for being so patient."

"No worries. See you in a few."

After ending the call, she dressed as quickly as she could, but didn't bother with her hair. "Sorry, Daddies. I gotta do this. Go back to sleep."

"Are you sure?" Bastian rose from the bed, all naked and gorgeous, with his cock coming to attention. Tania squeezed her eyes shut before she forgot what she was supposed to be doing.

"I... No! I mean, yes." She whirled around before she gave in to what she really wanted. "I'll be a few hours, then I need to get to the lab, and—"

"Shh, babygirl." Desmond folded her into his arms and kissed her forehead. "It's okay. I'll make breakfast for you before we leave you to do your thing."

"But—"

He turned her to face the door and swatted her butt. "Go. Don't worry about us. We won't disturb your work."

"Thank you." A few tears threatened, but she blinked them away and smiled. "Just... thank you."

She stretched up on her toes to steal a kiss, then scurried to her workstation and logged into the classroom. Thankfully, the software didn't include video conferencing, so she wouldn't have to explain her disheveled appearance.

Then again, it wasn't like she took the time to dress up on a good day.

Forcing herself to focus on the study guides, she ignored the sounds coming from her kitchen, but she couldn't help wondering what Desmond thought he was going to cook. It wasn't as if she had actual food in her apartment, but maybe he'd had groceries delivered.

God, how had she gotten so lucky? They rocked her world in the bedroom *and* cooked? How did that even happen in real life?

An alert announcing a new participant pinged from her speaker. She frowned when she saw Dr. Pappas's name and grabbed her phone to text her classmates.

Change of plans. Pappas just came in. Sending a video meeting link in a few.

Ignoring the replies, she set up the meeting, then texted the link to everyone. Jason was first in, followed by Theo.

"What the fuck is wrong with him?" Theo asked, scowling into his camera.

"Right? He's never bothered coming to study

sessions before," Jason replied as the rest of Tania's classmates joined the meeting.

Thankfully, none of them commented on her sex hair or the dark circles under her eyes.

"Especially when he barely bothers to keep regular office hours," Owen muttered. "Maybe he came in to see how to torment us with stuff he hasn't taught us yet."

"I don't know." Tania pulled up her textbook on her second monitor. "And I kinda don't care what the little fuckwit does as long as we all pass his stupid class. Let's move to chapter nine. That's where we're having the most trouble."

"Thank god," Hassan replied. "I fucking hate thermodynamics."

"You should have gone into civil engineering. The world needs more turd herders."

"Fuck off, Owen."

Tania laughed, then frowned when a dozen faces stared at her in shock. "What?"

Jason cleared his throat and cocked his head. "I know you'll hate me for saying this, but you're gorgeous when you laugh. Even when you seriously need to brush your hair and turn your shirt right side out."

Her lips parted in surprised embarrassment. "I—"

"Ooh!" Owen leaned closer to his camera. "She's blushing."

Her face heated even more, and she resisted the urge to turn off her camera. There was no way she'd let them see they'd gotten to her.

"Oh, my god! You're all assholes. Shut up, and let's get to work."

❧

DESMOND

"Eggs Benedict?" Bastian asked as Desmond whisked the Hollandaise sauce. Another pot contained simmering water, and a plate of Canadian bacon and toasted English muffins warmed on the back of the stove.

Tania's voice rose as she spoke over her class-mates' complaints about what they were studying, but he could hear the patience in her tone as she explained the concepts. It wasn't as if he understood what she was trying to tell them, but he liked listening to her.

"Yep. I figured I'd do something special for our first morning together." Desmond set the sauce aside, then cracked eggs into the poacher before setting it in the water. "You could pour the mimosas. The champagne is in the fridge."

"Des..." Bastian laid a hand on his shoulder and gently turned him away from the stove. "Tania is working, and she has to drive to campus later."

"Shit. I forgot." Desmond grimaced and decided it was the steam from the simmering water making his cheeks hot. "We'll do orange juice and save the mimosas for the weekend."

When the eggs were done, he assembled her breakfast and topped it with a healthy spoonful of sauce followed by a sprig of fresh parsley while Bastian filled a wineglass with orange juice.

"I'll take it to her," Bastian said, holding his hand out for her plate. "Along with this virgin mimosa."

"Thanks. Just make sure to stay out of view of her camera."

Bastian's expression darkened, but he nodded. "Good idea. No point in outing our relationship before we're ready."

"That's not what I meant." He touched Bastian's arm, then moved to block his path. "I'm ready, and I bet Tania is too, but you reminded me that she's working. Distracting her is the last thing we want."

Bastian sighed and pressed his forehead against Desmond's. "I know. I'm being an idiot."

"Join the club." Desmond stole a kiss, then

smiled. "You're not the one who made eggs Benedict and mimosas on a weekday."

"Right." Bastian returned his grin. "Makes me wonder what's on the menu for tomorrow."

"Blueberry pancakes." Desmond wrapped an arm around Bastian's waist and pulled him close for another, deeper kiss. His cock thickened with interest, but he forced himself to focus. They couldn't exactly grab Tania from her study group, and she was probably sore from their activities. "Well, assuming one or both of us don't lose our damned minds first."

"Damn. You're gonna spoil our girl."

"I'm certainly trying," Desmond retorted. "I hate knowing how much takeout she's been eating."

"Same." Bastian studied the path toward Tania's desk, obviously planning how to get there without letting himself be seen. "I'll take this to her before it gets cold."

When he laid the plate next to her keyboard, she flinched with surprise and shot him a beaming smile before lifting the wineglass to her lips. "Thank you," she mouthed silently.

Desmond smiled and edged to the side to watch her eat, careful to stay quiet and out of sight of her camera.

'Dude!" someone said. "She's got like a mimosa and shit. Tania is cheating on us!"

Coughing, she put the glass down and rolled her eyes. "Guys, focus on the work. My breakfast is none of your business."

"What is it?" Jason asked, leaning toward his camera.

"Eggs Benedict." She lifted a bite to her lips and stared at them while she licked sauce from her bottom lip.

Desmond bit back a groan at the innocently seductive gesture and surreptitiously adjusted himself in his slacks.

"Damn. No fair."

"I'm turning off my camera now. I'll demonstrate the seventh problem on the whiteboard while I eat."

"Hey, wait! Who's trying to steal our girl?" another young man asked. "No fair bribing her away from us."

Desmond tamped down a surge of jealousy. Tania was his and Bastian's, but he could almost understand their protectiveness because he felt it too. Didn't mean he wasn't still imagining Theo with a black eye.

"That is also none of your business." She clicked on the icon to disable her camera. "Also, you're all ridiculous, and the clock is ticking. Get to work."

Chuckling inwardly, Desmond shook his head. Tania definitely had some Domme vibes going on—at least toward her classmates.

She turned off her microphone, then faced him and Bastian with a brilliant smile. "Thank you for breakfast. It's delicious. How did you know this is my favorite?"

Desmond left his concealment and strode to her desk. After giving her a thorough kiss, he brushed his lips over her temple. "Lucky guess. I wanted to make you something special."

She stood and wrapped her arms around him, then kissed his cheek. "It's perfect. Thank you so much."

"It was my pleasure." He urged her into her chair, then added, "Finish your breakfast, then do the problem you promised before your peanut gallery revolts."

"Ugh." She scowled at the screen, then traded her mouse for a stylus. "I'm still working my way through this one too. Pappas is the worst instructor ever."

"You got this, babygirl." Bastian rubbed her shoulders, then kissed her cheek. "We'll leave you alone for now. Desmond will take you to campus when you're ready. I'll do a grocery run and take care of your laundry."

"You don't need to do that. I'm sure you have better things to do with your time."

"Not really, no." Bastian crossed his arms over his chest and gazed at her sternly. "You're our priority, and we're not leaving you alone unless we're absolutely sure Dr. Pappas won't be a problem anymore."

He tensed at Bastian's implacable tone but kept his mouth shut when Bastian held a finger over his lips.

"I—" She lowered her head and ate the last of her breakfast. "Yeah, okay. I'm not going to be that stupid girl who goes off on her own when she knows some asshole is trying to get up in her business. Thanks, Daddies."

"Good girl." Bastian turned her chair to face the screen. "We'll leave you to your work."

"Okay."

After she finished her juice, Bastian cleared her plate and jerked his head toward the kitchen. "We need to talk," he whispered.

Desmond nodded and followed. After looking to make sure Tania was occupied, he asked, "What's up?"

"I got a call last night after you and Tania were asleep." Bastian brought up a document on his phone, then passed the device to Desmond. "It seems Killian O'Rourke owed Victor a favor, and he's decided to give us a full background on Marinos Pappas. Before you ask, I already asked Ray for the same thing. We'll wait and see if Killian's information pans out before we do anything."

"What the fuck did Victor do to have someone like that in his debt?" Desmond scanned the document and frowned. "Not that I'm complaining, but Jesus. Did you catch Pappas's juvenile record?"

"Sadly, it's just a shrink's evaluation. He was never prosecuted, and we can't use it." Bastian hesitated, then added, "Whatever Victor did, it was a big enough favor that Killian has been watching over her. He already knew about Pappas."

"I was trying not to think about that, but as much as I hate him, Killian won't hurt her."

"No, that's not his style."

"Pappas is one sick bastard. Maybe I shouldn't look a gift horse in the mouth." Desmond closed the file and returned Bastian's phone. "Tania isn't going to like it, but she can't be left alone."

"Nope." Bastian's expression hardened. "Our babygirl isn't going to take a piss without an escort. I'm going to have Braden keep an eye on Mandy and Bee too."

"I doubt Pappas will bother them. He's banned from the club and wouldn't be able to get into that gated community without an invite anyway."

Desmond didn't need to ask to know Bastian would have been happier if he could convince Tania to move in with them—at least temporarily. Her building was reasonably secure, but he couldn't help the twinge of unease at the thought of leaving her alone.

"I'm probably worrying over nothing." Bastian hesitated, then added, "But better safe than sorry, right?"

TANIA

Whatever her Daddies had said to Dr. Pappas apparently worked. He barely looked at her and was actually polite and helpful for a change. His behavior made the class almost pleasant—well, aside from the subject matter —but she hadn't expected him to make it easier for them. They still had to learn the material, and he wasn't being purposely obstructive anymore. Instead of trying to accost her after class, he scurried from the room the minute his alarm went off and he hadn't shown up for any more of their online study sessions.

As she walked into the corridor, Hassan nudged her shoulder and jerked his head toward her Daddies, who, as usual, were seated on the bench across from the door. "Those dudes have been following you to and from class for two weeks. Who are they?"

*Nobody special. They're just the people who made me their priority.*

"I—"

"Hey, if they're bothering you..." He glanced toward the rest of her classmates, who frowned at Desmond and Bastian. "We'll get rid of them."

Tania wanted to tell her classmates who Desmond and Bastian were. She wanted to bellow, "They're my Daddies!" from the top of the clock tower. She wanted everyone to know how they took care of her.

Aside from cleaning her apartment and taking care of the laundry pile that was fast approaching sentience in her bedroom, Desmond packed fantastic lunches for her, and made breakfast and supper every day. They'd added her to their music streaming service and made a focus playlist that actually seemed to help her concentration.

Bastian even bought her a bookcase and organized her reference materials, so she didn't have to dig for them.

Hell, she had real dishes in her kitchen, along with pots and pans, which Desmond put to good use.

Not only had Bastian filled her gas tank when the idiot light in her car came on, but they'd even replaced her double bed with a queen, telling her it was from one of their guest rooms when she complained about them spending money on her.

And... they fucked her into a stupor every night, and usually in the morning before she got up for classes. She greeted each day with a tender pussy and kiss-swollen lips, filled with wonderment over how she'd gotten so lucky.

Unfortunately, they hadn't discussed taking their relationship public, and it was too new... no, it was too fragile to risk damaging it with her big fat mouth.

"No!" Her face heated and she shook her head. "They're fine. I mean—"

"We're Ms. Andersen's security guards," Bastian said, giving her classmates a smile as he held out his hand to Theo. The gesture reminded her that she still needed to cancel her date with him, but she wanted to do it in private with just her and Theo—not an easy task when Desmond and Bastian refused to leave her side.

At the rate she was going, Theo would have found someone else to date before she got the chance. Strangely, Theo greeted them as if he knew them, with a wide, knowing smile and a warm handshake. Of course, she hadn't known Theo that long. Maybe he was like that with everyone he met.

She breathed a sigh of relief at Bastian's sort-of fib and nodded. The explanation gave him and Desmond an excuse for staying close. In fact, judging by how the slimy little shit avoided her, Dr. Pappas wouldn't say a word either.

"And we very much appreciate all of you for looking after her," Desmond added.

"Tania shouldn't need guards to go to class," Jason muttered as he accepted Desmond's handshake. "But thanks for making the asshole behave."

"Yeah," Owen added, "he's actually doing his job instead of staring at Tania's—"

Hassan smacked his shoulder and scowled, making Owen flush. "Sorry."

"It's okay, Owen. It's not like you're wrong." She smiled at him to let him know she wasn't mad.

"Yeah, no. Anyway, we still on for Caruso's tonight?"

"I can't. I have other plans, but maybe we can do it Saturday?"

"Saturday works for me," Owen replied, making her return her attention to her classmates instead of her Daddies. "We on for six like usual?"

"Sounds good to me. See you then!" She waved at her classmates and smiled when Bastian shouldered her heavy backpack.

And boy, did she ever have plans. Desmond and Bastian were taking her to Club BDE for supper, and by all that was holy, she hoped for a scene too—or at least to be allowed to watch a few. Despite her questions, her Daddies hadn't really talked about what kind of dynamic they wanted, and she was dying to see what happened in real life.

Although she'd promised herself she'd never go there again, it was different now. She'd even offered to go with them when they went to see Mr. Braden for a business meeting, but her background check hadn't been completed. The background check hadn't been mentioned for her first visit, and Bastian told her she'd only been allowed to come so he and the Elliott brothers could ensure her safety. She wouldn't complain though. In fact, she liked how they protected everyone.

Dr. Pappas was banned from the property, and knowing the Elliott brothers and Bastian would be there soothed all her nerves. Well, sort of. It still blew her mind that they owned the club, and she felt some kind of way about knowing Mr. Braden and Mr. Damian might see her play with her Daddies.

The only thing that made Tania more or less okay with the idea was knowing that Mr. Braden and Mr. Damian were both engaged to women who were close to her in age. Neither of them would judge her for being with men so much older than her, and she doubted their fiancées would say anything either.

That was the other thing she looked forward

to. She couldn't wait to meet Emily and Lottie. Well, Emily anyway. Tania sort of remembered Lottie from growing up in the same neighborhood, but Lottie was a year or two older, and they'd hung with different crowds. She also wanted to properly thank the man in the gold pants for helping her.

"Are you ready to go, babygirl?" Bastian asked.

"Yep." Although she wanted to hold their hands, she kept her arms at her sides, but couldn't help the quiver in her core when she caught their masculine scents. In a softer voice, she added. "We have some time for fun before we get changed for supper."

"You have an appointment first." Desmond held the door and allowed her to exit the building after Bastian. They took their bodyguard duties way too seriously, and never let her enter or exit a building without one of them checking the area first.

"Um..." Frowning, she grabbed her phone from her pocket and studied her calendar. "I don't have anything scheduled. Did I miss something?"

"You have a dress fitting downtown." Bastian looped his arm through hers and hustled her to the parking garage. "We'll make it right on time if we hurry."

"A what?"

"A dress fitting," Desmond replied, opening the

passenger door of his SUV. "Then hair, makeup, and a mani-pedi while the alterations are being done."

She blinked. The last time she'd done anything so flat-out girly had been for her senior prom, and only at Mandy's insistence. Tamping down her surprise, she said, "Nah, I'm good. I still have that black dress Bastian fished out of the trash. I think it's back from the cleaners."

"No." Bastian lifted her into the back seat and fastened her safety belt. "When you walk into Club BDE on our arms, you won't be scared and desperate, and I guarantee no one will lay a hand on you."

Desmond squeezed next to Bastian and tipped up her chin with a finger. "You're going to walk in like a goddamned queen, because that's what you are."

## BASTIAN

When her lower lip quivered, he climbed into the back seat with her, letting Desmond drive. Without speaking, he pulled her into his arms, letting her rest her head on his chest. She sniffed a few times, then rubbed her eyes and straightened.

"Sorry, Daddy B. I'm okay." She gave him a watery smile and took the handkerchief he offered.

"Want to talk about it?"

He couldn't stand the idea of making her cry, but whatever it was, he'd fix it. No questions asked.

"I..." She finished wiping her eyes and crumpled the handkerchief in her hand. "It's just been a long time since anyone has done something so thoughtful for me. I don't know what to say."

"You don't have to say anything. You deserve a special night." Bastian stroked a lock of hair out of her eyes and lowered his head to kiss her. She tasted like the ginger hard candy she liked to suck on when she was studying, sweet and spicy at the same time, just like her personality.

"I actually don't know how to be like that either."

"Like what?" Desmond asked from the front seat. "Perfect and adorable?"

"Oh, my god. Daddy Desmond, do you need butter with that corn?" She flushed and pulled her backpack into her lap as if she needed something to hug, and Bastian made a note to find her a stuffie. "No. I mean, I don't know how to be, you know, someone who wears a custom-fitted dress and gets professional hair and makeup."

"Well, someone must have given you that cute pixie cut." Desmond smirked into the rearview mirror. "And you had to go somewhere for waxing, which Bastian and I very much appreciate."

"Lord, stop!" She laughed helplessly and reached forward to swat Desmond's shoulder. "If you must know, I go to the barber down the street when my hair starts to hang in my eyes, and I used the place Mandy recommended for the waxing."

"Well, this time you're getting the star treat-ment." Bastian touched her chin to make her look at him. "You deserve to be treated like the queen Desmond called you."

Her eyes got misty again, and groaning inwardly, he straightened the handkerchief she'd wadded in her fist.

"I'm good." She waved her hand in front of her eyes and smiled. "Don't mind me. I'm just being a big ball of anxious over here, but people get real haircuts all the time, right?"

"There's our brave girl." Bastian cuddled her close and didn't protest when she pulled out her tablet and focused on a homework assignment. Her coursework was never far from her mind unless she was in bed with them.

He studied the image she pulled up. "That's the Southern Cross," he murmured. "We're too far north to see it. I didn't know you were studying astronomy."

"It's an elective." She pushed her lower lip out into a pout then added, "Silly me. I was so focused on my major classes that I ended up a few credits short, but it's very cool you know about the constellations."

"You can get a good view of the night sky from the beach near our house."

Bastian wanted to take the words back the minute they came out of his mouth. Their relationship was too new to pressure her into moving in with them, and he really didn't want to make her uncomfortable, but it was too late to backtrack.

"Bastian has a telescope on our deck," Desmond said as he wended his way through downtown traffic to the dress shop where a personal shopper was waiting for Tania.

"That's amazing." She turned to face him and pressed her palms together under her chin, then gave him wide, beseeching puppy dog eyes. "Can I please touch your telescope, Daddy Bastian?"

Desmond snorted and nearly swerved left of center as he laughed uproariously, uncaring about Bastian's stare burning a hole in the back of his head. When he managed to calm down, he said, "I bet Daddy Bastian will let you touch all his hard and long things, babygirl."

Tania blushed a brilliant pink and put her hands over her face. "Daddy Bastian, will you spank Daddy Desmond for me, pretty please?"

"Hey!" Desmond stopped at a traffic light and

turned, scowling at them. "I can't help it if she just laid it out like that. No way was I letting that one pass by without a comment."

Ignoring him, Bastian sighed, then said, "I'd be happy to teach you how to use my telescope, sweetheart. We'll have to watch the weather, but just name the day."

She squealed happily and kissed his cheek. "Thank you, Daddy. I can't wait."

Before she could dive back into her homework, Desmond found a parking spot, then hopped out and opened her door. "We're here. Are you ready to put on those glass slippers, babygirl?"

# 19

# CINDERELLA MODE
# ACTIVATED

TANIA

The opulent dress shop was too posh to have a bell on the door. Soft music emanated from hidden speakers, and she inhaled the scent of lavender and vanilla as she walked inside. Instead of overcrowded sale racks, sumptuous dresses hung on mannequins spaced several feet apart. More mannequins wearing suits and business attire were placed deeper in the store.

"Oh, wow." She turned in a slow circle, taking everything in. "I shouldn't be here."

She'd been in expensive shops before, but it always seemed like a waste to spend money on clothes when she spent the majority of her time in front of a computer.

"Why not?" Bastian asked.

"Because..." She swallowed and forced herself to smile when Desmond crossed his arms over his chest and lifted an eyebrow. "I don't know?"

His gaze softening, Desmond pulled her into a hug and kissed her, then passed her to Bastian. Only when she was breathless and staggering did they stop.

"This is exactly where you should be." Bastian kissed her forehead. "Think of it as practice for when you're not a student anymore."

"And have fun," Desmond added. "We have some errands to run, but we'll see you soon."

"Okay, Daddies."

The door clicked shut behind them, and part of her wanted to run after them. She couldn't afford anything like the garments before her, and there was no way she could pull this off—no matter what her Daddies said about her being their queen.

A door painted red opened, revealing a curvaceous brunette, who gave her a huge, happy smile. "Ms. Andersen," she said, rushing to Tania with her hand outstretched. "It's such a pleasure, and holy crap, you're gorgeous. I can't wait to dress you."

"Um... hi?"

"Oh, sorry. I'm Lourdes Lopez. I'll be your style consultant."

"Tania. It's good to meet you."

She pumped Tania's hand a few times, then scampered to a rolling rack full of dresses. "Your Daddies gave me your dress size, and told me they're taking you to the club, so I picked out a selection. Do you want to see them modeled, or would you rather dive in and try them on?"

"I..." She glanced helplessly at the exit, but her Daddies were already gone. "Lourdes, I have no idea what to do."

"It's all good. Everything I chose for you is easy to get into and out of. You can scene without worrying about tearing anything." Lourdes snapped her fingers, and a young woman appeared with a bottle of champagne and a glass. "Sit down and have a cocktail, and we'll talk about what you like to wear. Think about what makes you feel beautiful."

"I'm an engineering student." Tania perched on the edge of a thickly cushioned armchair and decided not to be embarrassed over Lourdes knowing what she'd be doing with her Daddies. It didn't surprise her at all that they'd given Lourdes some idea of what they planned. "My stepmother tried to *My Fair Lady* me, but I'm lucky if my shirt is clean and right side out."

"You go, girl!" Lourdes poured champagne into the glass and put it into Tania's hands. "You have a forties-era pinup figure, but I'm thinking you prefer tailored and crisp instead of bombshell."

"Okay, yeah. That sounds like me, I guess." She took a sip of wine, resisting the urge to drink it all in one swallow.

"I think I might have something…" Lourdes's words trailed off as she rummaged through the rack. "Oh, yes. This will be perfect."

She turned and held up a gorgeous blue wrap dress with subtle beading on the bodice and a flaring, knee-length skirt. Tania gasped and stood, then fingered the decadent silk.

"Wow."

"Right?" Lourdes opened a door to reveal a large dressing room with a chaise longue and a three-way mirror, then hung the dress on a gilt hook. "I think you'll say yes to this dress once you put it on. It ties on the side, so you don't even need to worry about zippers."

"Thanks. Gosh, it's so pretty" She blushed and toed off her sneakers. "Well, everything in the store is beautiful."

"Glad you think so. The Elliott brothers and Bastian want me to put together a business wardrobe for you too." She tapped her chin with a manicured forefinger as Tania pulled her T-shirt over her head.

"Take off the sports bra. The dress is constructed so you won't need one."

"Okay." Tania's fingers froze on the front closure of her bra. "Wait. What wardrobe?"

"You know," Lourdes smiled at her, revealing a dimple in her left cheek. "A suit for interviewing, and enough separates to create several looks for your new job. We'll set up another appointment for the suit, and a third when you have an idea what your office dress code will be."

"But—"

"Face it, sweetie." Lourdes pushed Tania's hands aside and unfastened her bra. "Your inside-out t-shirt days are numbered. Now, get out of those leggings and put on the dress."

Tania almost said, "Yes, ma'am." Laughing inwardly, she wondered if Lourdes was a Domme. She definitely had the attitude down.

"I figured I'd just troll the consignment stores."

"That's always a good choice. You can find some great bargains, but I'd like you to find your style and learn to pick things that go with the foundation pieces I'll help you select. It'll save you money in the long run."

"Yeah, okay." Tania took off her leggings and laid them aside. Thankfully, Lourdes didn't comment on her plain black panties. "That sounds like a better plan."

Lourdes held the dress while Tania slid her arms into the sleeves, then tied it closed. Stepping back, she cocked her head. "You look good enough to eat. I'll be right back with some shoes."

"Thanks." Tania shivered, imagining her Daddies doing just that when they saw her all dressed up. As pretty as she looked, she could only picture the dress on Club BDE's floor while they did all the things she'd only read about. She bit back a whimper as heat pooled in her belly.

"Here we go. I think these will—" Lourdes lowered the shoebox she held and frowned. "Hey, are you okay? You look like you're about to pass out."

"I'm fine, thanks." Ignoring her inconvenient arousal, Tania smiled and took the shoebox. "It's my first visit to the club, and I guess I'm nervous."

"You'll have an amazing time," Lourdes promised. "Best of all, your dress doesn't need any alterations. You can take it with you when you head for the day spa. Now, let's see how these sandals work."

Unsurprisingly, they were a perfect fit, and after Lourdes bagged her selections, she walked outside to find a black limousine parked in front of the entrance.

"Ms. Andersen?" the driver asked. He wore a cap

and a tailored black suit, and his shoes were so brightly polished, she could have used them for a mirror.

"Yes. That's me."

He retrieved an ID badge from his inner jacket pocket. To her surprise, she caught a glimpse of a shoulder holster under his left arm. After passing the badge to her, he said, "I'm Steve Walters. Mr. Elliott and Mr. Carter arranged for me to drive you to your next appointment, then to Club BDE later. I'll also be acting as your security guard until they take over."

Christ. Her Daddies had been serious about making sure she was watched. Warmth blossomed in her chest, and she resisted the urge to hug herself.

"Um...sure." She checked his ID, then transferred her bags to one hand and tugged her phone from her pocket. "Let me text them first."

> Someone named Steve Walters is here with a limo and said you sent him.

> Bastian: Ask him to take off his hat. Tell me what color his hair is.

"Um..." She frowned at the odd request. "Bastian wants you to take off your hat."

Steve obliged, revealing a steel-gray buzz cut.

Dark gray.

Desmond: Good girl. Have fun at the day spa.

She sent them a smile emoji and slipped her phone into her pocket. "They say you're you."

Steve smiled faintly and nodded. "They said to tell you that you're a good girl if I didn't have to remind you to do that before getting into a vehicle with a stranger."

Tania lowered her head, her cheeks flaming. "So, the day spa next?"

"Perfect. Your chariot awaits."

## DESMOND

"Please remind me that asking a parent's permission to date their adult daughter is an antiquated social convention." Considering Mandy was young enough to be Tania's sister, it was more than odd, but he and Bastian didn't want her blindsided by the news.

"Very antiquated, and more than a little ridiculous. Tania would laugh her ass off if she knew what we were doing, and I wouldn't blame her." Bastian returned his phone to his pocket after answering Tania's text about the car they'd sent as Desmond gave their names to the guard at the entrance to Mandy's gated community. "But I don't feel right about not telling Mandy."

"Same." He gave Bastian a quick smile as he parked in Mandy's driveway. "Do we have our story straight? We met Tania at the pizza place she likes and got to talking, right?"

"Caruso's. There was instant chemistry." Bastian unfastened his seatbelt and ran a hand through his hair. "It's not entirely a lie. Best to keep it simple and as close to the truth as we can without mentioning the auction."

"Right." Desmond straightened his collar and gave himself a quick once over in the vanity mirror. "Guess we better get on with it. Do you think Mandy will punch us in the face like Emmett did to Braden?"

Chuckling softly, Bastian shook his head and got out of the vehicle. "Probably not. Tania had a point about her marrying Victor, but I think she would be upset if we didn't tell her."

"True." Desmond held Bastian's hand as they strode up the brick path to the front door.

Obviously expecting them, Mandy opened it before they could knock. "Bastian and Desmond, it's good to see you again."

"You too, Mandy." Desmond accepted her hug and kissed her cheek. "You look beautiful as usual."

"Thank you." After giving Bastian a hug, she stepped back into the house. "Come in. I just made fresh sweet tea and some cookies."

"Where's Bee?" Bastian asked as he followed Mandy past several framed photos of her, Tania, and Bee. A large portrait of her and Victor on their wedding day hung above the stone fireplace in the living room.

"I sent her to play with the neighbor's kids. They have a new puppy." She led them to an immaculate kitchen, where a frosty glass pitcher of iced tea waited on the breakfast bar, along with glasses, a bowl of lemon slices, and a plate of cookies. Lowering her head, she sighed wearily. "Before you start in on me, Braden and Damian have already been by to read me the riot act about how much money I've spent looking for Victor. I get it, and even though I don't think he's gone, I've contacted a lawyer to have him declared dead."

Although Desmond hated the fresh desolation in her blue eyes, it was past time for Mandy to move on. Of course, she wasn't the only one with unanswered questions. Maybe Tania was right, and Victor was hiding somewhere. The thought had occurred to him more than once over the last seven years.

After they were seated, Bastian reached across the breakfast bar and took her hand. "We're very sorry, Mandy, but that's not why we wanted to talk."

"Thank you." She blinked rapidly and gave them a weak smile. "But if you're not here to yell at me, what can I do for you?"

"Well..." Bastian hesitated, then let go of Mandy's hand. "It's about Tania."

"What about her?" Mandy poured tea into their glasses and pushed the plate of cookies toward them. "I'm kind of irritated with her for tattling to Braden, so I haven't talked to her in a few days."

Thankfully, it seemed Braden hadn't mentioned the auctions. Presumably, Mandy had gotten the emails about them because of her lifetime membership, but she probably didn't know about Tania selling her virginity. Desmond certainly wasn't going to enlighten her. After sharing a glance with Bastian, he said, "We met up with her a few weeks ago at Caruso's near campus. Bastian and I heard about how good their pizza is, and—"

"We got to talking," Bastian interrupted. "It was like instant chemistry, and—"

"Wait." Mandy rose to her feet and grabbed a bottle of scotch from a cupboard, then tipped a healthy shot into her tea and drank it without saying a word.

Bastian took his hand and gave it a quick squeeze while they waited for Mandy to process the information.

"Are you telling me you're dating my stepdaughter?" she finally asked. "I thought you were in a committed relationship with each other."

"We are," Desmond said. "We want to ask her to be our third, but we decided you needed to know how we feel about her."

"And?"

Desmond hid a laugh. It seemed Tania inherited Mandy's lack of patience for bullshit. Of course, as close in age as they were, it might have been the other way around.

"We're falling in love with her," Desmond replied.

"And if things work out, we're going to ask her to move in with us when she graduates," Bastian added.

Mandy studied them for several seconds as she sipped her iced tea. "What happens if she finds a job somewhere else? I know she's being courted by companies all over the country."

"Then I guess we'll move." Desmond took Bastian's hand and held his gaze steady on Mandy. "We go where she does."

"Well, I can't exactly throw stones. I was nineteen when I married Victor." After pouring a bit more scotch into her tea, Mandy corked the bottle and set it aside. "I want you both to promise me something."

"If it's within our power, yes," Bastian said.

"Good." Mandy folded her hands in front of her and pinned them with a steady gaze. "Promise me she'll finish college before you discuss a committed relationship with her. Promise you'll support her professionally and personally, and make sure she has everything she needs to succeed."

"We're already doing that," Desmond replied. "Bastian is taking care of her laundry and cleaning, and I'm doing the cooking. We also—"

"I'm not finished," she interrupted, her eyes glistening with unshed tears. "And I'm definitely not ready to be a grandmother before my thirtieth birthday. Swear to me you won't get her pregnant. Give her three years before you even discuss children."

"Tania made that decision without us and got a birth control shot," Bastian said gently. "We're also using condoms because the last thing we want is to have children before she's ready."

"She's always been smarter than me." Mandy dabbed at her eyes with a napkin, and Desmond nearly sagged in relief when she smiled. "I guess it's settled, then. Welcome to the family."

## 20

# TIME TO CELEBRATE

TANIA

After looking over the lengthy set of rules for behavior in Club BDE, Tania tucked her tablet into her backpack and looked up. To her surprise, Steve turned to head into Mandy's neighborhood.

"Where are we going?" she asked.

"We have to pick up a few people." He slowed to a stop and flashed the guard his ID, then continued past the first turn that would have taken them to Mandy's. "After that, I'll drive you to the club."

"Are we going to Mr. Elliott's house?"

"Yes, that's correct."

"Okay. Sounds good." Assuming he was picking up Mr. Braden and Lottie, she sent a quick text to her

Daddies to let them know where she was and smiled at the reply.

> We'll see you soon, babygirl. Are you enjoying your star treatment?

> I am. I can't wait to see you.

> Just a little longer.

She giggled at the heart emoji and put her phone away as Steve backed into Mr. Braden's driveway.

After turning to look at her, Steve said, "Stay in the car, please. I'll be right back with our guests."

"As if I would go anywhere. There's champagne and snacks here."

"Don't get carried away," he warned. "You won't be allowed to play if you overindulge."

"I know." She held up a bottle of water. "I don't want to miss a single detail."

"Good girl."

"Woof." She smiled impishly when he rolled his eyes.

"And also a brat. I'll be right back."

Without waiting for her to reply, he went to the door and knocked. A few seconds later, two women burst outside and hurried to the limo, then crawled into the back seat with her. Both were gorgeous brunettes, with perfect hair and makeup, and wore stunning cocktail dresses and high heels.

"Hi Tania! I'm Lottie. Please tell me you remember me, otherwise it's going to be really awkward when I hug you," the first into the limo said as she sat next to Tania. "Your stepmom lives close by. And god, your little sister is so stinking cute, I can't with her."

"I think so, but—"

"Squee!" Lottie squeezed her into a tight hug. "I knew you'd remember me."

Well, Tania mostly remembered her. They'd barely spoken in high school, and that was a long time ago—not that it seemed to matter to Lottie.

"And I'm Emily Graham," the second woman said as she sat next to Lottie. "Damian told me you're studying engineering. That's so cool. I'm going to school for accounting."

"Ugh. No shop talk," Lottie said, holding up a thermos. "I have cosmos!"

"Damian said we shouldn't drink before the club," Emily replied.

"It's about the only rule I follow." Leaning close, Lottie put a finger to her lips. "Shh. It's cranberry juice, club soda, and a tiny dash of Cointreau to make it smell right. Steve will tattle and we'll reap the rewards."

"Ladies, are we behaving back there?" Steve asked before Tania could figure out what Lottie meant by rewards. Of course, she had some ideas. It was a sneaky, bratty thing to do, and Tania was totally down for it. She was happy to outsource her bratting, and Lottie seemed like the perfect subcontractor.

"No!" Lottie shouted, as Emily said, "Yes, sir!"

With a heavy sigh, Steve put up the divider between him and his passengers as he exited the subdivision.

"So, anyway..." Lottie filled three glasses with the mostly virgin cosmos and passed them around. "Do either of you know what's going on?"

"I don't," Emily said. "Damian gave me my dress and said it was a surprise."

"Same here, but Braden picked this one out of my closet," Lottie replied. "Did Bastian or Desmond say anything, Tania?"

"Wait. How did you know I was with Bastian and Desmond?"

"Please. All anyone has to do is give Shane a bag of candy corn and he'll spill the secrets of the universe. Anyway, did they say anything?"

"Who's Shane?" Tania asked, trying to decide if she should be upset that they already seemed to know everything about her.

"He's a club submissive. He's usually dressed in

gold or lace, and always has a bag of candy corn," Emily said.

"Oh, I think I met him. Gold lamé pants and a corset?"

It sounded like Tania wouldn't have to work too hard to find her knight in shining... lamé. She wondered if she ought to have Steve stop for a bag of candy corn.

"That's him. And Shane always has the best gossip," Lottie said. "So, anyway, did Bastian and Desmond tell you about the occasion?"

"Nope. They just sent me to that nice dress shop downtown, then to the day spa."

"Ooh. I'm totally jealous." Lottie crossed her legs and sipped her drink. "I'm trying not to shop so much these days."

"I guess we'll have to wait and see." Tania hesitated, then added, "Sorry, but I'm feeling really weird. I haven't worn a dress since my senior prom."

For some reason, Tania felt comfortable with Lottie and Emily, even though she didn't have many female friends. Or, actually, friends at all. Maybe it was because they were also involved with men several years their senior, but she felt like she could talk to them. Even without knowing what the men had planned, she was already having a good time.

"I don't wear dresses either," Emily replied. "I

used to be a waitress, and I'm still surprised when my clothes don't smell like diner food."

"I like diner food." Tania turned to face them and lifted her glass. "Here's to big, greasy double cheeseburgers topped with a pound of bacon."

"Stop," Lottie complained. "I'm hungry now."

"But no burgers with fried eggs." Tania put a hand to her chest and sighed. "I love them. God help me, so, so much, but they hate me. Every time I eat one, it's like the eggs *know*."

"Umm..." Lottie shared a worried glance with Emily. "What do the eggs know?"

"It doesn't matter how careful I am. The yolks explode on me every time." When Lottie and Emily laughed, she added, "It's like a ballista with dippy eggs. No, it's Russian roulette, with every bite having a greater chance of yellow catastrophe."

"Ooh-kay." Lottie topped off Tania's drink. "Our gorgeous engineering nerd will henceforth order her eggs scrambled. It would be a crime to mess up that dress."

The limo pulled to a stop and Tania drank the last of her faux martini, before following Lottie and Emily from the vehicle.

Steve held the door for them and inclined his head. "Enjoy your evening, ladies."

Tania's heart stalled, then restarted when Lottie and Emily gasped.

Bastian and the Elliott brothers stood before them, all dressed in impeccable tuxedos and carrying bouquets of red roses. Tania's knees wobbled and her core clenched with arousal. Desmond and Bastian were bad enough, but the sight of all four of them...

"Holy Mary, mother of—" Emily staggered and grabbed Tania's arm. "Damian? Wow!"

"Dayum," Lottie smiled as she looked Braden up and down like he was a treat she wanted to devour. "Emphasis on the yum."

⚜

BASTIAN

"You were right," Damian muttered. "I hate the monkey suit, but the expression on Emily's face is worth it."

"I'd say I told you so, but it was Braden's idea," Desmond replied.

Surreptitiously, Bastian let his hand fall to Desmond's ass and squeezed in warning. Thankfully, he quit poking at his brother because Bastian was too busy looking at Tania to play peacekeeper.

Fuck, she was gorgeous, and that dress... Held to

her body with a tie at her waist, it would take a single tug to have her bare for them. His cock hardened and he forcibly stopped himself from snatching her up and escaping with her and Desmond.

She'd been working so hard and deserved a night out. He and Desmond could wait a few hours to debauch their babygirl.

Probably.

Instead of answering, Damian went to Emily and placed his bouquet in her arms, making her blush as he kissed her cheek.

"Thanks, Daddy. You look... Wow."

"Only for you," Damian said gruffly, appearing both uncomfortable and pleased. "Did my Sunshine lose her words?"

"Well, you do look good enough to eat, Damian," Lottie said, although her eyes were fixed on Braden. She sauntered to Braden and wrapped her arms around his neck. "I think you'd look better out of that tuxedo, Daddy, but I'm jealous."

"Oh?" Braden gave Lottie her roses, then tipped up her chin and kissed her. When she moaned and tried to undo his tie, he pulled away. "What are you jealous about?"

"Huh?" She blinked, then shook her head, and huffed irritably. "Tania has two Daddies. Why can't I have two Daddies?"

Braden gave her an evil smile and her eyes widened when he whispered something in her ear.

"Tania needs two of us to keep up with her." Desmond gave Tania her roses and kissed the tip of her pert nose.

"I do not. Bastian and Desmond think I need a keeper because I don't cook or clean." Tania shrugged, then added, "Or, you know, do anything but study. Desmond is a fantastic cook though, so I'm definitely not complaining."

"Hey," Emily said, "you're a student in a really difficult program. I think it's great that they're helping you."

"Me too." Tania turned her attention to the club, and her eyes brightened when she saw Shane approaching them in a royal blue corset vest and tight pants. "Will you excuse me for a second? I want to thank Shane for helping me the last time I was here."

Before Bastian could reply, she hurried to Shane and held out her hand. Instead of shaking it, he hugged her and gave her a chaste kiss on the cheek before escorting her back to the group.

"Look at you," Shane murmured, eyeing Bastian and the Elliott brothers. "Don't you look fine? And the ladies are chef's kiss. What's the occasion?"

"We're having supper to celebrate Braden's and

Damian's engagements to Lottie and Emily," Desmond replied.

"Congratulations to all of you." He tucked Tania's hand around Bastian's arm. "And it's wonderful to see you under better circumstances, Tania."

"Thank you. And again, thanks for helping me that night."

"It was my pleasure." He sobered, then leaned close. "Daddies, I know I'm not supposed to gossip anymore, but we have a situation in the princess room."

"What situation?" Braden asked.

"We have a new Dominant in Dom drop. He might need a little help coming out of it, and his sub doesn't know what to do."

"Thanks for letting us know, but that isn't gossip, so you're off the hook," Braden replied. "Do you think it requires all of us?"

Shane studied them for a moment, then said, "Desmond and Bastian would be better. It's a gay couple."

Bastian shared a glance with Desmond, and they nodded. "Tania, we're sorry to ditch you. This might take a few minutes."

"No." She took a step back and waved her hand for them to go. "If someone needs you, you have to help. I'll be fine. Maybe Shane can give me a tour."

"I'd be happy to," Shane replied, smiling at her.

"Thank you, Shane," Braden said. "Damian and I will be in the restaurant with Emily and Lottie if you need us."

Before Shane could whisk Tania away for her tour, Bastian said, "Are you sure you're okay without us, babygirl?"

"I'm good. I'll see you soon." She stretched up to kiss him, then Desmond. "Also, did I mention how freaking hot you both look?"

"You did not." Desmond gazed at her sternly, then cracked a grin. "But we got the idea when you started drooling."

"Oh, my god." She waved a hand in front of her reddening face. "Stop!"

"Nope. I'm going to tease you forever and ever, amen." Desmond stole another kiss. "We'll try to be quick."

"It'll take as long as it takes. You need to help." She turned him around and swatted his butt. "Now, shoo."

"Your ass might be paying for that later." He smirked but didn't protest when Bastian took his hand to lead him to the princess room.

"I hope so!" she called after them.

As they hurried to help the distressed couple, Bastian couldn't help looking back at her. Although he hated not being with her for her first visit to the club, Shane had already proven to be more than capable of taking care of her. Besides, after his visit with Mistress Rogue, he wouldn't dare gossip.

Well, that was what he told himself anyway. When they reached the princess room, he and Desmond turned their focus on calming the situation.

"She'll be fine," Desmond murmured as he wrapped a blanket around the trembling Dominant. "The club is perfectly safe."

"I know."

# 21

# COME INTO MY PARLOR...

TANIA

"It's like an adult amusement park," she whispered as she watched a flogging scene in the pit. The woman held a black suede flogger in each hand, and they blurred as she painted her submissive's bare back with faint pink stripes. The submissive wasn't even bound. Instead, she held leather cuffs mounted to the top crosspieces of the St. Andrew's cross. Perspiration gleamed on her body, and her head fell back as she moaned in pleasure.

"That's Mistress Rogue." Careful not to disturb the scene, Shane replied in an equally soft voice. "She's incredibly talented with impact play, and especially with those floggers. I swear, she's made more submissives come from a flogging than anyone else in the club."

Judging by the number of people watching, Tania could believe it. She'd had no idea Club BDE was so popular, but it was almost as crowded as the night-clubs around campus.

People of all ages, shapes, ethnicities, and genders roamed the club, dressed in a mix of casual street clothes, formalwear, and leather. Music with a thumping beat was loud enough to hear, but not intrusive enough to disrupt conversation or the ongoing scenes. The scents of perfume and leather tickled her nose, and she inhaled the pleasant fragrances deep into her lungs.

Mistress Rogue's blows softened and finally slowed. After trading her floggers for a soft blanket, she went to her submissive and covered her, then led her from the pit.

"Wow. I think I might need to try that."

In fact, she couldn't wait. Instead of one person with two floggers, she'd have Desmond and Bastian. Arousal sparked in her core and her breathing quick-ened as she imagined herself up on the cross instead of Mistress Rogue's submissive. Everyone would watch them and...

She squeezed her eyes shut in a desperate attempt to quell her desire before she hunted them down. Her

Daddies were busy, and she wouldn't disturb them while they were helping other people, but damn, they looked hot in those tuxedos.

"Lucky thing." Shane led her from the pit and toward the corridor where Desmond and Bastian had gone. "Desmond and Bastian are almost as good as Mistress Rogue. I think it goes without saying they'll be happy to help you with whatever you want to explore."

"I kind of want to try it all," she confessed. "I don't even know where to start."

"Perhaps I can assist," a faintly accented male voice said from behind them.

Shane paled and turned slowly, then inclined his head. "Master O."

Dressed in a well-tailored three-piece suit and a crisp white shirt with diamond cufflinks, Master O was gorgeous with thick black hair and a neatly trimmed beard touched with a bit of silver. He also looked vaguely familiar, but Tania couldn't place where she'd seen him.

"Be a good boy and run along, Shane." He took Tania's hand and tucked it in the crook of his elbow. "I'll be taking over Ms. Andersen's tour. You will give us at least fifteen minutes before you tattle to Desmond and Sebastian. Also, bring a bottle of my preferred whisky and two glasses to my usual table, please."

*Ooh-kay.*

The autocratic bullshit wasn't working for her, but when she tried to free her hand from his firm hold, he wouldn't let go. She bit her lip, trying to decide if she should force the issue, but he wasn't hurting her, and she didn't want to do anything that might embarrass her Daddies.

"I..." Shane swallowed and nodded quickly. "Yes, Master O."

"Good. Be quick with our drinks."

"Sir, I don't know you." Tania tried once more to free her hand from his arm.

"I hope to rectify that shortly." Master O led her from the corridor to a secluded table in a darkened corner. Although several women gave him longing looks, no one approached to rescue her, meaning she was on her own. Shane appeared with a bottle and two glasses almost before they reached the table, then seemed to levitate as he made his escape.

Her nerves sparking with disquiet, she jerked her hand and nearly stumbled backward when he let her go. "Excuse me. I'm going to find Desmond and Bastian."

"No." His eyes glittered as he claimed the chair

facing the pit, putting his back toward the wall. "I don't believe I will excuse you. Sit down, please."

The force of his voice was almost physical and seemed to press down on her shoulders. Although her knees shook, she held her ground. "I'd rather stand."

Thankfully, her voice didn't shake as much as her knees did as her brain set up a clamor for her to find her Daddies. Club BDE was supposed to be safe, and she'd been assured of that more than once, despite her first experience with Dr. Pappas. Master O might scare the stuffing out of her, but the Elliott brothers wouldn't have allowed him in if he was dangerous.

Master O laughed quietly, and his gaze softened. "You're so much like your father, little one. Did you know that?"

"He's dead," Tania snapped. "What do you want?"

Damn. It was getting harder and harder to remember the club rules. Of course, if he kept being a total dick, she'd ignore them altogether. If Bastian and Desmond decided to punish her for it, they were welcome, but she wasn't going to let Master O's behavior slide.

"And like Victor, your temper is short." He poured a few fingers of whisky into a glass and slid it toward her. "I'd love to get to know you better. I find you quite... fascinating."

"I'm not sure I can say the same about you," Tania

countered, still trying to control her nerves. "And I certainly don't know you."

"Ah, of course." He stood and bowed over her hand. "Killian O'Rourke, at your service."

The name clicked for her, and she bit back a gasp. Although he'd never been convicted, Killian O'Rourke was associated with organized crime all over the eastern seaboard. For him to be at Club BDE meant that maybe the Elliott brothers weren't as careful about vetting their members as they should have been.

She almost asked how he was connected to Victor, but decided she probably didn't want to know. Some things were best left hidden, and if her father had been dirty...

That definitely wasn't something she had the nerve to ask about, and thinking of it made her heart hurt. It also made her think harder about her relationship with Bastian and Desmond. She didn't want to jump to conclusions, but she couldn't help wondering.

If Victor was a dirty cop, did that mean Desmond and Bastian were too?

Before she could reply, he added, "I see that name means something to you."

"I might be an engineering student, but I don't

live in a vacuum, Mr. O'Rourke. I wonder how you managed to get a membership here."

"Aye. My entrance caused quite the disagreement between the Elliott brothers, but as I'm a very safe dominant, they have no complaints." He grinned boyishly and shrugged. "In fact, you would have no complaints either, Ms. Andersen. They call me Master O for a reason."

*Wow. Arrogant much?*

Maybe the salacious nickname was deserved, but he left her cold.

"Aside from your last name?"

"Indeed." He poured whisky into the second glass but didn't react when she left hers untouched. "I considered offering you employment following graduation."

"You can't afford me."

"Are you sure? My pockets... among other things, are quite generous."

"Not interested." She pushed the untouched whisky across the table. "Excuse me."

"What if I don't want to excuse you?"

She studied him for a moment, wondering if he'd force her to stay, then straightened her spine and smiled when she remembered the rules she'd studied.

He couldn't touch her without her consent. And if he did...

Tania almost hoped he would, just to have the chance to get his smarmy ass banned.

"Aw, bless your heart." Giving him her best *fuck around and find out* smile, she said, "This is Club BDE, Mr. O'Rourke. You don't get to take away my choices unless I let you, and frankly, you give me the creeps. Enjoy your evening."

She decided not to think about how strange it was to be able to stand up to a known mob boss when she couldn't do the same to Dr. Pappas.

Instead of trying to break land-speed records as Shane had done, she kept her steps slow and easy as she crossed the club to the staircase leading up to the restaurant. Killian's gaze on her as she walked away sent chills down her spine.

## DESMOND

"Stay here until you're both settled," Bastian said softly as he massaged the dominant's tense shoulders. "The room is yours for the rest of the evening, okay?"

"We can get someone to stay with you," Desmond added from his spot on the bed next to the sub. "And the minibar has water and snacks. You can also call for a meal if either of you are hungry. It'll be on the house."

Nodding, the Dominant crawled into bed next to his submissive and pulled him into his arms. "I think we'll be okay now. Thanks for talking me down."

"Happens to the best of us," Bastian replied as Desmond got up. "Dominants have as much right to aftercare as subs do, and there are several members who will offer it without a scene. You can even set it up before you start."

"We'll remember for next time." The Dominant yawned widely and rested his head on his sub's chest. "Thanks again."

"No problem. That's what we're here for."

As Desmond closed the door behind them, Shane rushed toward them, his face drawn with panic.

"Thank god I caught you! Killian—" He held a hand to his chest and tried to slow his breathing. "Master O said to wait fifteen minutes, but I couldn't. And then—"

"Shane, calm down," Desmond helped him to a bench and sat next to him. "What's this about Killian?"

"He's with Tania. They're at his usual table in the corner."

"He what?" Bastian shouted. "Shane, we left her with you. What the hell?"

"I'm so sorry I didn't take on a literal mob boss on your behalf. How silly of me," Shane snapped. "We all know he isn't going to hurt her, so stop busting my balls, okay?"

Grabbing Bastian's hand, Desmond raced toward Killian's little hidey hole in the club's shadows. Although it couldn't have taken more than a minute to cross the twenty or so yards to Killian's usual spot, it felt like forever.

Relief warred with fear when he didn't see Tania, but he forced himself to stay calm.

Killian lifted his glass to them and smirked. "Did you lose something, gentlemen?"

"Where's Tania?" Desmond tightened his fists and tried to keep himself from beating Killian's face in with the whisky bottle on the table next to him. "What did you do to her?"

"Oh, I quite cheerfully tried to steal her away from you. Such a lovely young woman shouldn't be with men who should have been put out to pasture years ago." Killian poured another finger of whisky into his glass. "I suppose retired is a kinder word for it. Such a shame."

"This from a man who claims he doesn't poach?" Bastian asked. "Not that I'm surprised. You've never been all that concerned about keeping your word unless it gains you something."

"Careful with that glass house, O'Rourke," Desmond added. "You're old enough to be her father."

"Well, she is very beautiful, but I'm afraid she'd strip the skin from my bones with that temper of hers." Calmly, he took another drink. "Then again, Victor's daughter would be quite a feather in my cap, don't you think?"

Desmond's jaw tightened and he forced himself to relax before he broke one of his hellaciously expensive crowns. "Where. Is. Tania?" he finally asked once he thought he had control of himself.

"Killian, if you touched a hair on her head..." Bastian's hand tightened on Desmond's. "Nothing in the world will save you."

"Do calm down before you have a stroke, Sebastian. If you must know, for the first time in my life, a woman has quite firmly shot me down." Giving them an enigmatic smirk, he added, "She said *bless your heart*, and I've lived in the south long enough to know what a woman means when she says that. I'm bloody astonished there isn't a knife in my chest."

"It's a crying shame she forgot the knife." Desmond didn't bother to hide his malicious glee at the thought. "Now, where is she?"

"She sauntered across the club like she owns it and went upstairs. As much as I enjoyed sparring with sweet little Titania, you may want to remind her to keep her temper more tightly wrapped in the club. Her only saving grace this time was the fact we did not have an audience for her... disrespect."

Knowing Killian was right didn't improve Desmond's mood. Tania had read the club rules, meaning she'd purposely disobeyed them. He also hated the idea of having to punish her during what was supposed to be a celebration, but hopefully she'd behave until they got her home. He didn't want her first scene in the club to be a punishment.

They strode across the club and up the stairs. Bastian's sigh of relief matched Desmond's when they found Tania seated between Emily and Lottie. Braden and Damian sat across from them, leaving the chairs at the ends of the table free for Desmond and Bastian.

Tania's smile seemed fixed in place as she chatted with them, and her hands were clenched in tight fists in her lap. She perched on the edge of her chair as if she was preparing to flee.

A small part of him wanted to paddle her ass for even thinking of talking to Killian, but judging from what Shane said, Desmond didn't think it was entirely voluntary on her part. Aside from that, she'd managed to extricate herself from the situation.

A situation he and Bastian should have protected

her from. They should have known better too. Killian had already expressed more interest in Tania than was comfortable for either of them.

"Trade us seats, ladies," Bastian said as he pulled the chair closest to Lottie out. "I'm sure you'd like to sit next to your fiancés."

Before she moved, Lottie leaned over to whisper in Tania's ear and didn't get up until Tania nodded. Ever the consummate hostess, she beamed at them as she seated herself next to Braden. "The server just told us that the chef has a tasting menu for us, but it won't include wine pairings in case we want to play later."

"Sounds good to me," Tania replied. "I'm starving."

"Oh, me too," Emily replied as she cuddled next to Damian.

Desmond took one of Tania's chilled hands and relaxed as he tried to warm her fingers. Knowing she was safe eased the tension from his spine, and with him and Bastian surrounding her, Killian wouldn't dare interfere again.

"It was so thoughtful for you guys to make this dinner special for us," Tania said, "but I have a question first."

"What's that, babygirl?" Bastian took her free hand and kissed her cheek.

She pulled her hands free and frowned as she crossed her arms over her chest. "Which of you knuckleheads decided inviting a known mob boss into a BDSM club was a good idea?"

Emily gasped, and Lottie burst out laughing while his brothers gave him meaningful looks. Apparently, Tania wasn't done being rude.

Desmond sighed and shook his head, wishing he could kiss her for being right.

# 22

# MASTER O'S DEMAND

TANIA

Bastian grimaced and rubbed his temples as if he was fighting a headache. "Do you even have a verbal filter, babygirl?"

"No. I poked holes in it with a screwdriver when it got clogged with f-bombs during my semiconductor class last semester. Answer the question, please."

Thankfully, Tania's fear was mostly gone, leaving enough room in her head for getting mad. What the heck were they thinking to let someone like Killian O'Rourke into Club BDE?

Lottie giggled, then rolled her eyes when Braden glared at her. "I love you so much, Tania."

"It doesn't matter who let him in," Braden replied.

His arm moved under the table and Lottie squeaked, then mimed zipping her lips. "Master O is an excellent, conscientious dominant and has never brought trouble into the club."

"As much as I hate to agree, Braden is right," Desmond said. Slowly, as if he thought she'd bite—which she was seriously considering, he lifted her from her chair and settled her on his lap. "He doesn't violate consent, and—"

"And," Bastian interrupted, "we'll discuss this when we get home. You're safe, and Killian won't bother you anymore. Let's enjoy the engagement party, but we'll be discussing your behavior when we get home."

"Fine." She glared at the Elliott brothers, then added, "At least tell me you're protecting yourselves if he decides to act up. You don't want to be on the wrong side of a court case because of him."

Braden sighed and shook his head. "As it seems you won't be satisfied without an answer, Master O is part of the reason we require full background checks on all members and their guests before they enter. And yes, that included you, Lottie, and Emily. Further, he is already aware that if he brings even a hint of his... business into Club BDE, I will call the police and testify against him after I ban him from the club. Does that satisfy you?"

Desmond's heat against her back soothed her, but she slid from his lap and tried to ignore the flash of hurt in his warm brown eyes. She couldn't accept his comfort when she didn't know if she could trust him. Bastian gazed at her as if he knew what she was thinking but didn't say a word.

*God, please let me be wrong.*

"Not really, but considering you've already let him in, it's the best I'm going to get." Knowing her bad mood was going to ruin Lottie's and Emily's celebration, she took a deep, calming breath, then added, "I'm dropping the subject now and I'm sorry for bringing it up. Congratulations on your engagements."

"Thank you!" Lottie held her water glass up in a toast and gave everyone a beaming smile. "Here's to the best Daddies in the world."

To Tania's surprise, she enjoyed herself. Lottie was the perfect hostess, and skillfully guided the conversation to more appropriate topics while making sure everyone was participating. There was no way Tania could have done that, considering she was socially awkward on a good day.

Unfortunately, she was also self-aware enough to know she'd be running out of peopling ability sooner rather than later. Even without Killian O'Rourke doing his best to ruin her evening, being around so many people was exhausting.

As they finished dessert, Braden checked his phone, then leaned close to Lottie. "I was going to take you into the princess room, but it's still occupied. Sorry, Lottie-bug."

"Oh no!" She hugged him and kissed his cheek. "I guess you'll just have to tie me up and have your way with me in the pit with everyone watching. Such a shame."

"Mmm." Braden smiled wickedly. "I'd like nothing better."

After folding her napkin, she laid it next to her plate and said, "First, Emily, Tania, and I are going to the powder room."

Emily bit her lower lip and looked at Damian. "But I don't have to—"

"Girl time," Lottie interrupted. "We all go together."

*No… Not the female group bathroom trip…*

"I… um—" Lottie pulled her to her feet before Tania could figure a way to refuse politely. Worse, Desmond and Bastian didn't lift a finger to help. "I guess I'm going to the powder room."

"Yes. You are." Taking her hand, Lottie hurried them across the restaurant. After closing the bathroom door behind them, she said, "Whew. Now, Miss

Tania. Tell us what went down with the deliciously dangerous Killian."

"Excuse me?"

"Come on." Lottie led her to a fainting couch upholstered in red leather and tugged Tania down to sit next to her. "You went ballistic, and I need to know what happened."

"He... Well, I guess he propositioned me, but..." She turned to glare at Lottie. "Wait. Deliciously dangerous? What the fuck, Lottie?"

"Well, he is!"

"Nope. Not doing this." She stood, then crossed the room to give herself some space. "Do you not even know who he is? He's like the leader of the Irish mob."

"He's the one who bought my virginity," Lottie shrugged like it didn't matter, but didn't look at Tania while she spoke. "And even though he won the auction fair and square, he let Braden have me without a fight and even helped Braden recognize I was the one for him. He's also helping Braden find out who is running the auctions."

"And Damian bought me," Emily added. "Neither of us knew the auctions aren't being run by Club BDE."

Tania wanted to rub her eyes but decided not to ruin the makeup artist's work. "I don't understand.

Isn't Braden doing the auctions? I got a callback from a number saying it was from Club BDE when I asked questions in the contact form."

"No. And trust me, Braden is pissed." Lottie went to her and took her hands, squeezing them gently. "I know what you think, but despite his reputation, Killian isn't the bad guy here."

Holy shit. No wonder Bastian and Desmond were so angry about her auctioning her virginity. If she'd realized the auctions weren't being run by Club BDE, there was no way she'd have done it. Whoever created the website was freaking smart too. Between the spoofed caller ID and the URL, they'd managed to fool her, and she'd actually taken the time to look.

It made her doubly glad she'd kept Mandy out of it.

"He's always been really nice and polite to me too," Emily added. "Damian says he's a good Dom, even if he's not always a good man."

Tania usually trusted her instincts about people but was willing to admit she might have been wrong about Killian. Maybe he was a decent guy—at least in the club.

*And maybe I'm trying to justify things, so I get to keep my Daddies without destroying my self-respect.*

Unfortunately, nothing Lottie said could explain

how Killian had known her father, and she still didn't know if she could trust Bastian and Desmond.

When several women entered the restroom, she said, "We need to go. Since Lottie used the chick bathroom trip to get me in here, I'm asking you both to cover for me. I need some time to think."

"Bastian and Desmond won't like it if you leave the club." Emily said, sharing a worried glance with Lottie. "Will you promise not to leave without talking to them first?"

"I promise," Tania replied. "They're my ride home anyway."

"Wait!" Lottie blocked the door before Tania could escape. "We'll help you, but you need to tell Braden about that callback. He's desperate for anything that might help him find whoever is running the auctions."

"Please, Tania," Emily said. "Damian is really upset too. If you can't talk to Braden, at least tell Desmond and Bastian."

"I will. Promise. But I need some time to myself first."

## BASTIAN

"It seems our girls are sharing all the gossip," Damian said. "I keep expecting Shane to duck into the ladies' room."

A group of women exited the restroom, and Bastian frowned when he didn't see Tania. His unease intensified when Lottie and Emily returned to the table without her.

"We're back!" Lottie said, giving Braden a brilliant grin as she perched on his lap. "Did you miss us?"

"Sure did." Damian patted his knee, and Emily didn't waste time sitting on his lap.

"Is Tania still in the restroom?" Desmond asked.

Emily looked at her hands and leaned closer to Damian. "Um—"

"She wanted to touch up her lipstick," Lottie interrupted. "I'm sure she won't be much longer."

"And she couldn't have done that in the fifteen minutes you were in there?" Braden touched her chin to make Lottie look at him. "Why do I get the feeling you're holding something back?"

"Emily?" Damian turned her in his lap. "Where is Tania?"

When she tried to look at Lottie, he wrapped her hair around one tattooed fist. "No, Sunshine. Look at me. Where did Tania go?"

Emily sighed and shot an apologetic look to Lottie. "She said she needed some time to think and asked us to cover for her so she can have a few minutes to herself. She promised she'd stay in the club though."

"And before you get mad," Lottie said, "she told us she got a phone call from whoever is running the auction when she signed up to participate. The caller ID said it was from Club BDE."

"Goddammit, Lottie!" His expression darkening with anger, Braden shook her gently. "You didn't think that was important enough to tell us first?"

Lottie's eyes widened as if she finally realized how much trouble she was in. "I—"

"Tell us where she is right now, or I swear by all that is holy I will cane your ass until you can't sit for a week."

"I don't know, okay? She promised to stay in the club, but she was really angry about Killian."

"She only said she needed time to think," Emily added. "That's all. We swear."

Deciding he'd heard enough, Bastian rose to his feet. "We're going to look for her. We probably won't be back, so enjoy the rest of your evening."

"I'm sure they will," Desmond muttered as he followed Bastian to the stairs. "They have two very naughty girls to punish for trying to lie to us."

"Take care of your own sub," Damian snapped. "We'll deal with ours."

When they reached the bottom of the stairs, Bastian laid a hand on Desmond's shoulder to stop him, "I'll find Shane and ask if he's seen her."

"And I'll ask Vivian if she's left."

"Good idea."

Before they could separate, Killian strode toward them from his usual table with a dangerous, angry glint in his eyes. "Gentlemen, I'm glad I found you."

"Why?" Desmond asked.

"I already mentioned that I wouldn't give your bloody terror of a woman a second chance. You need to deal with her now."

Despite his worry for Tania, Bastian glanced at Desmond and smirked. "Well, anything that upsets you is a bonus for us, but what are you talking about?"

"In the presence of several witnesses, she stole my personal table, then told me to be a good boy and toddle off." Killian took a deep breath, obviously trying to calm himself. "I swear, if she was mine, I'd have her over a spanking bench so fast her head would spin."

"Is that a threat?" Bastian asked, resisting the urge to punch Killian in the face.

Unfortunately, Killian was right, and as much as

Bastian liked to see him taken down a peg, Tania needed to learn that her actions had consequences.

"No, because she isn't mine." Killian bared his teeth in a smile, then added, "I know how much you must hate the idea of punishing your submissive on my behalf, but after such a public insult, I must insist."

"We'll deal with her," Desmond said.

"Good. I suggest you do it in the pit to extend the lesson to other submissives."

Instead of replying, he took Desmond's hand, and together they strode to what used to be Killian's spot in the corner. Tania had a bottle of water in front of her and studied it instead of looking at them.

"I see I've been found already," she murmured. "So much for having time to think."

Desmond scooted a chair close to her and sat down as Bastian did the same. "Babygirl, are you okay?"

"Depends." She picked at the label on her bottle. "Are you going to yell at me for being rude to Killian? Because I was, and I'll do it again if he doesn't learn to keep his distance from me."

"Yes," Bastian replied, deciding to deal with her misbehavior before he asked about the call she'd received. He doubted Killian would give them time for what would likely be a long conversation.

"Although we think you deserve a damned medal for telling him off, you know the rules for how a submissive should behave toward a Dominant."

"He is not and never will be my Dominant," she retorted.

"The rules still apply, and we know you read them," Desmond said. "We don't like him either, but you need to treat him with respect when you're in the club."

She sighed and nodded. "You're right, and I'm sorry. I just couldn't help it."

Tania's lips parted as if she wanted to add something, but she shook her head and didn't continue her thought. Although Bastian wanted to ask what she'd intended to say, he decided to keep the focus on her misbehavior.

"Thank you, babygirl," Bastian said. "That just leaves us with your punishment for being rude to a Dominant."

"Oh, hell no!" She slapped her hand on the table. "Does he deserve a punishment for scaring Shane, or for trying to make me talk to him when I didn't want to, or for hitting on me and refusing to take no for an answer?"

"Actually, no." When she tried to leave, Bastian caught her in his arms. "Tell me the rules you read about how a submissive should behave toward a Dominant."

She glared at him and rolled her eyes. "Fine. All Dominants will be treated with respect. Submissives may refuse any Dominant for any reason, but all refusals must be done politely. All submissives—"

"That's enough to know you understood them," Bastian interrupted. "You could have walked away. He wouldn't have stopped you because he understands the rules regarding consent. Instead, you stole a Dom's table and were publicly disrespectful in both your demeanor and word choice."

"And you've put us in a bad position," Desmond added. "As much as we hate Killian, he's within his rights to ask us to punish you. You were also very rude to Braden and Damian."

"Babygirl..." Bastian brushed his lips over her temple and tightened his embrace until she stopped struggling. "If you refuse the punishment you've earned, you won't be allowed to return to the club."

"Fine." She wriggled free of his arms and stood. "Let's get this over with. After that, I'm going home."

# 23

# (UN)JUST REWARDS

TANIA

**K**illian stood at the edge of the pit and smirked at her as Bastian and Desmond led her to a spanking bench in the center. Asshole.

She kept her eyes fixed on him as she untied the bow at her waist and let her dress drop to the floor. It might not have been what she'd imagined when she thought about undressing for her Daddies, but there was no way in hell she'd let Killian think for a moment she was sorry for her actions.

Because fuck that noise. She didn't even care that she was basically naked in front of dozens of people.

*Yeah, O'Rourke. Look at me and eat your heart out at what you'll never, ever touch.*

Judging by Desmond's and Bastian's comments about him, she wasn't sure she believed they were dirty anymore. They might have defended him regarding Club BDE's rules, but they'd made their distaste for Killian more than clear.

She didn't care about Killian's relationship with Victor anymore either, or that she was taunting a man who could easily have her killed.

All she cared about was letting him know she wouldn't put up with his bullshit. He could kiss her entire ass and choke on it.

"Sweetheart—"

"You don't need to restrain me, Daddies." Instead of letting Bastian distract her with his bare arms as he rolled up the sleeves of his tuxedo shirt, she knelt on the bolster and laid herself over the spanking bench as she kept her gaze on Killian. "I'm ready."

Desmond crouched and cupped the back of her head, making her look at him. "Do you understand why you're being punished?"

"Yes, sir." She returned her gaze to Killian. "I'm being punished because Master O is a big baby and got butthurt because a woman told him off."

Ignoring the gasps from the audience, she added, "You know, like a kindergartener."

"Tania! You need to stop!" Emily whisper-shouted from behind her.

"In fact, I hope more women tell him what he obviously needs to hear." She grinned at Killian as she grasped the leather wrist restraints. "Use lube when you fuck yourself, baby boy."

To her surprise, he returned her smile, then tossed something at Desmond. "Clearly she'll need that ball gag to remind her it's often better to keep one's mouth shut."

"Bite me, O'Rourke. You don't get to tell me to—"

Desmond slid the ball between her lips before she could finish and buckled it tightly when she tried to spit it out. "I'm sorry, babygirl, but you really do need to learn when to shut up."

Someone handed him a tennis ball, and after thanking them, he loosened her fingers from the wrist restraint and placed it in her hand. "This is your safeword, Tania. If your punishment gets to be too much, drop the ball. A dungeon monitor will be watching for it, as will Bastian and I."

He kissed her forehead, then sighed when she kept her gaze on Killian. The asshole was actually smiling at her, making her wonder if he'd baited her into misbehavior—which made her even madder.

Then again, she didn't have to engage him. There were plenty of other places she could have gone, including one of the unoccupied aftercare rooms.

She wasn't sorry for mouthing off, but knowing

how badly she'd disappointed her Daddies...

"You'll get ten from each of us with a leather paddle," Bastian said. "They're going to hurt, and if you move, we will restrain you. Nod if you understand."

The minute she jerked her head in a nod, she heard a snap of leather a split second before her ass lit up with the fires of a burning sun. A second blow followed from the other side, and she gritted her teeth, unwilling to give Killian even the smallest clue about how much it hurt.

*Whack.*

*Whack.*

She blinked back tears but didn't let her gaze leave Killian's face even when her ass felt like it was about to burst into flames.

*Whack.*

A flurry of blows fell to the tender spot where her thighs met her ass. Fuck, it hurt worse than the first time Bastian gave her a punishment spanking. She almost lost control and yelped, but that would have meant showing Killian she was affected.

"Tania..." Bastian crouched next to her head and tried to ease her fingers from the death grip she had on the tennis ball as Desmond removed the gag. "Apologize to Master O, and we'll get you out of here."

She let her hands relax and grimaced at the tendonitis flaring in her wrists. Slowly, she stood, even though the pain in her ass and thighs threatened to drop her to the floor. "I'm sorry you thought I was rude when I said what you needed to hear, Master O."

"Tania, please. Let it go. It's not worth it."

Emily's voice wafted over her, but Tania didn't take her eyes off Killian's.

"Gentlemen, may I have a word with your submissive, please?"

Bastian and Desmond shared a glance, then Bastian muttered a curse as he wrapped a blanket around her shoulders. "Make it quick. We don't want her to talk to you again."

"And don't even think we'll leave you alone with her," Desmond added.

"Very well."

Her legs shook, but she held her ground as Killian approached, ignoring the whispered comments from the crowd as Desmond and Bastian took a few steps away from her.

Killian leaned close, allowing her to inhale his citrusy aftershave. "You are definitely Victor's daughter, little love. He'd be so proud of what you've become. So strong. Powerful and willing to stand up for what you believe."

"What?" She tried to back out of his reach, but Killian took her hand and didn't let her go.

He smiled. A true, real smile that changed his whole face into something kind, making her wonder if he showed that part of himself to Emily and Lottie. It would certainly explain their opinions of him. "Don't let anyone steal your words, Titania. You should probably phrase them more politely but shout them to the world and make yourself heard."

"I—"

"Ah, my brave girl. Listen and let an old Irishman compliment you for doing what no one else would dare." He sighed and stroked her cheek. "God bless you and keep you."

Before she could reply, he walked away.

The tears she'd successfully held at bay during her punishment welled and she couldn't stop them. How the fuck had Killian known her most painful trigger?

Why did it hurt so much for an absolute stranger to see it?

"Let's go." Desmond wrapped the blanket more tightly around her and swept her into his arms as Bastian grabbed her dress from the floor. "We'll discuss this at home."

# DESMOND

Despite his care, Tania winced when her butt hit the leather seat in his SUV. Using a tissue, he dried the tears coursing down her cheeks, but decided not to question why she didn't start crying until Killian spoke to her. Not yet, at least.

He'd only caught a few words of Killian's whispered conversation and wished he'd heard it all. If Killian had threatened her...

"Your punishment is over, babygirl," he murmured, knowing he had to be patient before he demanded answers. "Close your eyes and rest until we get home. We'll wait until tomorrow to talk about what happened."

Instead of answering, she gazed out the window, and although she didn't protest when Desmond pulled her against his chest for a cuddle, she was stiff in his arms and held herself apart as much as she could. In fact, she didn't speak until Bastian took the exit for Isle of Palms.

"Where are we going?"

"We're taking you to our house," Bastian replied. "You said you wanted time to think, and the beach is the best place to do that."

"Oh. I... okay."

"You have to promise us something first," Desmond said. "We need you to talk to us."

"I'd rather not, if you don't mind."

"We do mind." Bastian backed the SUV into their garage and turned off the engine. "You wanted a relationship with us and being in a relationship means you talk about what's bothering you."

"No. Not until I think my way through it."

Desmond rubbed his eyes and sighed. "We said we'd give you time, babygirl, but Bastian is right. We need to know what's wrong so we can fix it. You can have as much time as you want after we talk."

"Fine. You want to know what's wrong?" She stumbled from the SUV and turned to look at him and Bastian as she clutched the blanket wrapped around her shoulders. "Killian told me he knew Victor, and now I'm wondering if my father was a dirty cop. Since you and Bastian were such good friends with Victor, I'm also wondering if that's true for you too. I don't really like thinking the men I wanted for my Daddies are dirty, so since you demanded to know what I was thinking before I was ready to share it, you might as well give me the explanation you owe me."

Fuck. Was it true? Desmond would have sworn Victor was one of the good guys, but Tania was right to be concerned. He and Desmond had no idea what

Victor had done when he went undercover, so they couldn't prove to her he hadn't been dirty.

Bastian's face hardened and he took Tania's arm to lead her inside. Ignoring her protests, he forced her to sit on the couch facing the fireplace, then took the chair across from her. "Desmond and I spent a decade trying to put Killian O'Rourke behind bars, Tania. He hates us almost as much as we hate him."

Desmond knelt, then unbuckled her sandals, and set them aside. "We don't know what his relationship with Victor was, but I don't think any of us like the idea of your father being a dirty cop."

"The only thing we know for certain is that Victor did a favor for Killian," Bastian said.

She lifted her head, finally meeting Bastian's eyes. "What kind of favor?"

"Killian wouldn't share the details." Bastian got his phone from his pocket and brought up the document Killian had sent them before passing her the phone. "It was a big enough favor that Killian decided to give us a comprehensive background check on Dr. Pappas."

"And it was big enough that Killian admitted to watching over you for several years," Desmond added. "He knew about Pappas."

She scanned the document and gasped when she read the most damning details. After returning Bastian's phone, she stood and went to the fireplace, then stared at the unlit gas log. "Well, that's just a whole 'nother level of creepy shit and pretty much confirms my father was a dirty cop."

"Why do you say that?" Bastian asked.

"Because I can't see a mob boss watching over a dead cop's daughter out of the goodness of his heart. Whatever Victor did was valuable to Killian, and I can't imagine it was anything good."

"We probably won't ever know for sure." Bastian went to her and wrapped his arms around her. "However, I don't think he was. Killian said something about giving Victor information that allowed him to arrest someone Killian claimed was a really bad guy."

"We also know there are things the O'Rourke family won't touch. He doesn't tolerate human trafficking, and his drug business is shut down because it's too easy to get legal marijuana. He refuses to deal in anything harder than pot."

She laughed softly and turned to rest her face on Bastian's chest. "I guess relatively speaking, that makes him a knight in shining armor. So, if he's such a paragon, why were you trying to arrest him?"

"Racketeering, weapons, some murders we were almost able to pin on him, gambling, a couple of brothels—"

"I thought he didn't do human trafficking," Tania

interrupted.

"He doesn't." Desmond rolled his eyes. "His sex workers are clearing two hundred an hour and have a better benefits package than most corporations. He calls them gentlemen's clubs, and we were never able to prove prostitution."

"Dang. Maybe I'm in the wrong line of work," she murmured.

"Right? And you have no idea how irritating it is." Desmond scowled, remembering all the times they'd tried to bust O'Rourke with nothing to show for it. "We also know Killian won't harm you."

"How can you say that, Desmond?" She extricated herself from Bastian's embrace and tugged the blanket more tightly around herself. "You know what he is."

"Well..." He shared a glance with Bastian. "He's not our favorite person, and I would die a happy man if I got to see him in an orange jumpsuit, but he's very careful with submissives."

"And we can't prove it, but we suspect he's made one or two abusive Dominants disappear after allegations of abuse in other clubs," Bastian said. "When the submissives tried to press charges, the police couldn't find the perps. Maybe they'd done something else to piss him off, but it was like they vanished off the face of the earth."

# 24

# A HEART TO HEART... TO HEART

TANIA

Maybe Killian was good for one thing at least. She'd been a cop's daughter long enough to know abusers didn't often get what they deserved. Worse, domestic calls were incredibly dangerous for responding officers. If she took the thought a little further, maybe he was doing the world a service.

*Doesn't mean I have to like the jerk.*

"Huh." Tania turned to face the fireplace again and chewed on her thumbnail. "I believe you and Desmond weren't dirty cops, but I'm still on the fence about Victor."

For a very brief moment, she considered asking Mandy, but changed her mind almost as quickly. It was better to allow Mandy to hold on to those illusions and let Bee grow up thinking her father was a hero.

Desmond pulled her hand from her mouth before she could do too much damage to her nail. "Honestly, maybe you should be. Victor was one of our closest friends, but we just don't know. If he was doing things he shouldn't have, he didn't involve me or Bastian."

"That's something, I guess." Although her butt still hurt from her punishment, she returned to the couch and tucked her legs under herself in an attempt to find a more comfortable position. "Can we stop talking about Killian and my father now?"

Mostly, she didn't want to think about what Killian had said immediately following her spanking. Maybe he'd been guessing about why she'd reacted so badly to him, but everything he said hit too close to home. She especially didn't want to think about the note of fondness she'd heard in Killian's voice when he spoke about Victor. It was like they'd been friends.

"Absolutely," Bastian said. "Do you want to have your thinking time on the beach now? We packed you an overnight bag."

"Um... why did you pack a bag for me?"

"We thought you might want to change into comfortable clothes after visiting the club," Desmond replied. "It's gotten chilly outside, so I'll loan you a jacket if you still want to sit on the beach."

She considered the idea for a few seconds, then shook her head. "No. Mostly, I wanted to figure out how to ask if I'd put my faith in the wrong men."

"We're glad you decided to trust us," Desmond replied quietly. "We know how it must have looked—especially when the situation forced us to defend Killian."

"Yeah, I get that." Knowing she owed them an apology, she added, "I'm sorry I put you in that position."

"But you're not sorry about being rude," Bastian said.

"I'm sorry for being rude to Damian and Braden. I'll apologize to them next time I see them." She lifted her chin and met his gaze. "I'll also walk away if Killian tries to talk to me again. That's all you're getting."

Bastian let out a breath, then sat next to her. After pulling her into his lap, he chuckled and kissed her forehead. "Hearing you say you'll ignore that asshole is the best gift you could have given us, babygirl."

"We want you to promise us something, sweetheart." Desmond squeezed next to them on the couch. "Promise you'll talk to us before you have another meltdown. Let us in and let us help you work through it."

What they asked sounded so easy on the surface, but she'd kept her feelings bottled up for so long...

Maybe it wouldn't be so hard to try—at least with them. They'd already proven they wouldn't run when her feelings got tangled and messy.

"I promise, Daddies."

"Good girl." They held her without saying anything more for several minutes, letting her relax in their embrace.

She yawned, hiding her face against Bastian's chest. "You know what the really weird thing is? I was totally willing to throw down with a mob boss, but I can't seem to do the same thing to Dr. Pappas."

"Well..." Desmond kissed her temple. "Might have something to do with him being able to affect your grades and ability to graduate. Killian doesn't have that kind of power."

"Maybe." She hesitated, then decided to do what her Daddies said and talk to them. "Killian told me not to be afraid to use my words, and that Victor would be proud of me for standing up for myself."

"Really?" Bastian snorted with laughter. "He actually said something productive? Shocking."

"I know, right?" She smiled at Bastian's amusement, then sobered. "But maybe he had a point. Why am I letting Dr. Pappas disrespect and threaten me? I shouldn't need bodyguards to make that creepy little fucker behave."

"No, you shouldn't," Desmond replied, "but we're still escorting you to class."

"Okay, Daddies." She yawned again, belatedly covering her mouth. "Sorry. I'm just really tired all of a sudden."

"Unsurprising. You've had a busy day." Bastian eased her into Desmond's arms. "Let's get you tucked into bed."

"And it's definitely a bed big enough for all three of us," Desmond added.

"Ooh." She let Desmond help her up and grinned. "Is it big enough for shenanigans?"

"I thought you were tired," Bastian said.

"Not *that* tired."

Bastian laughed as they led her upstairs and down a hallway dimly illuminated with a brass wall sconce, making her wish she could see their house in the daylight. She'd been too busy drooling over her Daddies to remember much from her prior visit when she was nineteen, but Mandy had raved about their decorating.

He opened a door at the end of the hall, then walked inside to turn on a lamp. Decorated in shades of warm terra cotta and peach, the suite was easily as large as her apartment. Thick cream carpet cushioned her bare feet as she inhaled the scent of their aftershave mixed with laundry soap and furniture polish.

A huge sleigh bed covered in a burgundy comforter sat across from expansive French doors leading to a deck overlooking the beach, and matching dressers flanked a large window on the other side of the room.

"Wow. This is beautiful."

"You haven't seen the best part." Bastian opened a pocket door and turned on another light to reveal a massive ensuite with a huge shower stall and a sunken whirlpool tub almost the size of a lap pool.

"Oh, my god."

"Exactly." Bastian untwisted her hands from the blanket and let it fall to the floor. "And that tub is definitely big enough for shenanigans."

## BASTIAN

He opened his mouth to ask her about the call she'd received before the auction, then shut it firmly. Braden had waited this long for a lead. Another night wouldn't hurt him, and it was more important to reconnect with Tania.

Judging by the look on her face as she gazed at the bathroom, it wouldn't be that difficult to convince her to spend the weekends at their house instead of her campus apartment. Not that she'd take time from studying to enjoy it. Tania didn't seem to understand the concept of a day off, but her obvious appreciation made every busted knuckle and sore muscle worth the time he and Desmond had spent renovating the en suite.

When she took a step toward the tub, Bastian turned her to face the bedroom and gently swatted her butt. "You can play in the tub tomorrow."

"Late tomorrow." Desmond loosened his bowtie, letting the ends drape to his chest as he took off his jacket and dropped it on a chair. "We'll be sleeping in."

"You think so?" Tania walked backward until she reached the bed, then turned the covers back before sitting on the edge of the mattress. "I'm not sure we'll be doing much sleeping."

"Which is why you won't be setting an alarm tonight." Bastian laid his jacket with Desmond's, smiling inwardly when she licked her lips as he began to remove the studs from the front of his shirt.

"See something you like, babygirl?" With warm,

callused hands, Desmond slid the shirt from Bastian's shoulders, then kissed a path down his chest before dropping to his knees.

Bastian's jaw tightened as Desmond unfastened his belt but couldn't tear his eyes from the desire on her beautiful face.

"I see lots of things I like." She scooted backward and lounged against the headboard; one knee bent as she stroked her gently rounded belly, coming ever closer to her bare mound. "I've decided something."

"What's—" Bastian groaned as Desmond nuzzled his cock before sliding his trousers to the floor. Fuck, he was a damned tease. "What's that, sweetheart?"

"Based on empirical evidence, watching men get out of their tuxedos is statistically superior to seeing men wear them." She licked a fingertip and circled her clit with the damp digit. "Daddy Desmond, I want you to suck Daddy Bastian's cock, but don't let him come. That's all for me to do."

Slowly, Desmond rose to his feet, still wearing his shirt and trousers. After sharing a glance with Bastian, they both stalked to the bed. It was time for their babygirl to remember she wasn't their Dominant—no matter how many switchy tendencies she had.

It was strange. If another submissive had pulled that shit with him, or more specifically, with

Desmond, he'd have walked away. Tania wasn't using it as a power play though. She just wanted to experience everything all at once. She wanted to see him make love to Desmond—and Bastian suspected she wanted that more than anything.

Of course, it wasn't the first time she'd asked to watch. He and Desmond had been too focused on her to allow it, but maybe it was time to give her what she wanted.

On their terms.

Desmond got rid of the rest of his clothes and crawled across the bed. Without warning, he grabbed her foot, then flipped her over to her stomach.

"Hey!" When she tried to roll over, Desmond swatted her ass, leaving a perfect red handprint.

"Don't you remember, Tania?" He spanked her again, adding to the color painting her backside. "Save your baby Domme tendencies for your classmates—not your Daddies, who you've already agreed to obey."

Laughing softly at her mulish expression, Bastian got leather restraints from the nightstand, and with Desmond's help, soon had her hands bound over her head, despite her efforts to escape.

"No fair," she muttered, giving up the fight.

"When did fair become a requirement?" Bastian gave her ass another stinging swat but was careful to avoid the reddened marks from her earlier punishment. "Des, did we agree to fair?"

"Well, I don't see any cotton candy or fried Twinkies, so I'm thinking no."

"Jeez. I thought I was the sarcastic one in this relationship." She stuck her tongue out at them. "Okay, already. I get the point. Will you let me go now?"

"No." Bastian jerked his chin toward the drawer containing all the toys they'd collected in preparation for Tania's first visit to their home. When Desmond returned with a few of the more diabolical instruments of sensual torture, he added, "We might not be playing fair, but you're definitely getting a ride."

# 25

# A LESSON WELL (L)EARNED

TANIA

One of these days, she'd learn to shut her big, stupid mouth.

It wasn't that she even wanted to be their Dominant. Tania loved submitting to her Daddies, and she especially loved how cherished they made her feel.

All of Desmond's special breakfasts he liked to feed her while she sat on his lap... Every time Bastian rubbed the tension from her shoulders when she hunched over her computer... The way they held her between them as they slept...

"The problem is..." Bastian turned her over and tucked a pillow under her head, then traced a path down her breastbone with a callused fingertip. "You haven't learned to ask for what you want instead of demanding it."

Desmond laid what he'd been carrying on the bed but didn't let her see what it was. Before she could ask, he said, "Don't worry though. Tonight's lesson will teach you."

"That sounds ominous."

*And also delicious.*

Despite her trepidation, her core spasmed with arousal and her nipples tightened into achy points as they loomed over her.

"It should." Desmond lifted something from the bed and held it over her. "Your first lesson will come from these."

"What is that?" she asked, trying to figure out the chain connecting two pieces of metal she didn't recognize.

"You'll see." Desmond circled her nipple with the cold metal, making the sensitive bud even harder.

Her eyes drifted shut as she arched into his touch. "Oh, yes. That feels good. I think I like this lesson."

Without warning, a sharp, squeezing pain erupted in her nipple. "Ow! What the fuck?"

She struggled to sit up, but Bastian held her still while Desmond decorated her other breast with the torturous clamp.

Smirking at her, Bastian tugged the chain, making

the clamps bite down even harder. Tears pricked her eyes, and she panted through the pain until it subsided into...

Something that didn't quite hurt anymore.

Every breath sent the pleasure/pain deeper into her belly, and she couldn't hold still enough to stop the chain from dragging over her flesh in an increasingly tempting tease.

"First lesson." Bastian tugged the chain, making her bite back a moan. "Patience is a virtue."

He moved to the side, effectively blocking her view of Desmond.

"How is this supposed to teach me patience?"

"Tell me something first. Did the pain from the clamps ease after a few minutes?" Bastian asked.

"Well, yeah, but..." She rolled her eyes and sighed. "Never mind. I get it."

"There's our good girl." He took a long piece of cloth from Desmond and didn't give her time to protest before he had it wrapped around her eyes. "The second lesson is to trust your Daddies to give you what you need."

"I wanted to watch," she retorted. "How is this giving me what I need?"

Between the ache in her nipples and her empty pussy, Tania was losing patience with them. What would it take to make them do what she...

Demanded. She'd never asked and hadn't said please—like a normal human with social skills would do. Tania blinked and the blindfold caught her tears. Her Daddies deserved better, and she'd been too greedy and impatient to give them the same courtesy she'd have given a stranger.

"I'm sorry, Daddies. May I watch you make love to each other, please?"

Soft lips brushed hers and she inhaled the scent of their shared aftershave. She almost wished they smelled different so she could differentiate between them without sight, but she liked their leather and pine fragrance too much. Aside from that, she could tell them apart by touch, and definitely when they fucked her.

Bastian's cock was longer than Desmond's, and Desmond's was thicker, but they both seemed to know how to hit all the best spots inside her.

"Thank you, babygirl," Desmond murmured. "Do you trust us to give you what you need?"

"Yes, Daddy Desmond. I trust you and Daddy Bastian."

"There's our good girl," Bastian said.

One of them kissed her again, slowly. Gently. Patiently asking her to open her mouth instead of demanding her surrender.

*First and second lessons acquired.*

She couldn't wait for the third.

Their seemingly random, whisper-soft touches all over her body only served to ramp up her arousal, and she nearly came when something cool and slippery touched her soaking pussy. Her lack of sight made everything doubly enticing, and she almost didn't want the blindfold to come off.

Tania really wanted to see them though. The lesson on patience might have been well and truly learned, but it didn't stop what she wanted, and it sure as hell didn't alleviate her deepest fear.

*God, please never let me come between them.*

"Such a good girl," Desmond crooned as he slid something thick inside her that pressed almost painfully on her g-spot. The pressure only increased when the object touched her clit, making her wonder if it was one of those vibrators from those old viral retailer reviews where the user said the toy made her come so hard she levitated.

The toy in her pussy sprang to life in a maddeningly slow rhythm that was too much for comfort, but not enough to get her to the finish line. She tried to move her hands, unsure if she wanted to rub her aching nipples or push the toy deeper inside her.

"Ah, ah, sweetheart." Desmond shifted next to her, and someone pushed her hands to the pillow supporting her head. "You don't get to touch yet."

"Oh, god." Breathing through her nose, she tried to relax and tamp down her spiraling need.

"How much longer do you think we can make her wait, Des?"

"Dunno." Desmond—at least she thought it was Desmond since he was speaking—stroked her inner thigh and jostled the toy in her pussy. "But she's been so good for us. Do you think she deserves a reward?"

"Hmm," Bastian said as one of them tugged the chain between the clamps. "I think we have one more lesson before she gets her reward."

"Oh, yes. I almost forgot those," Desmond replied. "Tania, the thing about nipple clamps is that they aren't so bad going on."

Bastian laughed softly and flicked her nipple, sending a fresh pulse of need into her core. "It's when they come off."

They removed the clamps at the same time, and she didn't manage a single relieved breath before circulation returned to the tortured buds with an instant rush of agony. Before she could scream, her Daddies each sucked on a nipple, somehow both worsening and easing the pain.

"Shit! Oh, shit! Ow, Daddies!"

They both laughed as one of them untied the blindfold. "Aw, poor babygirl. Was it so awful?" Bastian asked.

Tania almost stuck her tongue out at them, but the toy buzzing merrily away in her pussy made her rethink the rude gesture. Despite her earlier excitement about what they had to teach her; she wasn't sure she was ready for another lesson.

Aside from that, she still had to figure out how to tell them why she wanted to see them make love to each other so badly.

"No, Daddy Bastian."

## DESMOND

Smirking at Tania's disappointed whine, he turned off the toy in her pussy before removing it. She was being such a good girl for them, and it was time to give her what she'd wanted for weeks.

"Ask us for what you want," Bastian said, using the low, husky tone that never failed to make his dick hard. Not that he needed help there. Desmond's cock ached with desire and his mouth watered at the thought of what he and Bastian would do to their sweet babygirl.

She lowered her bound hands and sat up. "Would you please let me watch you and Daddy Desmond make love? I…"

When she hesitated, Desmond touched her chin to make her look at him. "What, sweetheart? Tell your Daddies what your heart desires."

"I..." She shook her head. "I don't know how to ask, but I mean it to be asking instead of telling, okay?"

Bastian knelt behind her and rubbed her shoulders, as he always did when she seemed tense. "Relax, baby. It's okay. Just let the words come out, and I promise we'll understand."

"You barely touch each other!" The words spewed forth in a rush as if she'd been holding them back. "It's always me. My pleasure. My orgasms. I love it, but I don't, and I don't know what to do."

Desmond met Bastian's troubled gaze and considered his words before he spoke. "What do you mean by that?"

"You and Daddy Bastian give me everything I want, sometimes before I know I want it, but you were a couple long before I came along."

"Tania, it's not like that." Bastian spread his knees, then pulled her against his chest and kissed her temple. "Des and I are in love. That will never change, but you're important too."

"I'm afraid, Daddies." She sniffed and Desmond frowned when she wiped her eyes with her still-bound hands. "I'm terrified you'll focus all your attention on me and forget about each other."

"Baby, no." Desmond cradled her face in his hands, making her look at him. "That will never—"

"But what if it does?" she interrupted, not bothering to wipe the tears darkening her hazel eyes. "I hardly ever see Bastian kiss you anymore, and I can't stand the thought of breaking you apart."

"Shh, sweetheart." Bastian rocked her gently as Desmond kissed her damp cheeks. "Seeing you come gets us both off. Your pleasure doesn't take away from ours."

"That's right," Desmond said, "and this is one of those things you should tell us. We want to know what scares you or makes you worried."

"And we didn't mean to make you feel like Des and I don't still love each other." Bastian got a tissue and wiped her eyes before kissing her cheek. "We're just stretching that love around you."

To Desmond's surprise, the l-word didn't make Tania try to escape. Of course, Bastian hadn't come out and said he loved her—not yet anyway—but it was coming. Maybe Bastian was trying to ease her into the idea. She was so damned young though. Desmond pushed the thought from his head. She'd made her choice, and he was done second-guessing her.

"And..." Desmond kissed the tip of her nose. "If you're not in class, you have this cute nose buried in homework. Bastian and I might be making out behind you all day, and you'd never know it."

Giggling softly, she wrapped her bound hands around his neck and hugged him. "I'm thinking that would be more than enough to distract me."

"Do you feel better now?" Bastian asked.

"I do." Smiling impishly, she ground her ass against Bastian's cock. "Can we get back to what we were doing before my unscheduled meltdown?"

"We'd like nothing better." Bastian slid from the bed after making sure she was stable without his support. "Des, take off Tania's restraints, then lie on your back in the center of the bed."

He was moving almost before Bastian finished speaking and soon had Tania's hands freed. With her help, he turned down the sheets and moved the comforter out of the way. Once he was positioned as Bastian wanted him, he crossed his arms behind his head and smiled as Tania crawled across the bed toward him.

"Om nom." Before she could touch his rigid shaft, Bastian pulled her hand away.

"Ah, ah, babygirl." Bastian kissed her hand before he pointed to the head of the bed. "Go sit there and don't touch."

"Mean Daddy."

Despite her cute little pout, she obeyed and knelt next to Desmond—close enough that he could smell the perfume of her arousal over the scent of her lemon soap. His mouth watered for a taste, but he'd already figured out Bastian's plan.

Their babygirl wanted to watch, and that was exactly what she'd get.

"I'm only giving you what you asked for." Bastian opened the top drawer of the nightstand on his side of the bed and retrieved a condom and lube. "How is that mean?"

She opened her mouth to speak, then shut it and shook her head. "Sorry," she finally said. "I'll be patient."

"Good girl." Bastian climbed to the bed and knelt next to Desmond's head. "You know what to do, Des."

"Yes, sir." He took the condom from Bastian's outstretched fingers and tore it open before quickly sliding the latex over Bastian's cock.

As Bastian coated his erection with a generous dollop of lube, Desmond gazed at his face. The need in Bastian's eyes startled him, and he couldn't help wondering if Tania had been right. Maybe they'd been too focused on her to remember what they were to each other.

It made him wonder if she was more emotionally mature than they'd ever given her credit for—especially since communication didn't seem to be one of her strongest skills.

Without looking away from his partner and best friend, Desmond bent his knee and tilted his pelvis in invitation.

# 26

# A VOYEUR IS BORN

## TANIA

Entranced, she couldn't tear her eyes away from the raw emotion in her Daddies' faces. She held herself as still as she could and barely dared to breathe in case she took their attention away from each other.

*Damn it, I was right.*

She didn't think they'd been purposely neglecting each other though. They were just too focused on her to pay attention to their own needs.

Ugh. She hated the thought of being such a needy bitch. Was she really so hopeless?

Considering she used to live on takeout and didn't do laundry until she absolutely had to... Yeah, she was.

It wasn't just the sex though. She needed to cowboy up and start doing things for them. Somehow, she'd squeeze something kind for them into her schedule, although she had no idea what she'd do for the men who had everything, and enough extra to take care of her too.

Tania decided to think about it later.

Much later because every fantasy she'd ever had about Bastian and Desmond was coming true.

Bastian knelt between Desmond's splayed thighs and kissed a path up his chest. He buried his hand in Desmond's hair and kissed him hard as he fisted Desmond's thick cock in his free hand. Her mouth watered and she bit back a whimper of need when a pearly drop of pre-cum slid down Desmond's hard shaft.

*No touchies. No touchies...*

"Yessss." The cords in Desmond's neck stood out in sharp relief as he gripped Bastian's shoulder. "Fuck me, Bastian. I need you so goddamned bad."

"Gonna fuck you so hard..." Bastian hissed his pleasure as he lined himself up with Desmond's opening and slowly eased himself in.

Desmond's hips jerked up and he groaned, his eyes fixed on Bastian. "Fuck, yes."

Her fingers tightened on her thighs before she broke her promise to herself, but her pussy clenched, and moisture trickled down to make a damp spot on the sheets. Slowly, careful not to catch their attention, she slid her hand between her legs and choked on a cry as she rubbed her clit in time to Bastian's thrusts into Desmond's ass.

For a moment, she wondered if she should feel like she'd been excluded, but that wasn't the case at all. They knew she was there, and she felt blessed, and maybe a little humbled to be allowed to watch them love each other.

Sweat beaded on Bastian's forehead as he pinned Desmond to the bed, and the veins in his muscular arms popped as he drove himself into Desmond's channel. And the sounds...

God, she'd never stop loving their animalistic grunts and growls, so different than the soft crooning whispers they uttered when they made love to her, but no less enticing.

Tania wanted to kick herself for not using her words to explain what she wanted days ago, but at least she'd figured it out sooner rather than later.

"That's right, Des." Bastian grabbed Desmond's hands and slammed them to the bed over his head. "Squeeze that gorgeous ass around me, but don't you dare fucking come until I say so."

He lowered himself until his chest touched Desmond's, trapping Desmond's cock between their bodies, then kissed the sweet spot under his ear, making him gasp out a breathless curse.

"Goddamn, Bastian!" Desmond arched his back as Bastian pulled almost all the way out. "Fucking tease!"

"That just cost you, lover." Bastian's lips trailed over Desmond's jaw down to his collarbone. "Maybe I won't let you come at all."

Tania's thighs quivered as she took her fingers away from her clit and pushed them into her needy pussy, obeying Bastian's order. She couldn't…

No, she *wouldn't* come without her Daddy's permission. Despite her promise to herself to keep still, her hips rocked into the penetration. Thankfully, Bastian and Desmond were too focused on each other to notice.

Exactly like she wanted.

Maybe time was the gift they needed. Well, time and acceptance. Maybe they needed to hear that she was okay with them enjoying each other. It was something she'd happily give them every day just for a chance to watch them together, because holy fuck, they were hot.

She allowed herself a small smile. As much as she loved the idea of watching them every day, they liked fucking her too much—not that she was sorry about it.

"Damn, Des. Look at our babygirl," Bastian said, surprising her from her thoughts.

Her hand froze and she bit her lip, but Bastian didn't stop his inexorable thrusts into Desmond's back passage.

Desmond turned his head to look at her and smiled. "That's right, sweetheart. Play with that sweet pussy while your Daddies watch."

"No." Bastian chuckled, and gave Desmond an evil, but oh so sexy grin as he straightened. "I have a better idea."

"Um... Wait!" She tried to scramble from the bed, but Bastian caught her wrist before she could escape. "This was supposed to be your time with Daddy Desmond."

"Sweet babygirl," Desmond purred. "We love that you care so much about us being together, but you're part of us too."

"Yes, but no." She pulled helplessly against Bastian's hold on her wrist. "You're supposed to—"

"Sit on Desmond's face, Tania," Bastian ordered. "You're going to let him eat your pussy while I fuck him, and if you're both very good, I'll let you play with his cock."

BASTIAN

Gingerly, Tania straddled Desmond's face, then squeaked when he tugged down on her hips to get her in position.

Bastian didn't know why he'd been so resistant to what Tania wanted. Actually, he did, and didn't like himself very much for it because it meant he hadn't been paying attention. In a way, she *had* come between them, although it definitely wasn't intentional. They'd been too busy spoiling her to recognize her worries about splitting them apart.

Hell, maybe she hadn't recognized what she needed until Killian started poking at her emotions with a fucking sledgehammer.

She wasn't interested in watching him and Desmond fuck because she thought it was sexy—well, not entirely. No, she needed proof of their love for each other, and had asked for it multiple times. Bastian just hadn't listened for what was behind the words—like a decent fucking Dominant should have.

"Oh!" Her eyes closed and she let out a breathless whine, clear evidence that Desmond was treating their babygirl right.

Desmond tightened around him, squeezing his shaft until he nearly went cross-eyed in a desperate attempt to keep himself from shooting his load before he was ready.

"That's right." He cleared his throat to get rid of the husky rasp, then grabbed the bottle of lube and squirted some on Desmond's erection. "Tania, jack Daddy Desmond's cock. Make him feel good while I fuck his ass."

She rested one hand on Desmond's chest and did as Daddy Bastian told her. When Desmond let out a muffled groan, she rose to her knees, yelping when he dug his fingers into her hips to pull her back where she belonged.

"Naughty girl," Bastian chided, encircling her small hand with his larger one to demonstrate how Desmond liked to be touched. "What made you think you could get up?"

"But he—" She tried to take more of her weight on her knees. "What if he can't breathe?"

"If I die, I die," Desmond said as he lifted her just enough to speak. "I'll go out with a goddamned grin on my face."

"Oh, my god." Her cheeks turned scarlet, and she squeezed her eyes shut. "Just fucking god, Desmond."

"Daddy Desmond," Bastian corrected, smirking as Desmond repositioned her where he wanted her. "Since he's being such a good boy and eating your pretty pussy, stroke his cock like I showed you."

Desmond jerked and tightened around Bastian's shaft as Tania tentatively squeezed Desmond's dick.

"Fuck, yes." Bastian eased back, then thrust home as his spine tingled with an impending climax. "Harder, babygirl. He wants it harder."

"I..." Her back arched and she threw her head back as her entire body quivered. "Oh, shit. God, yes, Daddy!"

Unable to help himself, Bastian cupped the back of her head and pulled her into a deep kiss. She trembled against him, but her hand never left Desmond's cock. She stroked him faster and faster, occasionally pausing to circle the swollen crown.

He smiled against her lips. He hadn't taught her that trick, but it drove Des crazy. Slowly, he gentled their kiss, but didn't move from her space.

"I want you to make him come, sweetheart. Make him come all over us."

"Shit." She blinked then shook her head as if to clear it. "Fuck, Daddy. He has me so close, I don't know if I can."

"Focus, Tania," Bastian urged. "You can come after he does."

"Yes, Daddy Bastian." Her brow furrowed and she dropped her head, fixing her gaze on Desmond's cock. Her tongue shot out and she licked her lips as she tightened her grip.

Bastian bit back a groan and tried to concentrate on Desmond's pleasure instead of his own, but nearly lost control when she leaned down and took Desmond's cock into her mouth.

Desmond let out a garbled shout and wrapped his arms around Tania's hips, holding her still as he redoubled his efforts.

The sight of her plump lips wrapped around Desmond's thick shaft proved to be his undoing. Unable to hold back, he spasmed and buried his dick in his partner's ass. Desmond clamped down on him, and his vision darkened as all the blood rushed from his head.

Tania lifted her head and fisted Desmond's shaft once more, then met his eyes and smiled when Desmond's cum bathed her chest.

Still looking up at him, she lapped the crown of Desmond's cock like it was an ice-cream cone, then rolled off him and fell to her back.

"That was amazing." She licked her lips as if she wanted the last taste of Desmond's cum, then yawned. "You can tell me I was right at any time, Daddies."

# 27

# CHANGE OF ADDRESS?

TANIA

The skin around Bastian's eyes crinkled as he eased himself from Desmond's channel. "You're a brat, but you were right."

"Mmm," Desmond murmured. He had one hand carelessly thrown over Tania's hip and the other rested on his chest. "Very right. We need to do that again sometime."

"Count on it." Bastian swatted Desmond's thigh. "Come on. Let's grab a shower."

Groaning, she rolled to the edge of the bed and sat up, her muscles still quivering from their activities. "No fun. I'm sleepy, Daddy Bastian."

Ignoring her protests, he pulled her to her feet

and led her into the bathroom. "You'll thank me in the morning."

He was probably right about that. She was sticky and covered with cum, which would make waking up really unpleasant—a fact she now knew from experience. Not that she'd ever complain. In fact, she kind of liked waking up with the evidence of their love on her body.

"I'll be right there," Desmond said. "Just going to change the sheets."

"Thanks, Des."

Bastian turned on the water in the marble and glass shower stall to warm it, then unwrapped a new bar of soap. When she caught a glance at the label, she gasped with surprise.

"You have my favorite soap." She inhaled the sweet lemon fragrance of one of her few indulgences. "That's so incredibly thoughtful."

"We got all your bathroom stuff." After giving her the soap, he nudged her under one of the shower-heads. "Just in case you might want to spend weekends here instead of your apartment."

She wondered if she should have been surprised by Bastian's invitation. Wasn't that where she wanted their relationship to go?

Yes, but also no. They'd been together less than a month, and it seemed way too soon to make a decision like that. Of course, she'd been spending almost every waking moment with them anyway, and their house was a heck of a lot more comfortable than her tiny apartment—even if she didn't count their spectacular en suite. Besides, they had enough room to give her a private study place where she wouldn't have noisy neighbors.

Moving in with them—at least for the weekends—meant they wouldn't be walking on eggshells in an attempt to stay quiet while she worked, and it would give them a chance to take care of their own business without worrying about her.

"I—"

"Don't answer that question without thinking about it, Tania." Shooting Bastian a glare, Desmond stepped under the showerhead across the stall from her. "We're not going to pressure you, and—"

"I did think about it," she interrupted. "I'd love to spend my weekends here, but I'll need a quiet place to study."

"We...um..." Bastian's cheeks turned ruddy with color, and he scrubbed a hand through his wet hair. "We kind of already turned one of the guest rooms into an office for you."

She bit back a laugh at the expression on his face, then said, "Wow. Were you that sure of me?"

"No." Desmond grabbed a washcloth and lathered it with her soap. "We were really hoping though."

She leaned back against Bastian's chest as he lathered her hair with her usual brand of shampoo, and she moaned as his strong fingers eased the tension from her body. "Honestly, you had me with this bathroom. I had no idea what I was missing."

Desmond drew the cloth over her body, washing the evidence of their love from her skin. "Oh, really?"

The gently abrasive touch on her sensitive flesh made Tania wonder if she had enough energy for round two, but after such a long, emotional day, she'd probably pass out. She took the cloth from him and returned the favor. "All three of us sharing a shower? I mean, duh. We'd have to be the size of toddlers to try that in my apartment bathroom."

"We noticed," Bastian said dryly. "It's barely big enough for one, and you have no idea how many times I've knocked my shins on the toilet trying to wash my hands."

"Poor Daddy." She turned to wash his chest, liking that they smelled like her. "I know it's tiny, but it's also cheap enough I don't have to have a roommate, and less than ten minutes from campus."

"And it's in a secure building," Desmond replied. "It's not a bad place, but our house is better."

"You'll get no argument about that from me."

Bastian detached the showerhead to rinse her hair as Desmond got thick fluffy towels for them. She yawned widely as she dried off, making them frown.

"Let's get you tucked in, babygirl," Desmond murmured. "You must be exhausted."

"Uh huh, Daddies." She yawned again as Bastian pulled a soft t-shirt over her head. Desmond got a pair of panties from the overnight bag they'd packed for her and helped her step into them.

"Sleepy babygirl." Bastian tucked her into the center of the bed, then climbed in beside her as Desmond took the other side.

She was out cold the minute her head hit the pillow.

## DESMOND

He glared sourly at Tania's phone, which buzzed merrily from the charging dock on Bastian's nightstand. It was well after nine, and he already had pancake batter mixed up, but he wanted to let her wake up on her own. When he silenced the notification, she sat up and rubbed her eyes.

"Morning, Daddy Desmond." She stretched and

cracked her neck, then smiled at him. "Where's Daddy Bastian?"

"He's on the beach fishing for our supper, but he'll be in before too long. I'm hoping for a fat spotted seatrout."

"Yum." She climbed out of bed and hugged his waist. "What time is it anyway?"

"Just after nine." He hesitated, then added, "I think you got a text. You woke up when I silenced the notification."

"Ugh." She trudged to the nightstand and frowned when she read the message. "It's from Theo, but it's not the number I have for him."

She sent a quick reply, and her frown faded when another text notification sounded. "Oh, that's a bummer. He says he lost his phone and is using a friend's but wants to know if I have a few hours to help him study for the midterm. He wants me to meet him at a coffee shop in North Charleston."

"You could invite him here. I'll make lunch for both of you."

"I... Give me a few minutes." Tania crossed the room and rummaged through her bag for clean clothes, then went into the bathroom. A few moments later, he heard water run and the sound of her brushing her teeth. He waited somewhat patiently until she came out but was beginning to wonder what had made her hesitate.

When she got out of the bathroom, he asked, "Are you okay, Tania?"

She nodded and as she dressed, she said, "I kind of want to meet Theo alone, Daddy. Do you mind if I borrow your car?"

He let out a breath through his nose, trying to control the sudden desire to chain her to the bed. "First, tell me why you want to meet him alone."

"Because he's a really nice guy, and he kind of asked me out. And I was fighting with you and Daddy Bastian, so I might have said yes, and now I need to tell him I can't, but I don't want to embarrass him, and—"

As much as he hated the idea of her spending time with the boy, he could see her point. Nobody liked to get shot down, and he knew what it felt like. If she wanted to break her date without an audience, he didn't want to stop her.

Well, as long as Theo understood he wouldn't be going out with Desmond's and Bastian's babygirl.

She took a deep breath and blushed. "Sorry. I babble when I'm nervous. That was way more information than you probably wanted."

"Why are you nervous?" He tucked a lock of hair

behind her ear, then stroked the silken skin along her jaw. "Does he frighten you?"

"Theo? Heck, no." She laughed and dragged a brush through her short hair. "He wanted to have our date after graduation on a day I can't even remember now."

*The twelfth of June, six o'clock at Caruso's.*

"Well, I've only talked to him a few times, but I suppose he seemed like a nice enough boy," Desmond replied. "Do you have time for breakfast before you head out?"

"I really want to get this done, so I'll grab a muffin at the coffee shop while we study." She wrapped her arms around his neck, then kissed him.

He took control, deepening their kiss until she whimpered and tried to move toward the bed. Chuckling softly, he smoothed her hair and kissed her forehead. "I thought you were going to help Theo study after you break your date with him."

She blinked at him, then touched her swollen lips. The lust faded from her eyes, and she shook her head. "No fair how you kiss me stupid, Daddy."

"I still don't see cotton candy or fried Twinkies," he countered, grinning at her.

"Ooh!" She stomped her foot, but he didn't miss the amusement in her sparkling hazel eyes. "I'm gonna bounce before you come up with another lame fair joke."

"First, text me the address of where you're going."

"No problem." She sent the message, and his phone chimed with the incoming text. "It shouldn't be too hard to find."

"Nope. I know the place. Your backpack is next to the door leading to the garage, and the keys to my SUV are in the blue ceramic dish on the counter."

"Thanks, Daddy!" She stole another kiss, then hurried from the bedroom.

He followed to make sure she found her bag and the keys. After tapping the button to open the garage door, he said, "Text me when you get there, and when you're on your way home, okay?"

"I will. See you soon, Daddy!" She got behind the wheel, then blew him a kiss before driving away.

## 28

# A VERY DANGEROUS
# ROAD TRIP

TANIA

Daddy Desmond had much nicer wheels than she did. She was especially a fan of his expensive sound system and how the vehicle linked almost instantaneously with her phone. Instead of listening to crappy broadcast radio, she got streaming music and a giant map on the dash screen to help her find her way to the coffee shop where she was supposed to break her date with Theo.

Dang. She really wished she'd invited him to her Daddies' house. It had been barely twenty minutes and she missed them already. Unfortunately, she couldn't bring herself to hurt Theo like that. He was just too nice, and even though there wasn't any chemistry between them, he deserved better than to have a date broken in her new lovers' house.

Maybe, as usual, she was overthinking things. It was possible he wouldn't care if she broke their date, and she would just look weird. She shrugged inwardly and decided she didn't care. It wouldn't be the first time someone thought she was weird.

She found the coffee shop easily, and even managed to snag a parking spot only a few dozen yards from the entrance. Man, she was beginning to love Daddy Desmond's SUV. The bigger backup camera was *nice* for city parking.

After gathering her bag and phone, she popped the locks to get out, but before she could exit the SUV, someone opened the passenger side door and got in. Thinking she was being carjacked, she didn't dare waste her breath on screams or pleading that wouldn't help. Her heart pounding in her chest, she scrambled to open the driver's side door.

As nice as it was, no car was worth her life, and bad things happened to people who got carjacked.

Before she could make her escape, the carjacker grabbed the back of her shirt and yanked hard, pulling her back into her seat. She turned slowly and froze.

"Dr. Pappas? What the hell are you doing?"

"I'm taking what belongs to me." A sharp,

metallic click filled the vehicle, and he smiled as he pointed a suppressed 9mm pistol at her face. With his free hand, he snatched her phone from the mount on the dash, then cracked his door open and threw it to the ground. "Start the car and drive, please."

Tania glanced around, praying for someone... anyone... to walk by, but even if they had, the SUV's windows were tinted, making it very difficult to see in. Maybe, if she was quick enough, she might be able to run before he got a shot off, but...

No. Just fuck no. He'd bullied her long enough and she was fucking done. She lifted her chin and stared him down. If she could hold her own against an actual Irish mob boss, she could certainly do it to the little prick in the passenger seat of her Daddy's SUV.

"Put the gun away and get out of my car. If you're very lucky, I won't press charges."

He laughed softly, but the sound jangled in her ears. Without warning, he backhanded her, catching her temple with the butt of his pistol. When she cried out, he slapped his hand over her mouth and put the muzzle of the pistol under her chin.

She closed her eyes, trying to will the pain from her head and the nausea from her belly as blood trickled down the side of her face. "I—"

"I asked you to drive, Titania, and don't bother

thinking your bodyguards will come after you." His dark brown eyes glittered spitefully, making her shiver. "If I'm forced to ask again, you won't like the next lesson on a young lady's proper behavior."

He was wrong. Her Daddies would come looking when she didn't text them. In fact, she doubted they'd wait much more than an hour before starting the hunt. Unfortunately, that would put her almost two full hours ahead of them if she started driving now.

Swallowing down her fear, Tania nodded, unable to bring herself to look at him again. Her hand shook as she stepped on the brake and pressed the starter button. "Where are we going?"

"Where are we going, sir," he prompted.

Bile filled her throat until she had to cough to clear it. "Where are we going, sir?"

He leaned close and muttered a soft curse. "Get on I-26, going north. It will be in your best interest if we have enough fuel to get to our destination, but I believe you owe me an apology for not having a full tank."

*Oh, I'm so sorry I didn't fill up the tank to make it easier for you to kidnap me.*

Christ. Pappas was off his rocker. And that made him even scarier than Killian O'Rourke.

"I'm sorry I didn't stop for gas, sir."

"Of course, you are. It was quite negligent." He turned in his seat and rested the gun on his knee, pointing it at her chest. "Now, as we both know you're a naughty girl who goes to sex clubs, I believe it's time to give you a new list of rules regarding your behavior."

When he paused, obviously waiting for a response, she said, "Yes, sir."

"Good girl. You're learning." She caught his smile out of the corner of her eye as she merged onto the expressway. "Now, regarding your master's program, I've taken the liberty of submitting your application to Dr. Ng. We'll start work together in the fall after I've had time to train you."

"Sir, may I ask who will pay for it?"

"You're a smart girl." He prodded her ribs with the pistol and chuckled. "I'm sure you'll figure something out."

"Yes, sir."

*That's right. Keep the crazy man happy and chatty. I don't have a spot on my bingo card for a gunshot wound.*

God, she needed her Daddies. Letting out a slow breath, she blinked back a few tears before Dr. Pappas caught her crying. If she managed to get herself out of this mess, she'd never leave their sides again.

She couldn't allow herself to think she'd never see

them again—especially since she hadn't told them how much she loved them.

Theo would just have to deal with having their date broken in front of witnesses. She didn't bother to ask where he was. He was probably safely, cluelessly in his dorm room. She should have known better than to trust a text without an actual phone call.

Dr. Pappas droned, filling her head with useless, contradictory, and frankly baffling rules until she lost interest and tuned him out in favor of finding a way out of her situation.

"Titania!" he snapped, just as she was about to floor the accelerator to pass a trooper in a desperate hope she'd get pulled over. "Quiz time."

"Sir?"

"How long did I say your hair should be?"

"I..." She tried to come up with the answer he wanted, but her voice stalled when he held the gun to her temple. He pressed it hard against the cut he'd given her, sending a vicious shard of pain into her face.

"To your lovely bottom, Titania. A young lady should never cut her hair." Slowly, he removed the pistol, then added, "Inattention will cost you dearly, my love. I suggest you focus."

## BASTIAN

"I've texted her dozens of times," Desmond snapped, scanning the streets for their missing babygirl. "She won't answer, we haven't found a trace of my vehicle, and Theo's roommate says he's sleeping off a night of studying."

Bastian cursed under his breath and tried to remind himself that Tania was a grown woman and perfectly capable of driving herself across town for a study session. Desmond had no reason to think otherwise—especially since Dr. Pappas had given up his harassment of her.

He could have almost thought she'd forgotten to text them—if not for Desmond's missing SUV, and the fact that the barista in the coffee shop Tania indicated hadn't seen her or Theo. His blood chilled when, not for the first time, he wondered if she'd gotten carjacked.

Worse, she'd been taken to a secondary location, and...

He stopped the thought in its tracks. If he went there even once, his panic would take over and he'd be useless.

"Okay." He cupped Desmond's cheeks and

brushed a kiss over his mouth. "It's okay. We'll find her."

"How?" Desmond asked, jerking out of his reach. "She's over twenty-one and you know we can't report her missing yet."

"We call in favors. All of them." Bastian tugged his phone from his pocket and scrolled to find Braden's contact before tapping to connect the call.

When it was answered, he said, "Braden, I need Killian O'Rourke's private number. Tania went missing this morning and we suspect foul play."

"Shit. Did you call the cops?" Braden asked.

"We reported Desmond's car stolen. She was driving it when she vanished. It would be different if she was underage, but as an adult, she hasn't been missing long enough for them to start a search."

"Are you sure she hasn't wandered off with a friend like Lottie did?"

"No, not like that." Bastian's jaw tightened, remembering when Braden asked him to have the police look for Lottie. "She went to a study session at a coffee shop in North Charleston and told us exactly where she'd be. She also promised to text us when she got there, but the barista hasn't seen Tania or her classmate."

"And you think Killian has the means to help you."

"I know he does."

"Bastian, I don't think you want to owe him a favor." Braden went silent for a moment, then added, "But if that's what you want, I'll text you his contact."

"If he finds our babygirl, Desmond and I will both kiss his ass in public."

"Thanks, but I didn't need that visual of my brother in my head. Let me know if I can help with anything else."

He opened the text with Killian's number, but before he could call, someone laughed behind him.

"I'm totally telling Uncle Killian you said that," a vaguely familiar man said. He was an indeterminate age, with gray eyes and silvery hair shaved on the sides. The hair made Bastian think he was over thirty, but his face didn't bear any lines or sun damage.

"Who the fuck are you?" Desmond asked.

"I'm crushed you don't remember me." His lips twisted and he pulled a dark brown wig from his jacket. He put it on, then added a pair of glasses. "Do you know me now?"

"Theo?" What the..." Desmond lunged for Theo, making Bastian scramble to catch him. "What the fuck did you do to Tania?"

"Chill out," Theo snapped. He held out Tania's phone, then added, "We tracked her phone here and found it in the gutter. Unfortunately, she isn't driving her own car."

"How the fuck do you know that?" Bastian demanded, still holding Desmond back.

"Please." Theo put his glasses and wig away and rolled his eyes. "We have a GPS locator on her car. If she'd been driving it like she should have been, I'd already know where she was."

"Son of a bitch."

*Just how big was the debt Killian owed Victor?*

"Why did it take you so long to help her with Dr. Pappas?" Bastian asked. "He's been bugging her all semester."

"My job was to watch her and not intervene unless she was in physical danger." Grimacing, he cursed under his breath. "If my uncle had let me, I would have made Dr. Pappas gator food weeks ago for being such a shit human being."

"You can tell him you told him so after we find Tania," Desmond said.

"I plan to." Theo pointed at the coffee shop where Tania was supposed to have met him. "Let's have some coffee while I narrow down where she might have been taken."

When they were seated with their drinks, Theo spread out a paper map. "I assume you reported the car stolen right?"

"Yes. Tania is over eighteen, so—"

"Yeah, I know. Cops won't look for her yet, but they'll look for the car." Theo produced string and a pencil from his pocket. "How much gas was in it? Need the make and model too."

"What are you doing?" Desmond asked. "Nobody uses paper maps anymore."

"Call it an affectation and get back on topic. How much gas was in your vehicle?"

"Maybe a quarter tank," Desmond said. "Less than a hundred miles."

"Finally, something actually helpful," Theo muttered, placing the string on the map. "Hold that there. It's where we are now."

Bastian laid his thumb on the end of the string, belatedly realizing what Theo was doing. Theo drew a circle on the map, then leaned back in his chair and took a sip of his coffee before returning the string and pencil to his pocket.

"I'm waiting for a contact to hack into video surveillance, but I'm betting they went north on I-26," Theo said as he folded the map and slid it and Tania's phone across the table to Desmond. "It's really close, and whoever took her would have wanted the fastest route out of town."

"That's a lot of territory to cover," Bastian murmured.

Theo shrugged and rose to his feet. "Yeah. Guess you better get moving but give me your number in case my contact can get a location for the car. I'm hoping they stop somewhere, so I can catch a ping when the car tries to connect to a Wi-Fi signal."

"Let me guess. Killian's generosity just ran out." Desmond rolled his eyes, then added, "Why am I not surprised?"

"I don't claim to know my uncle's thoughts, but I've been ordered to let you find her yourselves." He sobered, then added, "I genuinely like Tania. Not my type, but she's a sweet girl who managed to teach advanced calculus to a thirty-five-year-old with a geography degree."

"What is your type?" Desmond asked, still scowling at him.

"You, but a little younger and a lot more single. Good luck finding your babygirl."

Without waiting for Desmond to reply, Theo walked out.

"Let's go," Bastian said as he threw a tip on the table. "We need to find her."

He took the wheel, mostly to give Desmond a chance to calm down, but also to have something to do. Sitting idle while their babygirl was missing... Bastian couldn't do it.

As he got on I-26, his phone rang. He tapped the

button on the steering wheel to accept the call. "Bastian Carter."

"I got a surveillance video from a diner in Santee," Theo said. "That's within the range I plotted for you, and I'm calling in some favors to help us find the SUV."

"We're on the road now," Desmond replied.

"Good. I'll have more news in the next ten minutes or so."

The call dropped and Desmond pulled his phone from his jacket. "Calling Ray to get us a pass through. Don't worry about getting stopped for speeding."

"Good." Bastian pressed the accelerator to the floor, skillfully weaving his way through slower traffic, his anger growing with every car he passed. "Whoever took her is going to be so fucking sorry."

TANIA

"**I**nside, Titania."

As if she had a choice. The log cabin on the shores of Lake Marion was gorgeous, but she didn't mistake it for anything but a prison—especially after spending so much time listening to his freaking exhausting list of rules.

After his first warning, she'd listened. Oh, how she'd listened, but she'd learned very quickly not to question.

She ran her tongue around the inside of her mouth, praying he hadn't knocked any teeth loose, then swallowed a mouthful of coppery fluid before she gave in to the urge to spit it in his face.

*Dr. Pappas, rule fifty-two said I should only wear Petal Pink nail polish, but rule one thirty-seven says good girls don't polish their nails.*

Stupid, stupid, stupid.

What the fuck was Petal Pink anyway?

He'd set her up to fail. Well, assuming his crazy allowed him to remember all three hundred of his idiotic, nonsensical rules. It was like he'd taken everything that was beautiful about a consensual power exchange relationship and perverted it into an Escheresque parody.

"There's my good girl." Dr. Pappas ran his hands up and down her arms, letting his thumbs brush the outer curves of her breasts.

She shivered, barely able to hold her revulsion in check. "Yes, sir."

"And already so needy for your Master." He stroked the rapidly swelling cut on her temple, making her wince. "We'll have to get some sort of makeup to hide that mark. I hope you don't make me punish you again. You'd be pretty without so many bruises."

Not only did he have a criminally deluded misunderstanding about the nature of consent, but he was also tossing out the tired excuse abusers used to gaslight their partners into believing they were at fault.

He sighed happily and led her into an opulently appointed bedroom decorated in what should have been soothing shades of blue, then opened the closet. It was filled with...

Sheer nightgowns, all in pale pink.

*Let me count the ways I want him to die...*

"What was rule two hundred?" He kissed her shoulder, and she sucked in a breath to keep herself from throwing up when she smelled his stupid breath mints.

"Ladies should always wear dresses, sir."

The closet was in direct contradiction to rule one sixteen, which said ladies didn't wear anything revealing.

"Good girl. Choose one and show me you know how a young lady should dress."

"Yes, sir."

She picked one at random, knowing her choice truly didn't matter, then tried to ignore his avid gaze as she changed as quickly as she could. Despite her rush, it felt like ants were crawling on her skin.

*Please, God. Let my Daddies come before he touches me again.*

A sob crawled up her throat as she straightened the nightgown and turned to face Dr. Pappas. She couldn't give up hope. Her Daddies *would* come for her.

"So beautiful," Dr. Pappas murmured, stroking her bare back. "Perfect. A worthy mother for my children."

A block of ice lodged in her stomach, but the pistol in his hand stopped her from tearing his eyes out. Maybe if she was very lucky, he'd want a blow job. It would give her a chance to bite his dick off.

"Yes, sir," she finally said once she thought she could speak without screaming.

"Are you hungry, my love?"

"No, sir. I'm fine. Thank you."

"Silly girl." He took her hand and led her into a gourmet kitchen with a view overlooking the lake. "You'll find everything you need to create a delicious meal. You'll need to eat better for our children."

"Yes, sir."

Although she doubted she could make anything edible—even after watching Desmond—cooking meant knives. If she was very lucky, she could get her hands on a nice, heavy cast iron skillet—just like the one hanging on a rack over the kitchen island. Keeping her movements as slow and innocent as she could, she stretched on her tiptoes to reach it.

"Let me help, my love." Crowding her against the island, he pressed himself against her, letting her feel his hardening cock.

*So, so gross. Just ew.*

Shockingly enough, he set it on the stove, then sat at the kitchen table to watch. Taking a deep breath, she went to the fridge and grabbed a carton of eggs, plus some cheese. She'd probably burn the hell out of scrambled eggs, but that was okay.

She wanted that skillet as hot as she could get it without melting it.

"Are omelets okay, sir? I'm not a very good cook."

"I suppose we'll get you some classes," Dr. Pappas replied as he checked the action on his pistol. "A young lady should be able to cook very well."

*Ugh. Forgot the pistol, didn't you?*

She cracked eggs into a bowl and took her sweet time whisking them with a fork while the skillet heated. When a faint tendril of smoke rose from the cast iron, she dumped the eggs in, then screeched in faux surprise when they blackened.

"Oh, sir! I'm so sorry!" She wrapped a dishtowel around the handle and shook the pan. "I think I burned the eggs! Can you help, please, sir?"

"Stupid girl." Scowling, he laid the pistol on the table and stormed toward her. "I'm going to beat you bloody."

She let out a breath as she imagined Daddy Bastian's voice.

*Wait for it, babygirl...*

When Dr. Pappas reached for her throat, she swung the skillet at his head with all her might. It connected with a sick, meaty crack, not too different from the sound of a breaking egg.

He blinked once, then his eyes rolled back, and he dropped to the floor.

"Oh, hell to the no!" She kicked him in the ribs and raised the hot skillet over her head, ignoring the last bit of partially cooked egg falling around her. "You do not get to check out on me before I beat the shit out of you. Get the fuck up!"

Someone grabbed the skillet from her hands, and without waiting for them to catch her, she raced to the kitchen table and snatched up Dr. Pappas's pistol.

"Do not fucking touch me!" She lifted the gun, but it fell from her hand when she saw Desmond holding her skillet, its handle still wrapped in the dishtowel. "Daddy?"

He tossed the skillet into the sink, then opened his arms. "We're here, sweetheart. It's okay."

Her breath caught and she stumbled into Desmond's embrace as she burst into tears. "I knew my Daddies would save me."

## DESMOND

He took the blanket one of the local cops offered and wrapped his babygirl into a burrito before lifting her into his arms. As he carried her outside, he kissed her bloody temple and murmured, "Babygirl, you're a self-rescuing princess. You saved yourself, and I'm so fucking proud of you."

If he wasn't already coding, Desmond would have killed Marinos Pappas for what he'd done to Tania's face, and for making her wear that see-through nightgown. He kept walking, letting the paramedics decide if the sick fucker lived or died.

"No, Daddy. I needed you to save me, and you did."

"Sir, may we examine Ms. Andersen?" a female paramedic asked. "We'd also like to transport her for—"

"No! Nobody touches me but my Daddies!" Tania shouted. She struggled hard, nearly breaking free of Desmond's embrace.

"Shh, babygirl." Ignoring the startled woman, he found a bench in the garden fronting the cabin and sat with Tania in his lap. "You can make your own medical decisions, but if he touched you, the evidence will be important for his trial."

"He didn't rape me." She sighed and eased herself from his lap to sit next to him. "He was going to, but I brained him before he got the chance."

The tension in his back and shoulders faded and he slumped as tears threatened to fall. It wouldn't have changed his feelings for her, but he was so incredibly thankful she hadn't experienced that horrific violation.

"See?" He lifted her hand to his lips and kissed her fingertips, trying not to think about what might have happened to her. "Self-rescuing princess. Those are the best kind of princesses, you know."

"Yeah, I guess so." She touched her forehead and grimaced at the blood on her fingers. "No rape kit, but I guess I should do what everyone's told me for years and have my head examined. Probably ought to see a dentist too. I think he knocked one of my molars loose."

"We'll get whatever care you're comfortable receiving," he promised. "But if you want my honest opinion, you might want to consider having someone slap a little glue on that cut before it scars."

Laughing, she climbed back into his lap and nestled her head against his shoulder. "Your bedside manner sucks, Dr. Daddy, but you're right. Head wounds bleed like crazy."

When Bastian sat next to them, she moved to his lap and wrapped her arms around his shoulders. "Missed you, Daddy. Where were you?"

"I was convincing the local cops to give you a few days before they take your statement, and…" He hesitated, then added, "Dr. Pappas isn't responding to treatment. I don't know if he's going to live long enough to make it to trial."

"Dunno how I feel about that." She sighed and closed her eyes. "Is it awful to hope he doesn't wake up?"

"No, sweetheart. It makes you human." Making sure he had her nestled safely in his arms, Bastian stood. "Let's get out of here."

Desmond sat in the back seat of his SUV with Tania's head in his lap while Bastian drove them home. One of the officers from the local trooper post followed in Bastian's car.

He couldn't stop touching her, but he was almost afraid to. The bruises and cuts on her face…

In an attempt to ease his stress, he did some deep breathing, then laid his hand on her hip.

She was safe, and mostly unharmed. Their baby-girl hadn't been sexually assaulted, but he didn't delude himself into thinking there wouldn't be lingering trauma.

Whatever it took to help, he and Bastian would do it.

A gray sedan he didn't recognize was parked in their driveway as Bastian pulled in.

"Do you know that car?" he asked, careful to keep his voice soft so he didn't wake Tania.

"No." Bastian opened the door and strode to the strange vehicle as a woman got out. She smiled and held out her hand for him to shake, then turned and grabbed a large black bag from her car.

Shaking his head, Bastian returned to the SUV and helped Desmond with Tania. "Seems Killian isn't quite done with Tania. That's Dr. Gwen Santos. She's a plastic surgeon and is here to fix the cut on Tania's face."

"I really, truly hate owing that asshole a favor," Desmond muttered. "But I'm going to be kissing his ass in public next time I see him."

"Same." Bastian lifted her from the back seat and carried her inside. Tania woke just long enough to respond to Dr. Santos as she cleaned the wound and sealed it with surgical glue, then fell into a deep, restorative sleep.

He and Bastian didn't leave her alone. Not once was she left unattended, even when his irritating brothers and their women came by to drop off prepared meals. The only person they allowed to see her was Mandy, and only if Bee wasn't around to see the bruises on her sister's face.

She slept on and off for two days, only waking long enough to eat and let them help her bathe. Desmond spent every single hour castigating himself for letting her go to the coffee shop in the first place.

Desmond also made very sure to keep the television off. Although she slept most of the time, she didn't need to see the news reports, or the trouble brewing on campus. He didn't know what they'd have done if she demanded to return to class.

"It's not your fault, you know." Bastian leaned against the deck rail next to him as he stared at the sun rising over the beach. "We couldn't have known Pappas would become violent."

"Except we knew about his history of sexually motivated behavior," Desmond countered. "It was all in the file Killian sent, and she was alone when she needed us the most."

"No, Daddy Desmond." Wearing a hoodie, jeans, and thick socks, Tania squeezed in between them and wrapped her arms around his and Bastian's waists. "I decided to be too stupid to live and begged you to let me go by myself."

"Babygirl, don't blame yourself either," Bastian said.

"I'm not. I should have been able to meet

someone at a coffee shop without getting assaulted. If anyone is to blame, it's Dr. Pappas." She squeezed them tightly, then took a step back and smiled. "But there's something I need to do now, and I need your help."

# 30

# SHOWDOWN IN THE DEAN'S OFFICE

TANIA

"I'm not sure this is a good idea," Bastian said from Tania's left.

"I know it isn't," Desmond muttered from her right.

"This should have happened weeks ago." She pushed the door leading to Dr. Ng's office open and blinked at the crowd of women shouting at his assistant. It had probably been too much to hope the protesters outside were the only ones. "I should have made it happen at the beginning of the semester."

With her Daddies in tow, she pushed her way through the crowd until she reached the desk. The crowd noise died to near silence when she said, "Tell

Dr. Ng that Titania Andersen is here to see him, and that he doesn't get to refuse to talk to me this time."

The assistant glanced up, then quickly averted his eyes from the purple and red bruises on her face. "Um, yeah. Give me a minute."

He reached for the phone, then shook his head, and handed her a key from his desk drawer. "Actually no. I'm not giving him any warning. Go on in and give him hell."

She smiled as much as her swollen face would allow, then said, "Thanks. I appreciate it. Also, you might want to escape before the traffic around campus gets much worse."

"Yeah, thanks for the tip."

Bastian took the key from her and quickly unlocked the door, and without giving Dr. Ng a chance to protest, they went inside. Desmond closed the door behind them and locked it before anyone could follow them.

Dr. Ng stood behind his desk and glared at her. "What is the meaning of this, Ms. Andersen? I don't recall—"

"We're going to have that talk you've been ignoring for weeks," she interrupted. "And this time, you're going to listen to me."

"Fine." Dr. Ng scowled at her Daddies and folded his arms over his chest. "Who are they?"

Unwilling to let Dr. Ng focus on something that wasn't her, Tania didn't look at Bastian or Desmond. "They're my—"

"We're Ms. Andersen's personal security detail," Desmond replied.

"Which she needs because of your negligence," Bastian added. "Don't worry about us. Ms. Andersen requires your attention now."

When her Daddies insisted on coming into Dr. Ng's office with her, she'd been afraid they'd take over the meeting and not let her say what she needed to. Her heart swelled and she blinked back a tear at the proof they were willing to let her deal with Dr. Ng on her own.

Well, mostly. They still got weird about leaving her alone—not that she blamed them after what Dr. Pappas had done to her.

"Ms. Andersen..." He sat behind his desk and rubbed his forehead. "You've created quite the scene."

*Wow. Talk about screwed up. Is he really implying this mess is my fault?*

Not in this lifetime.

"With all due respect, sir. I didn't start this."

"Have you looked outside?" he asked, scowling at her. "I'd certainly call the whole of the female population of this university shouting outside my office a scene."

"Oh, it's a scene, all right." Ready to drop a few truth bombs on his head, she sat, then crossed her legs, and leaned back in her chair. "But you started it, and you're leaving the mess for me to clean up."

"I beg your pardon." He drew himself up and twitched his nose like she smelled offensive. "How do you justify saying that?"

"You obviously haven't bothered to read them, but there's a reason your name is on those signs," she snapped. "I came to you three times, begging for help. I told you what Dr. Pappas was doing. My class-mates reported him too, and despite the university's anti-fraternization policy, you did nothing. You let him keep threatening me, you let him assault me, and you still don't believe you did anything wrong."

A small part of her cringed at what she was saying, but she squashed it. The shy girl who was too afraid to speak up was well and truly gone.

"I did speak with him, but as you well know, Dr. Pappas has tenure. My hands were tied."

"Considering he decided to assault the daughter of a decorated police officer and is now breathing through a tube after I caved his head in with a cast iron skillet, I'm thinking Dr. Pappas better be unem-ployed by now. Aside from that, his tenure shouldn't have mattered. Your inaction put the women in this department at risk, and it's disingenuous to assume there wouldn't be fallout."

She leaned forward and put her hands on the arms of her chair. "In fact, I'd bet I'm not the first student he's hurt. I'm just the first one who made him stop."

"Be that as it may, he's made many valuable contributions to this university."

"Let me guess. He offered you a citation on the work he was going to steal from me during a graduate program I didn't want and couldn't afford. Speaking of which, he told me he submitted an application for grad school on my behalf. You might as well shred it. Even if I decide to attend grad school at a later date, it won't be here."

"Well…" He coughed uncomfortably. "That is to say—"

"It's all publish or perish, am I right? It must be so annoying when undergrads decide they don't want to be bullied into compliance." She laughed bitterly and shook her head. "How many of those contributions were actually his?"

He looked away and kept silent, letting her know her supposition had been correct.

Tania heard a soft, angry murmur from one of her Daddies and pointed at the jagged cut decorating her temple. "I'm thinking you'd have kept trying to brush his behavior under the rug if he hadn't decided assault and kidnapping was the solution to his problems. Sadly for you, that meant your negligence made the news."

"Well, that was unfortunate, of course, but I'm sure you don't wish to create so much trouble."

Dr. Ng said the words in a flat, irritated tone as if everything was her fault, and not once did he react to the bruising on her face. It was as if he was completely nonchalant about the abuse she'd suffered.

*Close your mouth and open your legs...*

"Actually, I wish I could create more trouble, and I really wish I'd done it when the harassment started." She met his eyes and didn't blink. "You can keep thinking it's my fault if it helps you sleep at night, but don't expect me to lie for you and tell those people everything was just a big misunderstanding when they can't even trust a department head to keep them safe."

"Well..." He stood and went to the window. "I suppose it will please you to know I've been asked to retire."

"It does, but you're still not going to apologize, are you?" When he didn't reply, she rolled her eyes and got to her feet. "Forget it. You're not worth it."

The crowd went silent when she exited the office.

Her Daddies took up positions on either side of her to walk her through the crowd. To her surprise, she saw most of her classmates huddling by the door. The only one missing was Theo.

Before she could take more than a few steps, someone asked, "What's going to happen to Dr. Ng?"

As if that one voice started a chain reaction, questions flew until she lifted her hand for silence. Unfortunately, Tania couldn't stop the phones being held up to record her, but maybe it was better that way.

Maybe whatever words she came up with would help other people.

"Dr. Ng has been asked to retire. I don't know the details or when it will happen." Tania took a deep, cleansing breath then looked at her Daddies and smiled. "I appreciate all of you for the support you've shown me, and I want to tell you a few things."

Bastian nodded encouragingly, and Desmond gave her a fist pump. God, she loved them. Finding two protective and supportive Daddies hadn't been on Tania's bingo card for her senior year of college, but she couldn't imagine her life without them anymore.

She just needed to tell them so.

"Margaret Atwood was once quoted as saying men are afraid women will laugh at them, and women are afraid men will kill them. Margaret was right, but it's so wrong."

She gazed at the young women surrounding her, taking in their fear and anger, then pitched her voice to carry over the crowd noise. "For anyone who doesn't know the story. Dr. Marinos Pappas began propositioning me a week after the semester started. He wanted me to be his graduate assistant with sexual benefits. When I told him I wasn't interested in grad school or a relationship, he threatened to falsify my grade and his scoring on my senior project unless I complied."

Tania paused, waiting for the angry murmurs to die down.

"I, along with my male classmates, went to Dr. Ng to report his behavior on multiple occasions. Our complaints were ignored. In fact, Dr. Ng just blamed me for causing problems."

"No fucking way!" someone shouted. "What a tool."

She laughed and nodded. "That's one way to put it, but you know what? If he'd just listened in the first place, I'd have gone about my business. It took Dr. Pappas assaulting me to make him pay attention, and he's still blaming me for what happened."

Her Daddies crowded close to protect her from the angry crowd, but she wasn't worried. They were pissed at her words—not her—and they weren't about to shoot the messenger.

"However, I will say I made some mistakes. I should have gone above Dr. Ng's head the first time he didn't listen to my complaint. I should have shouted it from the rooftops, gone on the news, or did something to make my voice heard before the situation escalated into physical violence."

She smiled wryly. "Society teaches women to be silent and not make waves, lest those men afraid of being mocked harm us. I even justified my decision to stay quiet and told myself I'd be okay once I graduated, but I shouldn't have to justify shit—not to myself or anyone else."

The women surrounding her nodded and looked at their feet but listened with rapt attention.

"My challenge to you, and to everyone watching the videos you're recording is to speak."

"What should we say?" someone asked.

"Well, people will call you weak if you don't speak up, and a bitch if you do. If they're going to call us bitches, then let us be bitches together. My advice to you is to speak your truth and your rage when you can."

When someone whistled, she smiled sadly and held up her hand. "Unfortunately, it's not always safe to do that, so get yourself to a secure location first. Bullies get power from our silence, and we get power by working together and letting our voices be heard.

We need to support each other, believe each other, and believe women when they speak. Men need to listen when a woman says 'no.'"

A slow clap sounded from beside her, followed by a second. Tania blinked and smiled as she watched her Daddies put their hands together for her. The crowd joined in, the applause and shouted encouragement deafening.

"One more thing. Men, we need you too. We need you to speak up when you see this happening to the women around you. Not just your girlfriends or moms or daughters or sisters, but your classmates, your acquaintances, the strangers you see on the street. Be like my classmates, who took it upon themselves to report him and then took it a step further by using themselves as a barrier between me and Dr. Pappas. Women cannot be the solution on our own because we are not the problem."

When the applause died down, she took a deep breath and smiled. "Anyway, thanks for letting me vent, but I need to bounce."

BASTIAN

They hustled Tania through the crowd of protesters and ducked behind the line of police to where Desmond's SUV was parked. Before Bastian got into the vehicle, he searched for his old friend Ray, then went to meet him.

Holding out his hand, Bastian said, "Thanks for letting us park behind the police tape, and for everything else you've done."

Ray shook his hand and smiled. "Nah, anyone would have done it for Victor's little girl. She okay?"

"Yeah. Anyway, we'll get out of your hair. Crossing fingers nobody gets violent."

Ray studied the crowd and shook his head. "I doubt it. The ladies are angry, as they should be, but this is more about making themselves heard. I think they'll wander off soon."

"Hey, Ray!" Another officer approached and held out his phone. "You may want to see this. Associated Press just picked it up. That's Victor's little girl, isn't it?"

"And two retired cops," Ray murmured as the video of Tania's speech played. "Damn. Atta girl."

He turned his attention back to Bastian. "I'm thinking once this goes viral, the protesters will find something else to do. Go on and take her home."

"Good idea. Are the roads clear?"

Thankfully, Ray nodded. Bastian didn't want anything slowing them down. Tania had been through enough already, and he didn't want to think about reporters hounding her. At least she'd be with them instead of at her apartment.

None of them had talked about it, but he suspected Tania would be moving in permanently. It was hard enough to let her go to the bathroom by herself, and he didn't want to think about her being alone in her apartment. Deciding to discuss Tania's living situation with her and Desmond later, he climbed into the back seat with her.

Careful of her bruised face, he pulled her close and let her rest her head on his shoulder. "How are you feeling, babygirl?"

"I'm okay. Kind of tired, but relieved too. I'm glad this is over, and I'm really glad Dr. Ng won't be there tomorrow when I go back to class."

"Excuse me?" Desmond said. "Did you just say you were going back to class tomorrow?"

"Well, yeah." She unfastened her seatbelt and leaned over the front seat. "I still have to work on my project to graduate, and it can't be done online."

"I don't like it."

"That's why you're coming with me." She

stretched forward and kissed his cheek. "I also want to go to the club tonight."

"It is really too soon for that," Bastian said as he pulled her back into her seat and refastened her seat-belt. "Maybe next month."

"Nope. I want some of those chicken wings I saw people eating." She chewed on her lip, then added, "I also want to give Killian a real apology and thank him for helping you find me."

Although he appreciated her willingness to make things right with Killian, the thought of taking her anywhere that wasn't under his direct control made Bastian's stomach clench with worry. Worse, he knew his anxiety was stupid. The club was perfectly safe—especially with Braden's new security measures.

"We can get wings anywhere," Desmond countered. "Hell, I can make you wings."

"Please, Daddy?"

"Damn it." Desmond sighed and glanced at him in the rear-view mirror. "What do you think, Bastian?"

"We can go, but we're doing it now before the club gets too crowded."

"Yay! Thank you, Daddies! Could we do a—"

Although he loved seeing her smiling and enthusiastic about a visit to the club, Bastian frowned and laid a finger over her lips. "Don't get too excited. We won't be playing."

"Mean." She pouted and stuck her tongue out at him, then shook her head and smiled. "Actually, I kind of just want to watch a scene or two."

"Any particular reason why?" Desmond asked.

She was silent for several seconds, then said, "I need to see. I want to remember what power exchange is supposed to be, so it can erase all the crazy shit Dr. Pappas told me. Does that make sense?"

"It does." Bastian hugged her tightly, and careful of her split lip, kissed the corner of her mouth. "And what our babygirl wants, she gets."

As he suspected, the club was nearly empty when they arrived, but Braden and Lottie hurried from his office to greet them the minute they walked in.

"Oh, my God, Tania!" Lottie pulled her into a gentle hug and sniffed, obviously trying to hold back a few tears. "I'm so glad to see you. Can I get you some ice? No, wait. Let me get you a chair."

"I'm okay, Lottie." Tania smiled and extricated herself from the hug. "We just came in for some chicken wings, and maybe watch a few scenes if anyone is playing."

"Do you need to use the accessibility elevator to go upstairs? I can totally show you where it is."

"I'm fine, promise. But thank you for making sure."

"You're in luck for the scene you wanted, Tania." Braden's jaw tightened, but he hugged her gently and brushed a kiss above the cut on her temple. "We have two happening shortly. Shane will be helping Mistress Rogue with her single-tail work, and Master O negotiated a scene with Cordelia and Ivy."

Bastian nodded his appreciation. Despite his dislike for Killian, he was a good Dominant, as was Mistress Rogue. Then again, he almost wished Killian hadn't been there. He wasn't looking forward to keeping the promise he and Desmond had made, but it was better to do it when the club wasn't crowded. There were less than a dozen people upstairs in the restaurant, and only a few couples seated at the tables surrounding the pit.

Deciding to get it over with, he said, "Babygirl, let's find Killian first, so you can talk to him."

"Okay, Daddy."

As usual, Killian was seated at his table in the corner of the club, with his back to the wall. He frowned darkly when he saw Tania's face but nodded when they approached. "Is there some reason you're interrupting my day, gentlemen?"

"Killian, we made a promise," Desmond said.

"We did," Bastian added.

"And what promise was that?" Killian lifted a glass

of water to his lips and took a sip before setting his drink on the table. "I'm all ears."

"For helping us find Tania, we both promised to kiss your ass in public."

"Ah, yes. My nephew, Theo, told me about that." He smirked and rose to his feet. "Follow me to the pit, gentlemen."

"Wait." Tania stepped between them and held up her hand. "Theo... my classmate Theo is your nephew?"

"Yes. He says you're an excellent teacher, but he's afraid the date he made with you is off."

"Son of a bitch." She put her hands on her hips and glared at him. "Did you have him watching me?"

"Of course. How else did you think your Daddies found you?"

"I thought..." She shook her head, then said, "Never mind. I wasn't really thinking."

"Very well." Killian stepped around her. "Shall we, gentlemen?"

When they reached the center of the pit, Killian announced, "Bastian Carter and Desmond Elliott have offered to kiss my ass in public."

"We did," Desmond said. "Right on his hairy backside."

The few people watching went silent when Killian unbuckled his belt. Bastian shared a glance with

Desmond and sighed, knowing the bastard was truly going to make them do what they'd promised. As awful as it would be, it was worth it to have Tania safe.

To his surprise, Killian stopped before opening the front of his trousers. His lips twisting, he said, "As much as I'd enjoy seeing you both on your knees for me in front of an audience, I'll settle for you keeping your woman in line. My debt to Victor is paid, and I won't be around to bail her, or you, out of trouble in the future."

"Master O..." Tania crossed the pit and threw her arms around him, then kissed his cheek.

Bastian's jealousy surged, but before he could protest, she said, "Thank you so much for helping me. I know I was mean to you before, and I'm sorry."

His gaze softening, he stroked her hair. "Apology accepted, little love."

She kissed his cheek again, then went to her Daddies and gave Killian a brilliant, beaming smile. "I'm so happy to learn what a really sweet, gooey cinnamon roll you are inside. I'm going to call you Master Cinnamon from now on so everyone knows how much I like you."

Killian gaped at her, and his cheeks turned ruddy. As if he was considering using it on her, his hands flexed as he buckled his belt.

Tania blinked innocently and her brow wrinkled. "Maybe it should be Master C. Do you like that better?"

"As I said, gentlemen, keep your woman in line." Without another word, Killian left the pit and returned to his table.

Desmond covered his mouth with his hand, trying to hold back his laughter. He turned so Killian couldn't see, but his shoulders shook with suppressed mirth.

"That was a textbook example of tactical bratting, babygirl," Bastian said, not bothering to hide the grin on his face as he gazed at Killian's table in the corner. "And Shane saw the whole thing."

"So did Lottie," Desmond snickered, then added, "Braden is in so much trouble."

She giggled and let them lead her up the stairs to the restaurant. "The look on Killian's face was so freaking priceless, and the best part is that he can't do a damned thing to stop me. I'm betting he never comes near me again."

# 31

# AN UNWELCOME MESSAGE

TANIA

Killian's scene with Ivy and Cordelia wrapped up as she finished the last of her chicken wings. She almost felt bad for picking on him so hard when she saw how tenderly he treated Ivy as he passed her off to Cordelia for aftercare.

Almost.

He was still a mob boss—and a supersized jerk—but she'd admit he was a good Dominant.

Watching them, and Mistress Rogue with Shane, went a long way toward erasing her memories of Dr. Pappas too. Power exchange wasn't gaslighting or abuse. It was supposed to be pleasurable for all parties—not make submissives too terrified of being hurt to find help.

The last of the people watching the scenes were gone, and they were the only ones in the restaurant aside from a server wiping down the tables. The sight of the empty club, and especially the vacant hostess podium, jogged something in her memory.

"Daddies, I completely forgot something!" She pulled out her phone and scrolled through her call list. "I got a call from—"

"Shh." Bastian laid a hand over her mouth. "Let's go to Braden's office. Des, will you ask Killian to join us if he's still here?"

Tania pushed Bastian's hand down. "Ew. Why him?"

"Because I said so." He swatted her butt to get her moving, then escorted her down the corridor to a wooden door and knocked softly. Desmond appeared with Killian while they waited for Braden to let them in.

"Has something happened?" Killian asked. "What possible reason—"

The door opened to reveal Braden working the buttons of his shirt. "Do you mind? I was busy."

Lottie appeared with his tie draped around her neck. "Ooh! I love having an audience!"

"Sorry, Lottie, but this isn't that kind of visit," Bastian replied.

Ignoring Killian's protests, Bastian pushed him into the room after Desmond and Tania, then shut the door and locked it. "With everything that happened, we forgot to discuss the call Tania got."

"Why do I care?" Killian asked.

"Because when I asked questions on the auction website's contact form, the person who called me spoofed the number to make it look like it came from Club BDE," she retorted.

"And I didn't know about this, why?" Killian asked, his expression darkening with irritation.

"I had no idea the auctions weren't sanctioned by Club BDE until Lottie and Emily told me the night I met you." She hesitated, then added, "Can we do this without Dom and sub rules? I get abrupt when I'm angry."

"Go ahead, Tania," Braden replied. "No punishments for anything you say."

"Good. Thank you." She whispered a virulent curse that made even Killian's eyebrow raise, then added, "Mr. O'Rourke, the only thing I knew about you at the time was that you're an arrogant bastard. Aside from being unaware the auctions were bogus, I couldn't have known you were looking into the situation."

"Fair enough." Killian nodded to acknowledge the point. "Continue, please."

"For what it's worth, I researched the website and the phone number. I even looked in places nice girls like me shouldn't go before I signed up. Both came up clean and were registered to Club BDE."

"A woman of many and varied talents," Killian murmured. "My people came up with the same information."

Tania sighed, wishing she had something more to offer. If nothing else, she'd really wanted to have one over on Killian. "I guess it's flattering to know I'm at least as good as a black-hat hacker."

"Touché."

"Anyway, whoever did this is really freaking smart, so unless we can find a way to trace the money..." Hating the idea of disappointing them, she glanced at Bastian and Desmond. "I'm not sure we're going to find him without getting a warrant and a good forensic accountant."

"Him?" Killian asked.

"A man called me, but I shouldn't assume. He might have been an assistant or something."

"You're definitely your father's daughter, but I doubt the Elliott brothers will approve of such an investigation."

"It isn't our preference, no," Braden replied.

"There's one thing we could do," Lottie said.

"What's that, Lottie-bug?"

"I can't believe you're overlooking the obvious." She rolled her eyes and sighed. "Call the number. Maybe one of you will recognize his voice."

"Dang, girlfriend. You're a freaking genius." Tania laid her phone on Braden's desk and tapped the number.

She touched the phone again to put the call on speaker. It rang twice, and she spun when she heard a tinny ringtone coming from somewhere outside Braden's office. Frowning, she asked, "What's on the other side of that wall?"

"That's my IT guy's office. His name is Martin Hall, but he's been out sick for several weeks," Braden replied.

"Are you fucking kidding me?" She jabbed her finger into his chest. "You didn't think to investigate the one person who has access to your banking, taxes, personnel, and your goddamned computers? What the fuck, Braden?"

"Both Killian and I did a full background check on Martin. He came up clean."

"Uh huh. Talk about overlooking the obvious." She rolled her eyes and ignored Desmond's attempts to shush her. "Pretty sure Sherlock Holmes said something about eliminating the impossible."

"And whatever remains, no matter how improbable, must be the truth." Killian murmured. "Little love, we did investigate him. I promise, there was nothing to find, and I daresay my investigation was more thorough than Braden's."

"A background check doesn't exclude him. It just means he's better than your investigators," she retorted. "Don't any of you find it at all suspicious that he's so conveniently out sick, and has been for weeks?"

Her phone stopped ringing, as did the one in the adjoining office, cutting off the rest of her meltdown.

"Hello, Elliott bastards."

"That's him," she whispered, slowly approaching the phone as if it would bite her. "That's who called me."

"You were right." Braden's face reddened and a vein pulsed in his forehead. "Fucking Martin."

"Braden, if you're listening to this, it means Titania Andersen finally remembered she has my number. She's cute, but just not that bright. Like father, like daughter, I guess. Such a shame the smuggling ring he was trying to bring down found out he was an undercover cop. Can't imagine how it happened. Anyway, I'm off to greener pastures. Thanks for making me a very wealthy man. Oh, and before I go, tell O'Rourke he needs to hire decent hackers. My senile grandmother could have done better."

Her fingers tightened into fists, and she blinked to halt the wetness burning her sinuses. If what Martin said was true, he was the reason Victor was gone. Slowly, she forced her hands to relax, then went to the window overlooking the club in a desperate attempt to control the furious tears threatening to fall.

Low conversation sounded behind her, and she heard footsteps approaching.

"Babygirl—"

She held up a hand to stop Desmond. "Give me a minute, please."

One greedy man was the reason she and her sister didn't have their dad and Mandy was a widow. How the fuck was she even supposed to tell her?

Her bones aching with a mix of worry, sadness, and hot rage, she turned to face the people surrounding Braden's desk "I want him."

"We're going to do our very best to get him for you," Bastian promised. Turning to Braden, he added, "We have to take this to the police."

"Yes. I should have done it weeks ago instead of trying to figure it out myself." Braden pulled Lottie into his arms and kissed the top of her head.

"If he's very lucky, he'll live long enough for the

police to find him," Killian muttered darkly. "If I catch him first, I'll present Tania with Martin Hall's hands on a silver platter. I'll be taking his head."

She lifted her chin and bared her teeth in a smile. "Thank you, Mr. O'Rourke. For that, I'll stop calling you Master Cinnamon."

## DESMOND

"Tell Damian what happened," Bastian ordered. "We're taking Tania home."

Ignoring Braden's protests, they ushered her from the club, not stopping until she was safely in their vehicle. She fastened her seatbelt and gazed out the window as Bastian drove home.

"I don't really want Martin's hands," she murmured. "I don't want Killian to have his head either, but I do want him prosecuted and forced to pay restitution before he accidentally on purpose dies in prison for causing the death of a police officer."

"We're turning the recording over to the police," Desmond promised. "It's time to get them involved, so we can get a warrant to shut the website down. We might not be able to catch Martin, but we can make sure he doesn't do this again."

"At Club BDE anyway. He'll start over somewhere else."

"Braden has friends in other clubs," Bastian said as he backed into their driveway. "He's going to make some calls."

"Good." She waited until the garage door came down before she got out. "I don't want to talk about Martin, Killian, or anything else except us."

"That's a wonderful idea." Desmond held her hand as they crossed the garage to the stairs leading into the kitchen.

"I thought so." She went to the fridge and got a bottle of wine, then three glasses from the rack. "I need to tell you something."

Bastian uncorked the wine and poured for them, then carried the glasses into the living room. She followed, then curled up in the chair facing the couch before accepting her glass.

He and Desmond sat across from her, and after she'd taken a healthy swallow of her drink, Bastian asked, "What did you want to tell us, babygirl?"

After taking another sip, she cleared her throat, then said, "I'm in love with you. I mean, both of you. I want to live here and get married, and..."

She set her glass on an end table and went to the couch to kneel at their feet. "Wow, I'm awkward, and I know it's too soon, but the whole time I was with

Dr. Pappas, I kept thinking I never told you how I feel. I never said what you mean to me, and I couldn't stand knowing I might not get the chance, and—"

Bastian silenced her with a kiss, and Desmond's cock throbbed at the way he plundered her mouth while being careful of her bruises. Before she could take a breath, he passed her to Desmond.

Instead of speaking, he kissed her more gently than Bastian, but no less ardently as he inhaled the perfume of her lemon soap mixed with the ginger candy she loved.

Desmond gentled their kiss and wiped a few tears from her cheek with his thumb. "You say all that like you thought we'd let you go."

"Because if you think you're going to walk out of our lives, we'll just have to work harder to change your mind," Bastian added. "In fact, we're going to take you upstairs and do some convincing right now."

"If you're ready," Desmond said, nudging Bastian with his shoulder when it looked like he'd protest. "If you're not, we know how much you love watching us."

"We want to be your Daddies," Bastian said. "We want you to marry us, and all the rest, babygirl. Will you say yes?"

"But not until after you graduate," Desmond added. "We promised your stepmother."

"Oof." Tania wrinkled her nose. "I bet that was an awkward conversation."

"A little." Bastian took her hands. "So, what do you say? Do you want us?"

"A million yesses, Daddies." She threw her arms around them as tears fell to dampen her cheeks. "I'm never letting you go."

"Then get your cute butt up those stairs," Desmond replied. "If you make us wait, we'll just have to spank you."

"You say that like it's a deterrent." Laughing, she whirled around and raced to the stairs.

They caught up as she was pulling her hoodie off. It went sailing across the room, followed by the rest of her clothes.

Aside from her face, no bruises or wounds marred Tania's gorgeous flesh, and for now at least, she seemed to be emotionally okay. Desmond made a note to find a kink-friendly therapist just in case.

Strangely, she seemed a thousand times better after her showdown with her college dean.

He and Bastian undressed just as quickly, and soon tumbled into bed after her.

"Slow and gentle," Bastian murmured as he kissed her belly. "No acrobatics."

"Yes, Daddy Bastian. I'll behave-ish."

"Ish?" Desmond turned her to her side and swatted her butt, making her laugh. "Behave-ish?"

"You'll just have to make love to me if you want to keep me in line."

Bastian tossed him a condom and he caught it out of the air, then quickly sheathed his erection and rolled to his back. "Ride me, babygirl. Let us watch you take your pleasure from us."

"Yes, Daddy." She bit her lower lip as she straddled him, then moaned in pleasure as she lowered herself on his cock. "Feels so good. I love you, Daddy Desmond."

Bastian moved behind her and played with her clit until she screamed out her climax. Desmond would never get tired of watching their sweet babygirl come, but it had been too long, and they'd come too close to losing her. Unable to hold his orgasm any longer, he grabbed her hips and surged into her as his cock swelled and erupted, filling the condom with his cum.

"God, Daddy..." She lowered herself and sank her hands into his hair as she kissed him. "I love you so much."

"Love you too, babygirl." He stole another kiss, then helped her sit up. "But I think it's Daddy Bastian's turn now."

"Mmm. Double my pleasure." Tania giggled when

Bastian spanked her ass, then climbed off Desmond. When Bastian opened a condom, she took it from him. "Let me."

Keeping her eyes on Bastian's face, she slid the condom down his shaft, then gently nudged him to lie next to Desmond. Straddling Bastian's hips, she said, "I think I like being on top."

"And I think I'm going to love playing with your clit while Daddy Bastian fucks you," Desmond said, taking Bastian's position behind her.

Tania shuddered and cried out the minute his fingers touched the swollen bundle of nerves. Instead of letting her come too quickly, he eased his touch as she leaned against him. Her head fell to his shoulder, and she gasped as Bastian grabbed her hips and surged inside her.

"Yes! Please, Daddy Bastian, fuck me harder."

"With pleasure." He sat up, and pressed Tania harder against Desmond's chest before hooking his arm under her thigh. After repositioning himself at her entrance, he thrust into her, making her scream in delight.

The cords in Bastian's neck stood out and he gritted his teeth, letting Desmond know he was close to the edge. He rubbed Tania's clit, hoping to make her come once more before Bastian lost control.

"Oh, God! Yes!" Her body spasmed and she cried out as Bastian slammed into her one last time.

"Fuck. Damn, babygirl." Bastian's head fell to her chest, and he let out a breath. "You about wore an old man out, but god, I love you."

"I love you too, Daddy Bastian, but you're not old." She kissed his sweaty forehead and wrapped her arms around him. "You're just well-seasoned."

"Brat."

"Tactical brat," she retorted.

Desmond shook his head, and despite the ache in his knees and back from supporting his lovers' weight, he chuckled. "Let's get cleaned up before my back gives out."

"Good idea." Bastian groaned as he climbed out of bed and went to the bathroom. Desmond followed, and after they'd dealt with the condoms, they returned to Tania with warm washcloths. Once they were cleaned up, they snuggled in bed with her in the middle, as usual.

"Our wedding might be a problem," Desmond said, rolling to face his lovers.

"What problem?" Tania asked. "We hire a planner, or just go to Vegas."

"Which of us do you want to marry?" Bastian asked. "That's where the problem is."

"Nope. Still no problem." She closed her eyes as a

faint smile blossomed on her lips. "There's a three-sided die in my backpack. One for Bastian, two for Desmond, and three you marry each other and make me a kept woman. We'll hire someone to plan a commitment ceremony for all three of us after I graduate. There. Done. Go to sleep."

"Why not flip another coin?" Desmond asked.

She opened one eye and glared at him. "Because there are three choices."

"I see," Bastian said, smiling at Desmond over her head. "Do you want to—"

"No. It's sleepy time for tired babygirls. Shh."

"Okay, sweetheart," Bastian said.

They each gave her another kiss, then held her as she slept. She was right. Tomorrow morning would be soon enough, and if he thought about it, the legal arrangements didn't matter. They'd be together.

No matter what.

The prosthetic nose and eyepatch itched, but he was too skilled to give in to the discomfort and scratch the sweat beading under the disguise.

They were part of his face now, as were the salt-and pepper-beard and shaggy hair.

His beard was real. The hair wasn't.

Victor didn't need the eyepatch, but it hid the scar left from the wound that had almost made it necessary. The disguise wasn't his only irritation, and it certainly wasn't the most annoying.

Of course, he wasn't Victor anymore. Victor Andersen was dead.

After too many years hunting the little fuckwit down while trying to maintain his cover with the crime ring he'd finally brought to justice, Martin Hall was gone and vanished to parts unknown after getting caught with his filthy little auctions in Victor's own fucking backyard.

It was like Martin was taunting him, and there wasn't much Victor wouldn't have given to catch him. Unfortunately, being dead meant Victor couldn't act without revealing himself.

Although Martin had never forced anyone to participate, and everything was supposedly consensual, Victor wasn't about to get over what had happened to Mandy—especially not when Titania had gotten caught up in the auctions too.

Club BDE was supposed to be safe. He might not have liked the idea of his daughter in a bondage club, but he wasn't worried about her being harmed. Although the Elliott brothers took way too long to find out about the auctions, they'd have protected Mandy and Titania with their lives.

He couldn't even bitch about Titania shacking up with Desmond and Bastian. After all, he'd asked them to watch over her, and they doted on her. Besides, considering Mandy was only a few years older than Titania, he didn't have much room to judge them for robbing the cradle.

God, he missed Mandy so fucking hard. It was like a spear driven into his chest every time he saw her and little Bianca. It was the same pain he'd felt after losing his first wife, Carina, when Titania was in kindergarten.

Of course, like Titania, Bee wasn't so little anymore.

Victor straightened his yellow vest and turned his stop sign toward oncoming traffic. "Did y'all have a good day at school?" he asked the children waiting to cross the street.

Most of them raced past him toward their waiting parents and caregivers, but one stopped and looked up at him.

"I made this for Mama, Mr. Androw!" Bee gave him a half-toothless hockey-player grin and held up a plastic vase covered in candy hearts. "It's her birthday tomorrow."

She'd lost another tooth, and he wished he could have put a silver dollar under her pillow like Carina used to do for Titania.

"Wow! That's a fine present, Buzzy Bee. I bet your mama is gonna love it."

Mandy would too. Despite being only a few years older than Titania, she'd stepped up to the plate and been a mother to both his girls. He might not have been Bee's biological father, but she was his daughter as much as Titania was.

"You think so?" Uncaring for the waiting traffic,

she cocked her head and frowned at the vase. "Maybe I should buy something from a store."

"No." He resisted the urge to pull her into a hug. "Your mama is going to adore that pretty vase because you made it. She'll cherish it more than all the diamonds in the world."

Just like he cherished her, Mandy, and Titania.

No, she was Tania now. Carina had loved Shakespeare, but Tania wasn't a fan. Damn, he was proud of her. Her little speech following her assault was still circulating around social media.

Fuck, he'd hated seeing those bruises on her beautiful face. Marinos Pappas was lucky he was already dead after she'd bashed his head in with a skillet, and he had to remind himself almost constantly that he risked exposure if he went after Dr. Ng. Best to let that asshole suffer with his forced retirement.

"C'mon, Bee!" Tania called. "Desmond and Bastian are making your favorite for supper, and we're having a campfire on the beach when your mom gets home."

He turned to look at the other side of the crosswalk. As usual, his heart skipped a beat at the sight of his eldest daughter.

His baby was all grown up. She wore an engagement ring, heels, and a light-gray pantsuit, meaning she must have just come from her new job. Like every day he saw her pick Bee up from school, he had to force his feet to stay still before he dragged her into his arms.

His girls had moved on. Mandy was back in school, studying biology like she'd been before Martin Hall convinced her to sell her innocence. Tania was working the job she'd dreamed of and would be getting married soon.

Well, close to it. She'd always sworn she'd work on the International Space Station, and every day took her one step closer to her childhood goal. Of course, maybe her aspirations had changed now that she had Desmond and Bastian.

"Bye, Mr. Androw! Have a nice day!" Carrying her vase, Bee raced to her sister.

All he could do was watch over them from afar.

❦

Want to know how the Cherry Popping Daddies all started? Check out Emily (By Golden Angel) and Lottie (By Stella Moore)

# ACKNOWLEDGMENTS

As always, my undying gratitude and love go to Engineer Hubby. Without your support and faith, I wouldn't be writing at all. Love you to the moon and back, baby.

Want to see what I'm up to next? Join my Renegades on Facebook. You can also sign up for my newsletter to receive a free short story delivered right to your inbox!

# ABOUT RAISA GREYWOOD

**USA Today bestselling author of filthy smut, empty nester, and cat snuggler.**

Raisa has worked as a teacher, an actuary (her husband called her a bookie—which isn't too far from the truth), mother, and scout leader. She's happily married to her husband of almost thirty years, and is now enjoying semi-retirement writing the books she always wanted to read with kick-ass heroines and sexy, sexy men. Sign up for her newsletter or visit her website at

www.raisagreywood.com

If paranormal romance is your jam, her alter-ego
Minette Moreau has just the thing. Sign up for her
newsletter or visit her website at
www.minettemoreau.com

You can also buy many of Raisa and Minette's books
direct from their websites!

facebook.com/AuthorRaisaGreywood

instagram.com/raisagreywood

bookbub.com/authors/raisa-greywood

goodreads.com/raisa_greywood

tiktok.com/@raisagreywood

**Cherry Popping Daddies (Multi Author Series)**

Emily (By Golden Angel)

Lottie (By Stella Moore)

Titania (By Raisa Greywood)

**Club Apocalypse**

Grim's Little Reaper

War's Peace

Pestilence's Cure

Famine's Feast

Death's Desire

Charon's Chaos

**Holiday Daddy Doms**

Jennifer's Christmas Daddy

A Valentine for Chelsea

Treats for Lucia

Zinnia's Solstice Daddy

**Black Light**

Black Light: Roulette Rematch

Black Light: Saved

## Dad Bod Doms

Henry

## Bridgewater Brides

Their Wanted Bride

## Cocky Hero Club

Sexy Scoundrel

## Anthologies and Standalones

Ladder 54: Five Firefighter Romances

Masters of the Castle: Witness Protection Program

Breaking Donatella

## Happily Never After (written with Sinistre Ange)

Demon Lust

Blood Lust